Cover Art by @alilyushka

Cover Design by Elliana Maggetti

Developmental Edits by Kay Morton @kmortonedits

Copyediting by Paisley McNab @perfectlywrite

Inside Art: @badeyart

SPARKS FLY SERIES

FOR THE Thrill of it All

A FORMULA ONE ROMANCE

ELLIANA ROSE

*For those who are still finding their way, and for those who dare
to be brave enough to embrace the journey.*

May you always trust in your own strength.

GLOSSARY

- **Chicane:** A series of sharp turns that alternate directions, used to slow down cars
- **Downforce:** The aerodynamic force that pushes a car down at high speeds, which helps the car grip the road
- **DRS:** Short for drag reduction system, which allows a driver to increase the car's top speed by opening an adjustable flap on the rear wing
- **Halo:** A cockpit safety structure that was introduced to Formula 1 in 2018 and has already been credited with saving the lives of several drivers. Resembling a horseshoe, the halo consists of a bar that surrounds the drivers head and is bolted to the chassis at three points.
- **Overcut / undercut:** Race strategies that involve a driver attempting to pass the car in front during a pit stop window
- **Paddock:** The area behind the team garages (or pits) at every Formula 1 circuit that is home to the teams' technical staff and equipment, catering, media, race officials and other important functions that contribute to the successful running of the race weekend.

- **Parc Femme:** Literally translated from French as 'closed park,' this is a secure parking area where Formula 1 cars must be left after qualifying.
- **Pole Position:** The first position on the grid at the start of the race. Pole position is earned by the driver recording the fastest time in the final period of qualifying.
- **Qualifying:** The one-hour session on Saturday afternoon that determines the order in which drivers start the race.

DEAR READER

Welcome to the Sparks Fly Series, a series of interconnected stand-alones. While these are sports romances they also will deal with heavier topics. One of my favorite things about the romance genre is being able to address the beautiful mess of being a human. Of life experiences, of traumas and how they affect someone's lives.The highs and lows of growth and healing. Sparks Fly series is a formula one inspired series. I myself love Formula One and have grown up watching races with my dad. That being said, you do not need to know Formula One to understand this book! I will do my best to describe things in an easy and accessible way, and hope you enjoy the fast paced spotlight driven world.

Next, there are some heavy topics discussed in this book (listed below). Lucia, our FMC is leaving an abusive relationship on page one and then we skip ahead in time. I will leave the exact content warnings below, but please put yourself first. My DM's are always open if you have any questions.

• Mentions of physical abuse and domestic violence off page. Dealing with the aftermath of someone leaving a DV situation on page.

• PTSD Symptoms

• Generalized Anxiety Disorder references with panic attacks on page.

• Postpartum Depression.

I know these topics are hard and heavy, if it is not something you wish to read, please put yourself first and take care. This may not be for you. I write these events with great care and love as someone who has experienced a version of the above myself.

If you or anyone you know may be in need of help or to talk please call the National Domestic Violence Hotline 1-800-799-7233 in the US.

CONTENTS

RACE SCHEDULE

Bahrain
Saudi Arabia
Australia
Japan
China
Miami
Emilia-Romagna
Monaco
Canada
Spain
Austria
Great Britain
Hungary
Belgium
Netherlands
Italy
Azerbaijan
Singapore
Texas, United States
Mexico
Brazil
Las Vegas, United States
Qatar
Abu Dhabi

1

BEFORE

LUCIA

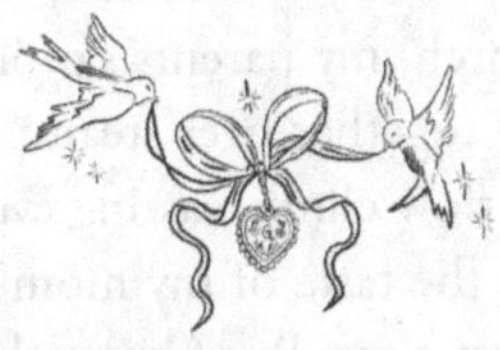

The thing about starting over is that it always sounds easier than it feels. At 3:00 a.m., I was driving through unlit Italian country roads. The headlights of my car sliced through the darkness, the air warm even in the early hours of the morning. My life was packed into the car, a haphazard mess of suitcases and boxes, and I was heading back to the rolling hills of my childhood, where rows of olive trees and grapevines stretched endlessly. Back to the family vineyard, where life was always slow and simple, the exact opposite of the city, and just what I needed.

It was 6:00 a.m. when I turned off the main road at a bend I could have navigated with my eyes closed, greeted by the ancient tree towering behind stone pillars and the ornate monument proudly spelling out *DeLuca Family Vineyards*. The shrubs lining the long drive to my parents' house were in full bloom, their sweet scent mingling with the crisp morning air as dawn began to break. Instead of continuing to the large stone building used for tastings and events, I veered toward the iron gates leading to the family home. Parking a little way down the lane, I stepped out, needing the quiet walk through the familiar landscape to gather myself.

Dust swirled in the distance as I got closer to the house. I imagined my older brother, Matteo, tearing around the backyard in circles in his old go-kart. The same one he'd had when he was twelve. All limbs and hunched shoulders, but he would laugh like a kid, kicking up clouds of dirt. For the first time in weeks, I smiled. A real, unguarded smile at the memory I had seen so many times over the years when he was home.

The house was just as I remembered—solid, comforting, and alive. On the front porch, my parents sat on the swinging bench, their heads bent close together over steaming cups of coffee. The sun was beginning its slow climb, casting everything in soft gold. I could already imagine the taste of my mom's cappuccino, the one she made just right every time. But I knew this wasn't going to be a regular morning. My arrival wasn't routine. My car, stuffed with everything I owned, told that story loud and clear.

As I rounded the big pine trees, the chatter on the porch grew louder, and it was Mom who spotted me first. Her eyes lit up, and she sprang to her feet, calling out with delight.

"Lucia! *Amore!*"

I saw Matteo's head pop out of the kitchen window, his dark brows lifting in surprise before he disappeared and reappeared outside, joining Mom and Dad on the porch.

But the warmth of the moment shifted in an instant. Matteo's smile vanished when he saw me up close. His face hardened, his jaw locking as his eyes swept over me. He was already moving, sprinting toward me before I could take another step.

"Lucia..." His voice cracked as his hands landed gently on my shoulders, like he was afraid I'd break under his grip. His eyes searched mine, and I knew the red eyes and the tears forming were the first signs he saw. I didn't cry. Even as a kid, when I fell out of the old olive tree by the lake and broke my arm, I did not shed a single tear. Matteo and I were inseparable as kids—where he went, I went. We had that twin telepathy thing, even though we were ten months apart. I wanted to tell him not to worry, that I was okay. But I wasn't. I'd moved mountains to leave, and standing here, under the weight of my family's concern, I felt impossibly small.

"I'll fucking kill him," Matteo growled, his voice shaking with anger. Mom was by my side in an instant, coffee cup discarded, her hands fluttering over me like she could fix it all with a touch.

"My sweet girl, what has happened?" she asked, her voice breaking.

My dad stayed rooted to the deck, his rage palpable, but there were tears in his eyes too. That undid me completely. He was never emotional, always the strong, steady presence. Seeing him like that, so broken for me, made me feel like my knees might buckle. A strangled sob bubbled up to the surface and made my sight blur.

Matteo steadied me, sinking us both onto the porch steps. He held me tight, his arms a fortress.

"You're okay," he murmured, over and over, like he could will it into truth. Mom knelt beside us, wrapping us both in her arms, and then I felt Dad's hand, solid and grounding on my shoulder.

"You're safe now," he said firmly.

For the first time in what felt like forever, I believed him. Because here, in this house, with them, I was okay. Or at least, I would be.

It was my mother who switched into fixer mode. As she did. My mother was quite the force. She shooed away the boys to bring my car up and unload my entire life back into my childhood bedroom. My brother kept glancing over at me while bringing my things in. I could see the questions swirling there. The million questions. His phone rang, and he walked outside to take it after giving me a small smile. My dad busied himself with getting my things sorted while Mom shuffled me upstairs into her bedroom. I sat on her bed, hugging a pillow to my chest with her next to me, brushing my hair down with her hand.

"*Stronzo*," she muttered under her breath, the Italian word for *asshole* cutting through the silence. "I never liked him."

It was the first thing my mother had said in what felt like

hours, her sigh carrying the weight of her anger and worry. We sat there quietly, the tension wrapping around us like a heavy blanket. Finally, I exhaled, knowing I couldn't avoid explaining any longer.

I hadn't looked at myself closely, but I didn't need to. The swollen ache of my eye was enough to tell me how bad it looked—surely an unpleasant mix of purple and blue by now.

"You loved him, Mom, so did I," I replied, feeling the weight of my words. We had all loved him. He and Matteo even got along, and Matteo hated everyone I had ever dated. But not Josh. Josh swept into my life like a perfect storm, sudden and all-consuming. He had been the perfect gentleman; he showed up, was interested in my work, and supported me in that. He was probably the most supportive and loving man I had ever dated. We had been together for three years. He proposed on the park bench we had sat on the first time we met. It had been such an easy yes. And it had been a blissful few months of being engaged. And I loved him. Truly, deep in my soul, I loved him. But the perfectness began to rot away. The controlling behavior, questioning me when I worked late, accusing me of cheating, of not loving him, were the cornerstones of so many fights. Then months had passed, I had hardly spoken to my family or friends, plans were canceled for some reason or the next by him. Then, what felt like suddenly, I was alone, with only Josh.

This rage poisoned and rotted away the man I loved, the sweet and kind man I thought I knew. The worst was when I realized no one would suspect it when he had convinced everyone that he loved me so profoundly it would be unfathomable that he would hurt me. I realized I had no one to talk to or confide in because we had gradually stopped seeing my friends. He never wanted to spend time with them, and if I left to hang out with them, it would make him angry—effectively cutting me off from the outside world.

It wasn't until last night that I left. He came home late and reeked of the bar. Had some choice words that turned to screams, but it was the first time he had hurt me.

After he left, I sat there, tears streaming down my face, lost in the weight of everything that had just happened. Hours blurred together before a stray thought pushed its way into my mind: *When was my last period?* The realization hit me like a jolt, and panic took over.

I grabbed my keys and headed to the store down the street, barely remembering the walk there. I bought a test and went straight to the drugstore restroom, hands shaking as I waited for the result. Then, there it was—one single word on the digital screen.

Pregnant.

That one word changed everything.

Something broke inside me after that. It wasn't fear, it was resolve. I walked home with fire in my veins and determination driving every step. Once inside, I grabbed the biggest suitcase I owned and as many boxes as I could carry, making two trips between the apartment and my car. I had no idea how long Josh would be gone, but the thought of him coming back, finding me, and pulling me back into that nightmare kept me moving faster. It wasn't just me now—I had another life depending on me. A tiny one that deserved so much better. I refused to bring a child into *his* world. I had always dreamed of being a mother, albeit not like this, but that one word on the test is what shook me to my core. I left my engagement ring on the counter without a second thought and drove ten hours straight to my parents' house, the weight of my decision sinking in with every mile.

"I'm pregnant, Mom," I finally said. She looked over to me, her lips quivering.

"It will be just fine, sweet girl. It will be just fine." She hugged me tight, and I knew it in my soul. *It would be just fine.*

2

BEFORE

ALEXANDER

"Hey, man." My best friend's voice came through the speaker on my phone.

"Hey, mate! I was wondering if I could take you up on your offer to spend the last week of summer break with ya?" I asked while packing a bag up. I had been bouncing around Europe all summer break and Matteo had offered his family's home up for me to land for some stability before we shipped out for the first races. In all honesty I could use the slow pace and the quiet. I had been all over for photo shoots and vacation spots and could use some time out of the spotlight. I should've listened to Matteo when he said it was an open invitation for the whole break. We still had six days before we had to gear up for the next Grand Prix, and while my blood buzzed with the urge to get back in the game, my body was begging for the rest I hadn't allowed myself since the break began.

"Yeah, man. There's just some things going on, my sister is in town."

"That's great, buddy, I knew you were hoping to see her over break! I thought she lived in the city?" I asked, still preoccupied with folding clothes.

"Yeah, she's, uh, home now." Matteo let out a gruff sigh. That was never good. I stopped what I was doing and grabbed my phone off the table and sat down.

"Is everything okay?" I asked. It was rare for Matteo to be anything other than happy and chipper, but he loved his family fiercely and was extremely protective of his little sister.

"Fuck no, Alex, it's bad. She's in rough shape."

"She and her man split?" I asked, rubbing my hand over my forehead. I knew his sister Lucia was engaged and lived in the city with her fiancé. We had met once or twice during hometown races for Matteo. She was strikingly beautiful, all long blonde hair and crystal green eyes, enough for any man to profess their love on the spot. Matteo had had some choice words for the boys after a few comments had been overheard during the first race she attended, and I had thrown a threat or two in for good measure.

And while I appreciated beauty, Lucia was an engaged woman and my best mate's little sister. So admiring her beauty was as far as it would ever go.

"Alexander, he should be six feet fucking under the ground." Matteo sounded angrier than I had ever heard him.

"The fuck you mean?" I asked, sitting up straighter. What had the fucking prick done to Lucia?

"It's a mess, mate, I don't know what to do."

"I could have someone figure that out," I suggested. Matteo sighed.

"No, Alex, you are not hiring someone to beat up my sister's trash fiancé."

"Ex-fiancé, hopefully?" I asked. Lucia was strong willed, but no one knows what's going on behind closed doors, or how manipulative some men could be. My blood was boiling now, feeling the immense need to run off the rage crawling under my skin.

"Fuck, yes, ex-fiancé, the piece of shit thinks he can lay a hand on my baby sister?" He seethes. I suck in a breath. *Fuck*. That man deserved to be dead for ever laying a hand on a woman, let alone my best friend's sister—the blonde windstorm who lit up rooms even brighter than Matteo's annoyingly contagious positive attitude.

"What did he do?" I asked lowly.

"She's fucked up, man, it's...it's awful." His voice cracked. *Fuck this. I would figure out where this scum lived, his security numbers, and make his life a living hell. I would—*

"Yeah, mate, come as soon as you can. We could all use company and distraction, and Luce loves you."

"I'll leave today, brother. See you soon." I hung up and immediately made a call to my "assistant".

"Alexander." Dante picked up immediately.

"I need information on Matteo's sister's fiancé."

"You going after your best mate's little sister, Wright? Not the best idea," Dante replied with his accent thick on most words.

"No, I am going after the piece of shit that thinks he can lay a hand on a woman and get away with it," I gritted out. The silence was deafening, and I could hear the tapping away at the computer.

"I'll send over everything I have," Dante replied. "Do you want me to ruffle some feathers?"

"Set the fucking bird on fire," I replied before clicking the phone off. I threw some more clothes in my bag, not bothering with the rest and texting Dante, requesting the jet be ready in one hour.

It was dark by the time we landed, Dante had arranged for a car to be ready for me to drive to the DeLuca residence. After driving through country roads lined with trees, the DeLuca residence came into view; a large house situated on a hill surrounded by rolling land. Rows of grapevines and some olive fields flanked the sides of the drive that winded through the hills to the house atop it all. Matteo had deeply undersold the little winery his parents owned. It was jaw dropping and went on farther than my eyes could see. I drove up to the large stone pilasters flanking the iron gate and pressed the button on the call box.

"The DeLuca Winery is closed to tours currently," a scratchy voice announced through the box.

"This is Alexander Wright, I am a family friend," I replied. There was no response, only a click and the gates began to slide open. I shifted back into gear and drove up to the estate. Pulling up next to a car I didn't recognize, I got out of the car and smiled toward the porch.

"Alexander." Matteo exhaled, sitting on the bench on the porch with his sister. I walked up to them.

"Hey, mate." I smiled and brought him in for a hug. Lucia looked up, and I tried not to suck in a breath. Deep purple and black bloomed around her right eye, and there was an angry red splotch on her check. A split lip. *Fuck*. Her eyes were sunken, looking like something had sucked the life right out of her.

She smiled up at me, her split lip tugging up regardless of the discomfort.

"Hey, Luce." I smiled back and brought her in for a hug as well. She felt so small in my arms it was almost alarming. She was much smaller than she used to be, not that I gave a single shit how many kilos someone weighed, but this was clearly in a *something is wrong* way. That man deserved to die for this. No, not die, *rot*.

"You should see the other guy!" she lamely joked, shrugging her shoulders and sitting back down.

"I sure as shit would like to," I replied with a grunt. "I wouldn't be using my words."

"Does it look that bad?" she asked, again seeming so damn small and fragile, her eyes welling up, making my damn heart break. This wasn't the Lucia I knew, the Lucia that Matteo talked about daily. She was a spitfire, throwing sass and shade like it was her goddamn job. She demanded attention when she walked into a room and glowed—she fucking glowed. This, this was not that. I fucking hated it.

"Nah, Lucia, you're still beautiful—as always," I replied.

"Watch it." Matteo shoved my arm. I rolled my eyes at my best mate.

"Don't be so sensitive." I laughed and sat down on the chair across from them.

Mr. and Mrs. DeLuca were long asleep, but we stayed up late talking. Matteo and I even got Lucia to laugh, and that alone made Matteo visibly relax. The cool mountain air was glorious as we talked over beers and Matteo and I swapped race stories. After a while, Lucia's smile faded, as if the exhaustion was taking over or the weight of the day. She smiled sadly and said good night before trudging inside and leaving me and Matteo staring off into the open night sky.

"She's pregnant," Matteo whispered. The beer in my hand froze at my lips. *Fuck.*

"I won't ever let that fucker near her, or the baby," Matteo said, looking into the stars. "Ever."

"He'll have to go through us both, mate." I could feel the rage simmer low in me. I did not take well to any man fucking with my family, and Matteo was family. So if anyone even thought about messing with his sister, they'd have to go through me first. No exceptions. I fired off another text to Dante, making it clear that deadbeat wasn't welcome.

Now or ever.

THREE YEARS LATER
LUCIA

"**C**ome on, Lucia!" Matteo groaned. "It's just the last circuit! Ten races! It's a vacation, all paid for!"

"Matteo." I sighed, bouncing Gianna on my hip. "I can't just take a vacation, what am I even going to do, the only people who attend race after race like that are the girlfriends and wives!" Also coined as the WAGS: Wives and Girlfriends.

"Not true!" Matteo practically whined. I swear he's worse than Gia is when she's hungry.

"Matteo, I have a toddler, I barely remember to shower. How would I even do that?"

"I have people for that!" he called, following me from room to room.

"Like who?" I shot back.

"Alexander will be there!"

"Yes, Alexander, the five-time world champion who will be busy racing just like you, Matteo!" I laughed out loud at my brother's idiocy. He was the embodiment of a golden retriever. Sweet, goofy, and much too good for this world. I loved Alexander, he's practically family to us, but he would be zero help when it came to any type of childcare, he was even busier than Matteo was.

"I'll hire someone! A nanny! Gianna will come with us, obviously, but then you have someone to take her and we can go out and party!" Matteo typed vigorously on his phone.

"Matteo," I shouted at him. "Matteo!" He stopped typing. "I'm not just leaving Gia with someone I don't know!" I rolled my eyes, bending to put Gianna down. She happily ignored us and walked over to her kitchen set. "Also, it's not exactly easy to travel with a kid, she needs all her stuff!" I said, brushing off my jeans.

"We can use Alexander's private jet! Bring it all!" Matteo called back, now in the other room.

"Stop using Alexander as the solution for everything, Matteo!"

"Why is everyone yelling, and what are you using me for?" Alexander appeared, wearing an oversized hoodie and his braided hair pulled back into a knot at his neck. The tattoos on his hands peeked out from the sweatshirt. The wings marking his neck were relatively new, and very, very distracting. Alexander had countless tattoos, each a piece of art, a piece of him, etched onto his skin. If his British accent wasn't enough of a swoon, the man was just straight-up stunning. He was tall for a Formula One driver; I only came to just below his shoulders.

I rolled my eyes and threw my hands over my face at his remark. Alexander had been Matteo's friend for a while now. They karted together when they were little, and Alexander signed with Belen years before Matteo. But when Matteo finally got a spot on Moretti Racing's team, they were thick as thieves all over again. About three years ago, he started making his yearly summer break trips out to the vineyard with Matteo, spending them with us. The summers were filled with sunshine and swimming in the small lake on my parents' land. The pair of them kept me sane through being pregnant and having a baby while they were here, but once the season began again, the days were long and lonely.

Alexander had this uncanny ability to make me relax, like his presence alone was a calming draft through the air. That or the cologne he wore, which was intoxicating. It became a sense-memory for me. After being my anchors all summer, they would finish out their break with me, assuring me I could do it and I wouldn't be alone. Matteo and Alex had shown up, and I never had to worry about Gianna having a role model to look up to because these two would rope the moon for her if she asked.

I looked at Alexander, his dark skin was so glowy and perfect, it was such a waste on a man who had never touched skin care once in his life. Long lashes and the most perfect lips.

Good god, I need to snap out of it.

"It's too much, Matteo, I can't do it all. I am so tired, I could literally sleep for, like, four days straight and still not be rested." Warm arms wrapped around me and the scent of leather and pine cologne that was so familiar now, so very Alexander, flooded me. I indulged my tired limbs and melted right into him.

God, I am so starved for affection, this is pathetic.

"You can sleep for four days! We'll watch Gia while you sleep!" Matteo yelled from the other room.

I let out a sigh into Alexander's chest, who squeezed his arms around me. I tried not to let out an actual groan. *I really need to calm down.* "I love him, but I hate him," I grumbled.

"I know the feeling," Alexander replied. I could hear the smile in his voice. "You should come, though, it would be good for you *and* Gia." His voice was so soft and gentle, reminding me of when he and Matteo got on the first flight to come meet Gianna when she was first born. The "You got this" whispered in the middle of the night when Gianna was only four months old and the sleep regression hit like a freight train. Alexander woke up to a crying baby and a crying me. He stayed up with me, in the moonlit nursery, as I rocked her back to sleep, and when she finally went back down, I closed the door and slid down the hallway.

Am I fucking this up? I had asked, tears leaking from my tired eyes.

No, he'd said simply, as if it was this known fact. No, I was not fucking this up. Simple and to the point. Then his shoulder knocked mine and he whispered with full confidence, *You got this.*

It became a mantra after that, over and over again. *I got this.*

Even on days where it was the furthest from the truth.

Alexander had been around constantly after that first summer, following my brother home. My parents adored him, he sent photos in a group chat that included all of us on race days, he was just a part of our lives. As if he just slotted himself into it so seamlessly.

"The only people who will be there will be models or celebrities or wags who look like models or actually are celebrities." I pulled myself out of Alexander's arms reluctantly and saw Gianna looking at me. Her room was pink but race car themed, thanks to Uncle Matteo, who surprised us with a little nursery makeover right before she was born. She even had a custom plushie that was the pink version of Matteo's own Formula One race car. Alexander had then of course found someone to make a Belen version for his own team, it was black with bright blue and pink racing stripes, and much to Matteo's annoyance, it was Gia's favorite.

"Up, up!" Gia's small voice drifted over to us as she walked to Alex, her favorite human. Alexander ruffed up my hair before leaning down and picking her up. The absence of his warmth and arms was sorely missed. But it only took a moment for my heart to swell again when I watched them.

"Yes, love?" he asked, peering down at my daughter with the biggest smile on his face, giving all of his attention to my girl.

"I just, I don't trust people enough to watch her. It should be me. And you know how it is on the circuit. There are so many people and the cameras." I sighed. "I don't know if I want to expose her to that."

Alex turned to me, Gia resting in his arms and staring up at him like he had hung the moon just for her. He probably would if she asked.

"What if I ask Anna?" he asked. Anna was one of his personal managers, she handled PR and media and all around scheduling. She was incredible and could figure out anything you asked. Unlike Dante, who scared the shit out of me. "No one will bother you, we will make sure of it. Plus, some of those hot wives are rather nice." He smirked, and I immediately rolled my eyes and mouthed, *Yuck*, because yes, they were nice, but Alex was the definition of a playboy and was constantly being berated by the media about it.

"And if you don't want cameras on her, I'll make every photographer allowed in the paddock sign an NDA." His eyes were gleaming with sincerity, like he was planning it all out in his head. I couldn't help but smile at him and the thought of being in the paddock with Gia. Letting her see that world was such an exciting thought. She would be obsessed with the real-life version of Alexander's car, I knew it.

"Dante is never allowed to watch her," I said quickly as the thought entered my mind. If Anna was Alexander's right-hand woman, Dante was the left. He was a sort of fix-it man—could do basically everything and anything at the drop of a hat—however, I did not trust that man to watch my daughter; he would probably hire someone else to do it or something.

Alexander chuckled. "Christ, no. I rarely see him, myself. He keeps to himself."

"I want full background checks," I said, hands on hips. Alexander nodded, as if that was a given. Honestly, Alexander was probably as protective as me when it came to Gia. It was jarring to see that love pour out of him when Gia was born; if only the media moguls saw this side of him, they would maybe stop the relentless rumors and invasions of privacy.

We all loved Alexander, of course, but he was a bit of a wild child, he had loads of money, more than I could fathom, and loved extreme sports—like driving a car at two hundred–plus miles per hour for his job, or skydiving in Abu Dhabi. An adrenaline junky who loved fame and the spotlight, but after eight years in the high-paced sport, the spotlight was becoming too much, and he had begun to slow down.

Alexander had really calmed down from his bachelorhood over the last year, even bought some land on the mountains only twenty minutes up the road from my parents' house. Matteo could've done the same, but he preferred to be here with us on his breaks instead. He had an apartment in France and a home in New York, but he would always pick the family home here in the Italian countryside first for summer break. We loved summers here growing up, and I wanted Gianna to love it as well.

I started picking up around the room while Alexander held Gianna and looked out the window with her, pointing out trees. I stayed in the doorway, a hip leaning on the wooden frame of my baby's nursery that used to be my own room as a child. The door was chipped and painted over hundreds of times, pencil marks on the edges to show my and Matteo's heights over the years. And now a pink pencil marking little Gia's height at only two-and-a-half years of age. My parents adored her. They were so supportive and wonderful about everything. With so much land, Gianna could have a wonderful childhood here, I knew that, of course, because my own had been the same. Dad had even offered to split off some land for me to build my own house on and have my own space, but that step felt so big and scary. I felt safe here, with my mom down the hall or my dad waking up and rocking Gianna back to sleep on hard nights. That's why I loved it here; it was the only place that I had ever felt entirely safe. And after everything, I wanted to give that to Gianna too. A safe place to call home, to dream up anything she wanted, and to be anything she wanted. Places to go explore, endless trails, a creek to swim in, trees to read under.

"Okay, Lucia, you're added to all the flight schedules and Anna has already booked rooms next to ours for all the stays. Also, you have been emailed a list of options for how to help with Gianna on circuit, and she even offered to help watch her and has a friend who might be able to help out too!" Matteo called out from across the hall. Alexander looked at me, offering me a smile as if to say, *if Matteo wants it to happen, it's going to happen.* Alexander knew damn well I couldn't say no to my brother.

"Anna is a wonder woman," I shouted back. Matteo had sort of adopted Anna as his own assistant, so she now somehow juggled both Alexander and my brother. She was also one of the nicest people I had ever met. Sweet and kind, but so strong and fierce. I was never sure whether to be scared of her or in awe of her. It was a little of both, if I was being honest.

"Make sure you tell her that. She eats that shit up," Alexander said while poking at Gia's cheeks to get her to giggle. My own smile dropped. The circuit isn't made for babies; this would not be easy for her *or* for me.

"I don't know—"

"You are coming," Matteo said, walking into the room. "End of story. Mom and Dad want their house back," he added, including the guilt trip card. "And you can run DeLuca Family Vineyards from anywhere!" After going to university for business, it was an easy decision to take over the dealings and marketing for the family business. My parents wanted to tend to the winery and the tasting rooms, creating an experience. I did the backend, the marketing, helped pick events to sponsor, and made deals with markets all across Europe. Alexander would send a proud photo from whenever he saw an end cap at the market with DeLuca Family Vineyards wine bottles on display.

"Don't listen to him, darling, we always want you here! But you *can* work from anywhere, why not get out there!" My mom piped in from another room, eavesdropping on the whole conversation. It was a huge house, but somehow the whole family seemed to move in a small pack, always inhabiting the same section together. My mother, the wonder that she was, walked past holding a basket of laundry. Her light brown hair was in loose, natural waves down her back. Even into her sixties she had not one gray and kept her hair long. My dad always said he loved it wild and free, like her.

Her eyes softened when she looked at me, then glanced behind to see Alex with Gianna, a knowing smile playing on her lips as she gave me an arch of her brow. "And Matteo got us tickets for the Italian Grand Prix!" Mom added before going back downstairs.

"You leave in like three days. How am I supposed to be ready in that amount of time?" I threw my hands up.

"Whatever you forget, I'll buy you a new one!" Matteo answered like it was the most obvious answer ever.

"I don't want your money, Matteo!" I reached for Gianna out of Alexander's arms. She lunged for me the minute I got close, mumbling a tired "Mama."

"Yeah you do!" he called after me as I walked out of the playroom, upstairs to my own room.

It's a huge undertaking, traveling with an almost three-year-old, let alone traveling with an F1 driver and his team, and being on the circuits on race days. Alexander and Matteo drove for different teams, but as far as I remembered, their paddocks were always close to one another, since they ranked closely. That was a plus for Gianna to be able to see Matteo and Alexander the whole time. I smiled at her and kissed her forehead.

"Want to go on an adventure, G?" I asked. She smiled and cheered an enthusiastic "Yeah!"

It was a huge convenience to live with my parents. Sure, I could take my father's offer up on eventually building my own place on the land, but I liked not being alone, having my own mother when I felt like I was failing at being one myself. She was an angel on earth, that one. I loved it here, *this was home*. At the same time, it was deeply lonely to be here in the countryside. I felt so stuck. I had grown used to working all day and dedicating every other second of my life to Gia. I missed going out, having friends besides my annoying brother. I used to love traveling with my family, going to races, but between leaving an ex who isolated me from everyone and having a baby, there just wasn't time for any of it.

Being alone, having so many changes thrown your way, and becoming a mother—it was hard to explain, especially to the two boys in the room with me who were so fiercely cheering me on. I needed a change, needed to do it for myself but also for Gia. She deserved a happy mother, she deserved a good life. And I knew I could give it to her. Maybe this was the start, the start of saying yes to things, to getting out of my comfort zone. My sweet girl was everything to me; blonde curly hair, bright eyes, a contagious smile, and the most bubbly personality. My mom would constantly mention how similar she was to me when I was young. My own childhood had been so bright, my parents the eternal beams of sunshine that they were, my father a sturdy rock of the family. I wanted to give that to my girl, a happy childhood, an exciting life.

"Guess we're going on the road, G," I whispered to her, looking into the mirror at our reflections. My blonde hair was long and wild now. The curls were doing exactly what they wanted today. If someone showed me a picture of myself from three years ago when I showed up on my parents' doorstep so afraid of the future, I wouldn't recognize myself. I had gained weight, finally gained some curves back, and my face wasn't hollow anymore. It had been years since anyone had hurt me, and since I'd seen *him*. I was always shocked he never reached out. I expected him to maybe even show up one day. But he never did. I lived with a small amount of fear that he would, and that he would take Gia away from me. My father had walked in one day when Gia was just born, signed custody papers, Josh's signature right there, granting me full parental rights. It hadn't felt real, I only nodded at him with teary eyes when he leaned down to kiss my forehead. We hadn't talked about it, no one had; I didn't know if I even wanted to know. I just knew he was gone, according to the men in my life.

"What's going on in that head of yours, sweetheart?" Mom asked, leaning against the doorway.

"I think some days I expect him to show up out of nowhere," I replied honestly with a shrug.

"Oh, honey, he wouldn't make it far." She jutted a thumb out behind her to Matteo and Alexander.

I waved her off. "Oh please, Mom."

"Those two would do anything for you."

"Sure, Mom," I replied.

"I mean it, Lucia." She turned and left with a smile. I knew it was true, too, they loved Gianna something fierce. Any of us would move mountains for her. But it didn't distinguish the constant fear that lingered in the back of my mind.

⚙

"Hey, Luce." I looked up to find the brown eyes I'd come to obsess over staring back at me. Alexander was dreamy by anyone's standards. There were thousands of fan accounts dedicated to his eyes alone, unsurprisingly.

"What's up?" I asked.

"I have to leave early, Anna says they want to add another interview before the season," he explained. I felt the knot of disappointment since that would mean I wouldn't see him before his first race back. We had a bit of a tradition, the three of us, before the end of break, would sit around the campfire and pull out a vintage from the wine cellars and swap stories all night before they had to leave. I was told they did it for me in the beginning to cheer me up that first summer, but Matteo and Alexander had come to love the tradition as well.

"Oh."

"Okay, I'll be seeing you then." He rubbed a hand over his

forehead. "Just find me before start, when you get in?" His eyes softened and he looked over to Gia. "And bring my girl with ya."

I smiled so brightly. "Of course," I said softly, looking at Gia, who stared at Alexander with big eyes.

"Promise?" he asked, his voice smaller than I was used to as he knelt to Gia and kissed her forehead before looking up at me. And if my heart didn't burst at the sight of him on his knees with my daughter being so gentle and kind. I was so in over my head with this one.

"Promise." I nodded.

4

ALEXANDER

It was Saturday morning, and the last place I wanted to be was sitting on a plane, flying away from the people who had somehow become my family. I knew I had to start getting my head in the game and ready for racing, my usual pre-race rituals started on the plane. I watched old race videos, went over notes from my strategist and studied the map of the next racetrack.

But my mind was miles away. Solely focused on the rolling Tuscan hillsides, endless rows of vineyard, and a house perched on top of it all. By the end of the last season, I knew I wanted to make a home of my own in the small region near the DeLucas. I had just closed on a property next to the DeLuca Vineyards. It was about a twenty minute drive down the country road and our properties touched at a small lake in the middle, where the DeLucas had built a dock that we would spend the summers diving off of. I had plans to build more on the land, the small building could be used as a guesthouse or an artistic space, then I would build my perfect home. But the moment I closed on the property I had compiled a list for the perfect home. I wanted it to be warm, truly feel like a home. A stark difference against my apartments in London and New York, but that one felt the most like home. I knew I wouldn't have much time throughout the season to focus on it, but closing on the property felt like a huge milestone in itself.

My manager, Anna, had called and told me she had a magazine photoshoot scheduled for the day before our first practice for the Dutch Grand Prix. I knew training was going to start and I had to get my head down and morph back into my race self. My summer self was rather relaxed, letting the days pass and doing things on whims. However, when I was in the race season, I was purely focused on my career. I couldn't risk anything getting in my way. Seemingly every minute of my day was planned down to the second by someone from my team. Sure, I had allotted downtime, but I was never truly at ease when we arrived on the circuit. The fan base expected me to be prevalent on socials, at events, and doing interviews. They wanted me to keep the persona of a playboy. One I was growing more and more tired of by the second. I had cleaned up my act, I partied less, focused on my career more, but the fans liked the old me. Anna mainly focusing on the PR management side and some scheduling of events, and she had pushed to switch the narrative, had worked to get my reputation to match who I was now. It was an uphill battle.

I knew I had a good chance of qualifying for pole position here in the Netherlands, due to our car being pretty solid this year. But Matteo was giving me a run for my money. Last Grand Prix he knocked me out of first at the last minute, and a penalty from an incident with another driver knocked me down to P3. It was still a podium, but I wasn't going to win my sixth championship by getting P3. I was sitting in second place in the Drivers' Championship currently, Theo Brauer of Kaze Energy Racing just barely above me in points. There were a few championships, split into team rankings and individual driver rankings. My teammate was in fourth place. Matteo behind him in fifth.

The Dutch Grand Prix was one of my favorite tracks, and I knew Mateo would be a formidable opponent. He put up quite the fight last year during his rookie year. But Matteo was a seasoned driver now, according to the Formula One world—he was still a rookie in my eyes, though. Sitting in fifth place for the Drivers' Championship, the other teams were already offered contracts, trying to get him on their own team. He raced for our biggest competitor, Moretti. I doubted he would leave the Italian team of his own volition. It was his childhood dream to race with them and he was blowing past everyone's high expectations as a new driver.

I fell asleep on the plane with my phone in hand. Only when the stewardess tapped my shoulder notifying me we had landed did I realize I slept the whole flight, my pre-race flight routine ruined. I stretched my tight limbs knowing I shouldn't have stayed seated all flight and I'd pay the price with my trainer tomorrow. The plane door opened with a loud pop, revealing Anna standing at the bottom of the steps, dark brown hair pulled into a tight bun, a leather jacket in place over a black dress. My savior.

"Hey." She beamed as I walked out, squinting at the sun and wishing I was back on a vineyard. "All right, we have a shoot at three p.m. and an interview at five, and then I have a meeting set up with the team principal at six, dinner with your manager at seven." She rambled off my schedule and I tried not to outwardly wince. She responded in tow.

"Okay, scratch that. Photoshoot at three, and meeting with the team principal at six. The rest I'll move." She tapped her long nails on her phone, typing away. Anna had the ability to read an emotion in five seconds flat. She managed my entire schedule and could somehow read one glance from me and adjust accordingly. In the last two years I've been avoiding interviews and doing fewer shoots, enjoying time off the track to rest and not be in the spotlight.

"Thank you." I sighed, pulling my bag up and slinging it over my shoulder.

"When does Luce get here?" I asked.

"Last day of practice, I have a car picking her up and bringing her straight to the track. Someone will handle her bags and set up her hotel suite for her and Gia." Anna nodded then broke her focus, a bright smile breaking through. "Who I am so excited to finally meet!"

"She's grown so much." I couldn't help but smile wildly as well. Gia was this little ball of blonde sunshine. A mini version of her mother. Same gleaming green eyes and the ability to make me stop anything for them.

"I need any and all photographers who are allowed in the Belen and Moretti paddock to sign NDAs. No photos of Gia, no exceptions. If something gets leaked, we sue," I said sternly. Anna nodded and jotted down notes.

"I'll make a call now, and get in touch with the media handlers, no one in the circuit," she said, stepping aside and pulling the phone to her ear. We walked to a waiting town car and got in. My phone pinged with a message as soon as the door shut. I pulled out my phone from my hoodie and was greeted with a text from Matteo—a picture of Gia smiling brightly and holding the plush version of my exact Formula One car.

MATTEO

Is it wrong to want to rip a kid's plushie in half? Why does she hate the one from me? They are literally the same thing!

ALEXANDER

Mine's better, obviously.

ALEXANDER

Make the kid cry, I make you cry, mate.

MATTEO

I would never. You land yet?

ALEXANDER

Yeah. Principal already wants to meet

MATTEO
I'm sure it's nothing, just start of season shit.

ALEXANDER
I hope so. Wish I was there.

MATTEO
So does G!

Another photo came through. G was wearing a Moretti Racing shirt, looking like she was about to cry.

ALEXANDER
Stop torturing her. I'll fly back right now.

MATTEO
You wish

Matteo's face filled my phone screen, a big grin and an equally grinning Gia, who was now holding a large piece of bread. I rolled my eyes at it but the smile stayed. I missed them already. *When did I get so soft?*

The photo shoot was a blur. I liked fashion and working with designers. Breaking the mold of wearing Belen Racing branded items that my teammate, James, wore into race days, I preferred to wear something interesting. One of the designers showed up on set and I was greeted with smiles and excitement. Their designs were fresh; I dug the blue velvety chunky sweater so much I asked if I could buy it. The designer sent me on my way with it at the end, refusing to accept any money for it. I messaged my stylist to place an order for some other items as I left the shoot, planning on wearing them for walk-ups.

Anna shot me off some emails, having me read over a few items and sign releases. I was eventually shuffled into the town car again and driven to the hotel I'd be staying at this weekend. It was posh, and vintage elegance dripped from every corner. I smirked at the old-fashioned details, odes to the original architecture here, and Lucia invaded my thoughts. There were golden framed paintings that I knew she loved. There was one weekend last summer when Matteo dragged us to Florence, determined to cheer up Lucia after a particularly hard week. It was the first time she had left Gia overnight. I had caught her with tears in her eyes on the train as she read a book in the window seat. When we wandered into a museum, there was a room with impressionist paintings in large golden frames, and it was the first time she had really smiled in months. That memory had burned into my head somehow.

"Okay, here are your hotel suite keys." I jumped at Anna's voice. She had a bad habit of suddenly appearing, I swear the woman moved silently.

"Fuck, you scared me," I muttered under my breath, rubbing a hand over my face.

"Get yourself a nap. You need to be fresh for the meeting tonight."

"Do you know what it's about?"

"No. But there's some weird energy going on throughout the team. So head down and focus."

"Aye aye, Captain." I was met with a roll of the eyes as she trailed over to a bellboy carrying her luggage.

"Anna," I asked, "you got Matteo and Luce suites, right?"

"Yeah, across from you. We basically have the whole hall."

I nodded and sent her a wave, trudging myself and my luggage to the elevator. Anna had fussed over me bringing my own things, but I desperately needed to take a nap, and being woken up by a bellman bringing it up just sounded awful. Plus, I liked things in my control. After fucking up my own pre-race flight routine, I just needed to do this myself.

The sun was glowing over the paddock, casting a warm glow across the sea of team trailers and racing equipment. My meeting with the Belen Racing team principal a few days ago had gone as I expected, no new contract yet. This year was the last one on my current contract, meaning I was about to be a free agent. While other teams had shown interest, I didn't care. I wanted to stay at Belen Racing.

I was still lost in my thoughts zipping up my race suit for the day when I heard it—an unmistakable, joyful shriek that sliced through the usual din of engines and chatter. My head snapped up, searching for the source.

And there she was—Gia, a bundle of energy and joy, barreling toward me. Her tiny legs carried her faster than I would have thought possible, her blonde ringlets bouncing with every step. Her laughter rang out like a bell, everything else faded into the background. She spotted me and her face lit up with pure, unfiltered happiness.

I dropped to my knees, arms wide open, my racing suit crinkling as I stretched out to catch her. I could see her tiny fists clenching in excitement as she made a beeline straight for me. My heart swelled, an overwhelming wave of affection washing over me. Nothing prepared me for this—the real, tangible joy of her presence here in the paddock. Gianna DeLuca was a whirlwind of a kid. After summers with her over the last few years, she had decidedly picked me as her best friend. She used to scream "OW OW" before she could even make out my name, demanding my attention. I loved it, though. Feeling so important to someone was something I wasn't used to. On the track, people saw me as a champion, but to Gia, I was just Alex. She didn't care about wins or titles, she was just a kid who thought race car driving was super cool. That simple, pure love made me want to be better, to be someone she could look up to, to be good.

During the season, I would make time to FaceTime Lucia after races, just to see the little gremlin's smile. Matteo and I would fly back occasionally when we were a short flight away. For her first birthday, we snuck away and flew to the DeLuca's home. We were both fined excessively for missing some media days. We stuffed the private jet with presents, I bought her a stuffed bunny rabbit that year, which she now keeps with her always. The two days we snuck away were worth every penny of the fines. We did the exact same thing for her second birthday. She had the DeLuca spunk, the sassy attitude and the same blonde hair as her mother. It dawned on me that for the next few months at least, Gianna would actually be here for races. She talked endlessly about wanting to be a race car driver like her "Ow Wex" and Zio. It made Lucia roll her eyes and Matteo beam with pride.

"Alex!" she cried, throwing herself into my arms. I caught her easily, her small body pressing against my chest. She clung to me, giggling as if she'd just conquered the world. I couldn't help but laugh, the sound coming out as a genuine, deep chuckle. "Well, if it isn't my favorite little whirlwind," I said, hugging her tightly. "Look at you!"

"Hi, best friend." She giggled in my ear, squeezing her little arms around my neck. My heart squeezed.

Over Gia's shoulder, I saw Lucia approaching. She was dressed in an oversized Belen Racing jacket that practically swallowed her, but in Lucia fashion, she paired thigh-high, heeled boots with it, a purse slung over her shoulder, and just under the sleeve of her sweatshirt were colorful beaded bracelets, the ones Gia loved to make. God, she was a vision. Her long blonde hair fell in waves over her shoulders, and her smile was soft, warm, like a cozy blanket on a chilly day. She watched us with a mixture of amusement and affection washing over her features, her eyes crinkling at the corners as she took in the sight of Gia nestled in my arms. I waved at her, still holding Gia, who seemed to have no intention of letting go anytime soon.

"Hey, Luce!" I called out. I tried to keep my voice easy and casual, but seeing her *here. In my team's sweatshirt.*

Fuck.

Something had changed over this last summer break with Lucia. Like something clicked in my brain, sorting her as *Lucia,* this strong and amazing woman and not just my best friend's sister. She was bold and brave, with this exceedingly bright energy. She had become a constant presence in my thoughts.

"This feels surreal, having you guys on the circuit. I think G is going to be my good luck charm, huh?" I leaned down and tickled Gia, who giggled in turn. Gia was wearing a miniature version of the same jacket, Belen pink and blue colors splashed onto the dark fabric.

"Love the sweatshirt, G," I said to Gia, who beamed up at me.

"We made bracelets!" she announced, pushing up a sleeve clumsily and showing off her pink and blue bracelet. She turned her wrist, revealing two white beads and two numbers.

One and four.

Fourteen.

As in *my racing number* fourteen. My heart picked up speed as I looked up to Lucia, standing there with the corners of her mouth ticked up. She had her arms crossed, but she casually pushed one sleeve up, revealing a matching bracelet, the same pink and blue with two white beads.

They were both wearing my number.

"She insisted we wear your number today, to go with the jackets. We have Matteo's, too, in red, of course."

"Of course," I replied, the smirk growing.

Lucia laughed, a sound like tinkling chimes. "She's been so excited. I think she's convinced you're a superhero."

"Well, I'll take that." I grinned, finally setting Gia down but keeping a hand resting gently on her back. "But Matteo's gonna be pissed when he finds out you're not wearing Moretti gear on day one."

Lucia rolled her eyes, but her smile didn't falter. I laughed again, this time more softly. "But don't worry. I'm sure he'll find a way to forgive me once he sees how happy she is."

I could see Lucia's relief, the way her shoulders relaxed as she watched Gia interact with me. She wore her emotions right out in the open, and had never been good at hiding them away. It was like this small slice of normalcy, and joy was something she'd been looking forward to. I hoped being out at the track would help her find pockets of joy again. It was thrilling to be here, you couldn't help the buzzing and exhilaration of it all get to you.

For a few minutes, it was just us: Gia, who was now chattering excitedly about all the things she'd seen, Lucia, who seemed to be soaking in the moment, and me, enjoying the rare opportunity to connect with the people I cared about in my space, in my world.

Life on the circuit could be a whirlwind of adrenaline and intensity. The summers had been a needed break, calming and so removed from high-paced life. As I watched Lucia and Gia together, it struck me just how important it was to hold onto these simple, genuine connections, no matter how fast the world might spin around us.

"Excuse me, why am I seeing *my* family in the enemy's colors?" Matteo's booming voice broke through the Belen garage. He was dressed and ready for practice, as I was. His red racing suit looked so out of place in the Belen's trademarked electric blue and pink.

"Zio!" Gia screamed, turning and running to Matteo. His faked annoyance quickly dropped, replaced with a wide smile.

"*Principessa!*" Matteo said, bending down and holding out his arms for Gia. She quickly threw herself at him, a blur of blonde curls and *my* racing colors.

"What is this?" Matteo asked, pointing at her sweatshirt.

"Ow Wex," she said, a stern look on her little features. I

couldn't keep the smirk from my face when Matteo's eyes met mine. He rolled his eyes.

"That's fine on practice days, but race day?" He focused back on Gianna. "What colors do we wear on race days?"

"Red!" she cheered. He beamed and shot me a glance as if to say, *I win.*

I only crossed my arms in reply, and proceeded to look busy. I was the one winning, with both his sister and niece wearing Belen gear, but whatever made the man feel better, I guess.

"You in the zone yet?" Lucia asked quietly, stepping close to me while Matteo and Gia had their moment and people walked by saying hi.

"I fell asleep on the plane," I grumbled.

"No!" She mock gasped. "Not the pre-race flight routine!"

"Listen, every part of a ritual is important," I replied.

"I think missing one more review of races you have one hundred percent already watched back is okay, Alexander." She smirked at me.

"I might have missed something."

"No, you drove a perfect race, the team choosing to undercut was not on you." I tried to keep my heart from jumping out of my damn chest at the comment. I knew she watched the races, for her brother obviously, but it did something to my head to know she was paying attention to my own team and their strategies.

"Better get you on the payroll, because my engineers could learn a thing or two from you."

"About time." She smiled and turned, walking back to her daughter. Gianna had been waving while in Matteo's arms to every single person who passed by. A few crew members from surrounding teams had stopped to say hi. I, however, could feel the glare on my brow. I pulled out my phone, texting Dante.

ALEXANDER:

Are the NDAs signed?

DANTE:

Yes.

ALEXANDER:

And fucking ironclad?

DANTE:

Your possessive prick complex is showing

I put my phone back down on a nearby ledge with a huff. Like Dante was one to speak, the man was like a Doberman all wrapped up into a scary Italian man who had some insane connections. He was also as loyal as they come. And I paid him enough to do whatever I wanted, so there was that.

"Where is Anna?" Lucia asked, looking between Matteo and myself.

I shrugged as Matteo spoke. "Regretting taking me on as another client, probably." His lopsided smile was ever present. A constant on and off the track. Lucia was just as bright, her soft smile in place as she turned her attention to Gia, who was half explaining about how she saw a puppy and wanted to find who had the puppy and also could they get a puppy. I took a mental step back, enjoying the mundaneness of it all. Of my people all together. I didn't have much of a family. My dad was all that was left, but his memory had begun failing years ago—early-onset Alzheimer's. I saw him as much as I could, had him in the best facility money could buy. He had worked his whole life to give me my future, to build karts, spend every weekend on a track, or driving across the damn country for certain races. He worked harder than anyone I know, and I would be forever grateful to him. As for the rest of my family, it was easier to pretend they just didn't even exist. My mother had left long ago, not wanting to be a mother at all. Years passed, I worked my way through lower-level racing up to F1. I found out through one of those trash magazines I saw one day walking in London that she had a new family. I pushed it as far down as it could go, and visited my dad that same day. It was a bad day, no memory of who I was. The good days were far and few between now.

Matteo on the other hand, his family had such an abundance of love and support to give. I even received a text message from his parents today wishing me luck. They had sort of adopted me against my will years and years ago. They would make sure to come say hi to me when visiting Matteo in the Moretti paddock, always inviting me to come stay with them during breaks. But I was too busy going to parties, dating celebrities, and being a grade A asshole. That life felt far behind me now, much to Anna's relief. Probably why she had the bandwidth to take on Matteo as another client— not to mention I had practically begged her to take him on after his last manager had fucked him over.

"We're going to scout out the lounge and find some snacks," Lucia announced, pulling me from my thoughts.

"Mine has better food," I noted.

Matteo shot me a glare. "Fuck off." He laughed as they walked away.

Lucia mouthed, *Bye*, and Gia waved, still in Matteo's arms as they walked away. My stomach growled right on cue. I couldn't wait to get to the Belen Lounge to eat after; their food was genuinely really good. My phone pinged loudly through the quiet garage; the crew had dispersed when Lucia and Gia came in, giving me some privacy I was extremely thankful for.

ANNA

10 minutes, meeting at the lounge deck

Right, back to work.

5

LUCIA

$\mathcal{B}$eing on the circuit was like an extreme sport for someone who hadn't traveled in three years. I had really leaned into the homebody lifestyle. Gianna loved the noise and excitement, but I also knew how overstimulating this was for her. Naps would be extremely necessary, and pulling her away from her Zio would be nearly impossible. But that was a problem for later me.

Gianna was happily bouncing in Matteo's arms as he led us to the Moretti team lounge. Apparently today was a quiet day. But everywhere I looked was still busy. Luckily today, no cameras yet. I had my very own ID tag hanging around my neck, making me feel very official. I was jittery and anxious for qualifying and race day; it was the first taste of what life on the circuit would be like. I was thankful for the progression into chaos rather than being attacked headfirst by people and cameras and all the questions. I felt the pang of a headache starting. *I could do this. Everything would be okay.*

"Mama, they have nuggies!" Gianna announced as Matteo held her, pointing out the different food options behind a glass counter.

"Perfect, Bug!" I replied. The chef looked to me with a smile, I ordered the pair of us food as Matteo declined. The boys were on strict diets, when and what they could eat was all managed by a nutrition specialist. Matteo stayed with us for some time while we ate, until being called away for a meeting with some of his engineers.

We finished our meals and left the lounge. I was excited to be in the paddock. When Gia and I watched races from home, she would point out the people in the paddock and their "big headphones." She couldn't wait to wear her own pair during races. I looked for the red Morretti-branded things and followed the path toward the paddock.

"Mama! Puppy!" Gia's hand slipped out of mine, leaving my heart rate to leap out of my chest. She was running full force toward a tall woman with a small dog on a leash.

"Gianna Rose!" I shouted after her, jogging to keep up.

"Hello, darling! This is Monty!" The woman leaned down to Gianna with a smile.

"I'm so sorry! She saw your sweet dog and just made a run for it!" I quickly apologized. "Amore, you have to ask first, okay?" Gianna paused and nodded up to me then looked to the woman.

"Go ahead, It's no problem!" The woman looked over to me with a perfect smile. She was stunning. Long, dark brown hair, perfectly straight, wafted down her back. She was dressed like a royal, and if her beauty wasn't shocking enough, she was actually glowing. The sunlight directly behind her made her seem aglow.

"I'm Nicola!" She stood and held out a hand. "And this is Monty." She nodded toward the golden, shaggy-haired dog Gianna was petting. I stood in small shock for a moment, she was holding out perfectly manicured nails, golden rings adorning her fingers.

"H-hi," I stuttered. "Lucia. This is my daughter, Gianna."

"Are you with Belen?" she asked, nodding to our matching sweatshirts.

"Oh, actually, Moretti!" I said. "I'm Lucia, Matteo DeLuca's sister. Gianna is his niece. He talked us into joining for the rest of the season."

Nicola smiled warmly but eyed the sweatshirts.

"The sweatshirts, are, um—" I stuttered under her gaze.

"Alexander Wright?" she asked, seeing the number fourteen clearly displayed.

"Yeah, I—"

"Matteo and Alexander are inseparable." Nicola laughed. "If you know one, you know both."

I beamed. That was my brother, all right—a pain in the ass but so damn lovable. "Yes!"

"Well, since you're family, I'll actually introduce myself," she said, pushing her hair behind her ear. "Nicola Moretti."

"As in?"

"Mm-hm, so we will be seeing a lot of each other! And thank God because I need another girl here who isn't a wag." She waved a hand. Then paused. "We do have some badass women on the Moretti team, but they're all so damn busy."

"No interest in being a wag then?" I laughed.

"Absolutely not! God forbid it." She placed a hand on her chest dramatically. "But I do want to work in motorsports, so I'm here this year and hopefully from now on. I've been floating around helping whoever needs help!"

"That's great! Have you met Anna?" I asked.

"The most beautiful, intimating person alive? I want to be her when I grow up."

"She's amazing." I sighed. As if we conjured her, Anna appeared in my view and waved, walking over.

"Oh good, you girls have met!"

"Baby G, how are you so big!" she said to Gianna, who was still enamored with Monty the dog. Gia looked up, looking unsure.

I crouched down. "You remember Anna, she helps Zio and Alexander with work." Gianna only nodded and went back to petting the dog.

Anna smiled. "It's a lot of new things."

"Hoping it doesn't overwhelm her too much, but I know it will only get busier."

"True," Anna said and reached out a hand, squeezing my arm gently. "But you are here." Her sincerity took me aback. Her eyes are so genuine. I had assumed Alexander and Matteo had spoken about my decision to join them on the road, but this felt deeper.

"My Olivia is almost eight. She was super intimidated by everything here in the beginning but begs to visit me at work now."

"I didn't even know you had a daughter!" I beamed.

"She lives with her father." There was a hint of sorrow in her eyes. "But she's everything to me."

I smiled, glancing to Gianna.

"Well, I need to meet Alex, but find me later. I'll show you the secret entrance and introduce you to my favorite security guard here. You can completely avoid the main entrance and all the paparazzi," she said, and I let out a relieved sigh. *Thank God*.

"Perfect," I replied.

Anna left us and Nicola walked with us into the Moretti paddock just in time for practice to get started.

The racing was loud and exciting. We got to watch as Matteo got into his car. Gia got to wear the big headphones and we watched the screens from the garage as all the cars zipped around the track during free practice. Moretti was looking really strong this year, and Matteo just signed on for another two years. Despite being in the Moretti garage, I couldn't help but keep an eye on the familiar blue and pink car with a *14* painted on it for the rest of the day.

By the end, Nicola had cemented herself as my new best friend, which she had announced after practice, linking arms with me and showing me some of her favorite quiet spaces around the club and lounges in case Gia or I needed a break at any time. Nicola and I clicked right away; it was like we had known each other for years.

Making friends as an adult felt like this huge, impossible task. I was lucky to have such a supportive family, a semi-intrusive, albeit loving brother, and his very attractive best friend who had this unmatched ability to make me smile. We were a hodgepodge, mismatched bunch. While I loved my family and the boys, it was a breath of fresh air to have a girl friend to talk to.

"All right, give me your roses and thorns," Nicola asked while we walked around, letting Gianna walk Monty in the most chaotic way.

"My what?" I asked.

"Roses and thorns, the good and bad of the day."

"Oh," I said, slightly stunned, and racked my head for them. "Well, a rose is being able to do this. I can work remotely, I just need my phone to do socials and marketing for my parents' vineyard. That's a huge privilege. Today was super exciting, but a thorn is that I am a little overwhelmed. I think once I get the hang of the schedule, it'll feel less overwhelming, and maybe even start to feel like more of an escape. Another rose is how excited Gianna is about this whole trip."

"And meeting me." Nicola smirked.

"And obviously meeting you. What are yours for the day?"

"Rose, I just bought these boots and they're so comfortable. I made *two* new girl besties." She looked at Gianna with a smile as she laughed and Monty licked her face. "Honestly, no thorns today, today's been really good."

"No thorns, wow." I sighed. When was a day that had no thorns?

"You'll have them too." She nudged my shoulder and looped our arms together. We had trauma dumped already over coffee earlier, just full force jumped into this friendship. She knew my baggage, and I knew about her on-and-off again relationship with a very problematic man. She added her phone number into my phone as *your F1 Baddie (Nicola)*. I loved her already.

The day was chaotic and new, but something about that felt

endlessly exciting. So in contrast to my life at home. I was so nervous about it all, but meeting so many nice people today and knowing I had the boys and now a new friend in my corner gave me some fortitude to take on tomorrow.

By the time we made it back to the hotel, Gia was asleep in my arms, didn't even stir as I set her down in her crib. Our bags were strewn among the large suite. I took a much-needed long shower, feeling myself reset, put on my comfiest oversized sweater and leggings, and curled up in bed with a book.

I woke up to my alarm, an instrumental version of "Mirrorball" by Taylor Swift. Gianna stirred but stayed asleep. She was a good sleeper—honestly would happily stay home and chill all day if we needed to. So I got ready while she slept in. I looked at myself in the mirror. My hair was so long now, the blonde highlights I had done before leaving home were fresh and bright. I looked like myself again, like the *before* me. My cheeks had filled out, and I no longer had hallowed out, dark circles under my eyes. My eyes seemed brighter, my skin more olive from being in the sun over the summer. Freckles kissed my cheeks, making me not want to cover them with makeup. I had painstakingly picked outfits for the track. I loved clothes. Back when I had my own place, I had taken over the closet in my own room and the guest room. Slipping on a long-sleeved, brown, knit dress and boots, I reapplied my lip gloss and was about to get Gia up when a light knock was at the door.

Our room was a huge suite, an attached living room to the bedroom with a table and couches. This hotel was stunning. It was rich and luxurious, paintings hung in the hallways with these ornate golden frames. I wanted to remember to look at all of them before we left for the next race. I walked into the attached room, gently closing the bedroom door behind me after I glanced at my daughter, unfazed by the noise, and smiled to myself. I opened the door to our room to reveal a man with a tray of food.

"Miss DeLuca." He nodded. "Your room service."

"Oh!" I said, taken aback. "I'm sorry, I did not order anything!"

"It was ordered last night by a Mr. Wright to be delivered at seven a.m. sharp to room 489 for a Miss DeLuca." The man's thick accent slowed the words down as I let the information sink in. *Alexander had ordered us breakfast.*

"O-okay," I said, holding out my hands for the tray.

The man shook his head. "Allow me, Miss."

I moved out of the way, and he walked into the suite, setting up the food on the table and placing out the plates. My mouth watered at the array of breakfast foods. Steaming pancakes, waffles, plain eggs, and an omelet. Coffee and tea options, and a juice for Gia. He really did think of everything.

"Thank you so much," I said to the butler as he left.

"Mama," a groggy Gianna called from the other room. I peered in through the cracked door and dark room, only the dim light of the bathroom giving me some light onto my daughter.

"Hey, Bug, guess what we have?" I said, walking over and picking her up. She yawned and rubbed her half-awake eyes.

"What?" she asked.

"Breakfast pancakes!" I cheered. She wiggles out of my arms and onto the ground, dragging her bunny plushie with her, pink unicorn pajamas blurring into the other room in one blink.

"This is amazing," she announced loudly. I followed after her to find her already sitting in front of the seat with the pancakes, looking at me expectantly. I giggled at her, all bright eyes, blonde curls smashed and going in every direction.

"Go ahead," I said, and she dug in. I poured myself coffee and pulled over the omelet and waffles for myself. Taking out my phone, I snap a photo of her and send it to Alexander with one sentence:

LUCIA

You did good.

By the time we were out the door, Gia and I had perfectly coordinated denim jackets on. Gia was clad in a matching black sweat set to fight off the chill of the day. We were introduced to a driver as we exited. Anna had coordinated a private driver just for us so we could come and go as we pleased, or if Gia needed a break from the chaos. The sun was peeking through the clouds, the chill in the air making my nerves skitter and stir. I hoped there would be no rain for qualifying today—for both my brother and Alexander's sakes. Rain always made races tricky, but according to what I overheard yesterday from the race engineers, no rain was forecasted for race day, only today for qualifying. Which promised a chaotic day of racing.

My hand found its way to my necklace, a small butterfly charm Matteo had given me after he won his first race. It was his rookie year, the big paychecks were beginning to roll in and he bought everyone in the family something nice to celebrate. The simple but gorgeous golden butterfly necklace had become somewhat of a talisman for me. I found myself sliding it through my fingers to combat any stints of anxiety that would hit me. Below it was my heart locket, a cursive *G* on the front for the one who had my heart. My mini sunshine girl, my Gianna Rose.

Once we arrived at the gates, Gia was bursting with excitement to see her Zio Matteo and Alexander. The security at the front gate smiled widely and waved hello to us as we scanned our badges into the paddock. Upon crossing said barrier, the excitement of the day began to unfold. Anna found us rather quickly, and explained how the day would go, what time Q1 would begin, and how it would progress to the final formation for the day of racing. The drivers were doing some promotional things for the morning, so we made our way to the Moretti lounge. Nicola appeared as we walked through the door, basically jumping up and down, a shit-eating grin plastered on her face.

"I have a surprise!" she sang and ran up to Gia with a big smile. "Hi, cutie girl!" She crouched down and held her arms open. Gia giggled and ran into them, then immediately after gave Monty her attention, who wagged his little tail in response.

"Okay, so follow me." She waved her arms all big over herself, making Gia giggle again and run up to her, tugging on her arm. Nicola paused to look down at my daughter, who was holding out her hand, silently asking to hold Nicola's. Nicola looked back at me, her eyes slightly bewildered and excited. I gave her a reassuring smile. Nicola didn't have much experience with children, but it did not stop her from making Gia feel loved and included. Gia on the other hand was quick to love anyone who gave her attention. She was a lovebug. I picked up my pace, falling into step with the two of them.

"I think she likes me!" Nicola whispered to me.

"She totally likes you. So, does Monty go with you everywhere?" I ask.

"Basically. He's actually my dad's. My mom thought it would be a good idea for him to have an animal as he slows down from the day-to-day operations, but I am kinda obsessed with Monty, so when we started the season, I asked if he could hang with me too. Other times, he's with my dad. Monty is very, very spoiled." She scratched his ears, earning an adorable little eyes-closed snuggle from the dog.

"I think he was meant for track life," I said, reaching out and petting him, too, as Nicola held him in her arms. She had a Moretti-branded dog leash for him and a crimson red collar around his neck. He was the cutest thing to ever exist.

We walked past a sea of red: crew members, team members, all donned Moretti red. Nicola pushed open double doors to reveal a small room, a couch, a table and chairs, and to my great surprise, a corner of toddler toys. A princess tent with sparkles and a wand leaning against it. Gia stood mouth agape for one whole second before letting out a screech and sprinting into the princess tent. I stared in awe, watching her, then looking to Nicola.

"You did this?" I asked, not knowing how I got so lucky to meet this woman.

"I had a little help, and did some recon with two certain boys to make sure Gia would love it." She shrugged and sent me a smile.

I shook my head, beaming a smile that could not be contained.

"I figured you both might need a place to decompress during the weekends, so I simply used my power to secure a room for you at every lounge set up for the rest of the year. Nepotism really works for me."

I let out a laugh. "Really glad you forced your friendship on me, this is going to work out."

"Damn right," she replied before grimacing. "I mean, darn." I waved a dismissive hand and we sat down on the large couch, which had cozy blankets and very cute throw pillows. Yup, this was all Nicola, and not the work of a single man. I loved it.

"I can't believe you did this in a day."

"I've got people." She smirked, then her expression softened as she looked to Gianna, who was already playing with the toys. "Races can be long, so if you want me to hang with Gia in here for any time at all, I am happy to!"

"Oh my god, no, that's too much!" I insisted.

"It's actually doing me a favor, I would love to chill with G and Monty in a quiet room from time to time. Plus, I have, like, every princess movie at my disposal."

"You're about to be her favorite person ever." A sigh made it out before I could continue. This was so nice, so thoughtful. It was honestly a little jarring to have someone find a quiet space. Life at home was very different from here and on the road. I was used to the silence on the vineyards, long walks through the hills with Gia, playing in the lake or the grassy meadows, or sitting on the porch with a cup of tea. But I wanted this, wanted the change of pace and the new, exciting adventure. I knew that. Nicola, thinking I might still want a quiet place among the fast-paced chaos of the circuit, cut my heart right open...in the best way.

"This is..." I paused, turning to my new friend. "Thank you." I hoped the sincerity was there because that was about all the words I could muster at the moment.

"It's half for me too. Dealing with a male-dominated industry all day makes me want to scream. We need more women in motorsports." Nicola shrugged and walked over to Gia, leaving me to my thoughts. I walked to the tinted windows, thankful for the privacy, and looked out to the main walk that had grown twice as busy in the time we had been in the lounge area. A knock rang through the room, then a familiar brunette poked her head into the room. Anna.

"The boys are back in the pit if you want to say hi before everything begins!" she announced. Gia jumped up immediately, abandoning her new toys.

"Zio!" she cheered her answer. We waved goodbye to Nicola, who needed to go back to work, and followed Anna to the Moretti pit. Gia walked next to me, hand in hand, her excitement was evident by her big smile as she took in all the big posters and bright red colors. Crew were hustling around us, the buzz of the pit was unlike anything I had experienced. Turns out, yesterday *had* been the quiet day.

"So this is the pit, where all the exciting things happen. The car is getting ready here." She pointed, and Gianna's eyes got even bigger seeing the car up close. Her bedroom was lined with little model Formula One cars, both Belen Racing and Moretti ones.

"Mama, it's so shiny." She beamed, her little hands were clenched at her sides. I had talked to her about how important it was to not touch anything while in the pit. Gianna had nodded seriously and answered with a stern, *Otay.*

"Does it look like the one in your room?" I asked her. She

shook her head and walked around the back end of the car, pointing her little hand, red sparkly nails shining.

"That's different," she said. I looked at it, noticing the new design on the back wing, and nodded. Gia had an attention to detail that constantly shocked me.

"Principessa!" a familiar voice boomed through the pit. My brother walked across the space, clad in his bright red racing suit.

"Zio!" she squealed as he picked her up and spun her around. "You are so red!" she noted after they spun around and he held her on his hip. Her little hands poked at his uniform.

"Matches your nails perfectly." He smiled, poking at her fingers. She giggled. Matteo turned to me. "No pink and blue today?"

"She makes the rules, and it was black and red today." I pointed at my outfit, a little Moretti Racing embroidered patch on Gia's and my denim jackets.

"They're perfect," he whispered to Gia, who kept giggling. I looked around the paddock, at the screens in the back, where people wore large headsets and looked at screens, analyzing whatever was on them.

"Oh, that reminds me, I got you both your own personalized noise-canceling headphones to wear during races, they'll be out for you at every race. The small ones with sparkles are G's. Obviously."

"Thank you, that is so thoughtful of you," I answered.

"Thank you, Zio," Gianna mimicked. Matteo smiled proudly and began introducing Gianna to everyone. I tried not to get emotional at the sight. "This is my niece, Gianna!" he repeated as they walked around the whole room. He pointed at screens and described what people's jobs were. The whole crew seemed to light up as she came around, showing her what they did and what things meant. Gianna was in absolute heaven, and so was Matteo.

"They're adorable," Anna commented as she reappeared. She

held out the headphones to me; they were Moretti red with little butterflies on them and Gianna's name in black bubble letters.

"He seriously is the best uncle." I took the headphones from her and pulled out my phone to snap a picture of the two of them.

We spent as much time with Matteo as we could before he needed to get back to work. The pit began to fill with more people, all getting ready for qualifying that started in two hours.

"Did Gia want to say hi to Alexander?" Anna whispered to me once we are in the back rooms, a TV in front of us of the circuit, which will play the live video once qualifying begins. Gianna was given another mini race car from one of the crew members, so she was happily making zoom noises and pushing the car along the floor.

"Probably, but I wanted to give her a little time to decompress before we go back into the loudness," I whispered back.

"You know you can take a moment to decompress for you too..." Anna mentioned, then added a soft, "if *you* need to." Her smile was soft and warm. When first meeting Anna, she was terrifying. After knowing she's a mother, too, something about that alone was so comforting. That I was not alone in that version of life, and that finding myself and trying to be my own person along with being a mother was okay. It was a hard balance, one that I felt endless guilt for at times. But as my own mother had told me, *taking care of yourself and your mental health is what will make you a good mother. A happy mother is a good mother, so go find your happy.*

I smiled remembering the conversation we had had on the porch that day. It felt like so long ago now. Gianna was only slightly over a year old at the time, and I was not doing well. Getting up in the morning was hard; I felt like my entire life had been turned upside down. I didn't have anything for me anymore, and it was chipping away at me slowly. After many months, it was my mother who sat me down and talked with me, told me how she had felt the same way after I was born. How postpartum depression is common and how it was okay to feel all the things I was feeling and to try doing things for myself again. Gianna was my whole world, the biggest little bundle of joy, and despite everything I had been through that gave me her, I would not change it for the world. Because that was my path, that was my choice. It was that morning when we made a list; my mom and I took out an old notepad that had been stuffed into a kitchen drawer and wrote down how to find my spark again. On the top of that list was to do new and exciting things, to say yes to experiences.

When Matteo came home that summer, Alexander had been with him. They both spent the entirety of their break on the DeLuca vineyard instead of flying around the globe and attending lavish parties and skydiving or doing whatever it was the adrenaline-addicted racers did on breaks. It was the summer that my healing began. I was determined to keep going, to keep being more present, to keep fighting for my own happiness, and being the best mother I could be.

A giggle from Gia brought me back to the present.

"Yes," I replied to Anna. "I am trying to be better about that."

She gave me a reassuring arm squeeze. "Me too," she agreed.

6

ALEXANDER

It was two hours before the race started. Raining conditions only made my heart race more, but not in the *I am about to race a car at ridiculously high speeds,* heart-racing way, in that thundering, *I can't hear my own thoughts* way. It was new, and I hated it. I pushed the thoughts down. I had driven in rainy conditions before, that was not new. It just was not ideal. One of my engineers reported to me that the storm was passing through today, and tomorrow there would be bright skies, which only meant more chaos for formation. Tomorrow would be ideal for the Dutch Grand Prix, but a rainy track was a dangerous track. It also meant that formation was a toss-up. Middle-ranking teams could find their way up, crashes could happen, safety cars would surely be abundant.

My thoughts continued to pound, a dull pain behind my eyes forming. I pushed my hands into my eyes, trying to rid myself of the thousand thoughts running through my brain. The music in my headphones was doing nothing at this point. Then came a tap on my shoulder. I turned, and my mind silenced.

"Hey, stranger." Lucia smiled up at me. My body seemed to let out a full sigh, muscles relaxing as I pulled my headphones from my ears.

"Alex!" A little blur of curly blonde was bouncing next to Lucia.

"Hey, kiddo." I smiled and reached for her. Gianna threw herself into me, I caught her easily, and she squeezed her arms around my neck.

"Mama said to say good luck today," she whispered in my ear.

"Thanks, G!" I replied and snuck a glance over to Lucia.

"You see Matteo already?" I asked.

She nodded, her smirk sharp and teasing as her green eyes gleamed. "Yeah, he said he hopes your tire management is finally as good as you keep bragging it is."

I raised an eyebrow, leaning a little closer. "My tire management? Please, he almost burned through his practice ones and slipped right off the track."

She shrugged, the corner of her mouth twitching like she was holding back a bigger smile. "Maybe I'm just trying to see if the five-time champion knows how to handle a little pressure."

I chuckled, crossing my arms as I tilted my head at her. "Bold move, throwing down a challenge. Should I be flattered or worried?"

"Depends," she said, brushing a strand of hair behind her ear and pretending to study me. "Are you better at handling tires or trash talk?"

I grinned, leaning just enough to close the space between us. "I guess you'll have to stick around and find out."

Her cheeks flushed, but she didn't back down, rolling her eyes instead. "We'll see, Wright."

"I got a new sports car!" Gia interrupted and reached out her hand.

Lucia laughed. "Oh, you'll love this one." She reached into her bag, pulling out a small Formula One model car, bright red in color. I tried not to groan out loud, I really did.

"You really brought that into my pit, on qualifying?" I kept my voice light for G, but covered the car with my hand and pushed it back into her bag, hoping no one in the pit saw it. Sure, everyone knew Matteo was my mate, but the boys here were a superstitious bunch. Bringing a rival's colors into our sacred space, not great. I was letting the whole wearing Moretti gear slide, but no cars—even tiny toy model versions. Not here.

"I like the pink one better," Gia said, making my ego expand tenfold.

That's right. As she should.

"I'll get you an even better one, okay, G?" I said to her. Gianna cheered, her little arms swinging in the air.

"She has too many already." Lucia groaned.

"Not *with* her, and now she only has the traitor's colors."

"What's a traitor?" Gianna asked.

"Nothing, Alexander is being mean," Lucia assured her.

"Don't be mean, Mama says that's not allowed." Gia looked at me, little eyebrows scrunched together.

"I apologize." I nod sincerely and try not to let the smile break through. From the corner of my eyes I could see Lucia doing the same. *Fucking rude.*

Simon walked over, all smiles. "Wright, this your girlfriend?" he asked. My heart lurched and Lucia's eyes widened dramatically.

"No-no!" She smiled. "Just friends. I am Matteo's sister, Lucia." She held out her free hand to shake his. Simon was a blunt man. He asked things straight up, said things how he saw them, which made him a strong race engineer, and I was lucky to have him. But I never had people in the pit *for me.*

"Just a friend, mate." I reinforced, hoping to make Lucia's alarmed look recede. Simon only nodded, shook her hand, and walked away. Lucia looked to me, our eyes locking before we both burst out laughing at the interaction.

"Gosh, is everyone going to think that? Do you bring girlfriends around at races?" she asked, a slight blush on her cheeks.

I shook my head. "Bloody hell, no," I said. "Never brought anyone in here except my dad back when I was a rookie." I missed my dad. Lucia nodded and reached out a hand, placing it gently on my own arm. The small act was comforting and grounding, all the things Lucia exuded. She and Matteo knew all about my dad's diagnosis and how much worse it had become. It was one of the main reasons I slowed down; reality had a way of knocking you back down. I wanted to be more present, spend time with those who mattered. Nothing was guaranteed.

Lucia and Gianna stayed with me until one of my engineers needed me and prep was beginning for qualifying. After they left, I noticed the loud noise filtering back into my surroundings. I guess it had been there the whole time; we were standing in a pit, after all. But those fifteen minutes of quiet was enough to get my brain to reset. It was time to focus.

As I lowered myself into the car, pulling down the steering wheel and clicking it into place, I felt the adrenaline rush I always felt right before a race. My blood was pounding in my ears, but in the best way.

"Checking, one two." Simon's voice crackled alive over the radio.

"Copy, you are clear," I responded.

"All right, mate, we're going with plan A unless there is a crash and a safety car, then we switch to plan B. Rain in thirty."

"Top five, baby," I said, getting myself into position as they rolled out the car from the garage.

"Top five," I heard back over the radio.

We got out early into Q1, trying to outpace the storm as only a trickle of rain was coming down at this time. Pulling out of the pit lane, only one thought was rattling around in my brain.

Let's fucking go.

"And that's a P2, Wright," the voice over the radio sounds as I finish my last lap in the last leg of qualifying. I knew it would be a fight, but the strategy was top fucking tier today. We managed to stay out of the extreme rain. Two crashes from the lower teams gave us an advantage and knocked me up a few places. It really was all about timing, and on the last lap I had pushed with everything I had, going with barely any time left on the timer. I slowed my car and pulled in behind the second place marker. A familiar white car pulled up next to me, taking the spot behind the first-place marker, Theo Bauer. Kaze Energy Racing team was a formidable opponent. It was Belen and Kaze, neck and neck for the Constructors' and the Drivers' Championships. But then, pulling up in third was a bright red car, and as soon as the helmet came off, a beaming Matteo threw his fist into the air, his team cheering. I took off my own gear and made my way to him.

"Fuck yeah!" I shouted over the crowd as we hugged. "About damn time you joined me up here."

"Godamn luck was what it was." Matteo shook his head, his smile firmly in place as we pulled away from each other. I patted his back as we went through our routine of cooldown and semantics. Anna appeared by my side, giving me the rundown of the rest of the day, and I tried to hide the grimace on my face. I had been hoping to spend some time with Matteo and Lucia today after qualifying, but it seemed like there wouldn't be time for that. Anna, ever aware, stopped her list mid-sentence.

"You know what"—she waved a hand and put her phone away—"one interview, the same one Matteo is doing, then I'll clear the rest. Enjoy the day." She smiled and walked away before I could even respond with a fake *No, it's okay.*

I swear that woman could read minds. I let out a sigh of relief, as if it had been balled up in my throat. And right as I did, I saw Lucia across the way, Gia was throwing herself into Matteo's arms. A pang of something hit me. I never had that tight-knit family like the DeLucas did. I admired it truly, hoped one day to even have my own. God, if I could hear myself three years ago. Settling down? I would have laughed at myself. Those thoughts had never crossed my mind before seeing how the DeLucas were. How much I felt like I missed out on. The gaping empty hole in my chest faltered as I looked up, familiar green eyes colliding with mine, and a soft smile forming over her expression as our eyes met.

Good Job, she mouthed at me. I put my hand to my heart to say thank you, and I felt a warmness inside me slowly creep over and dull out the emptiness. Having someone here who wasn't being paid to care about where I placed or how I was racing.

Fuck, that was nice.

It only took another second for Gianna to see me, her eyes growing to giant orbs before her mouth opened and a screech cut through the noise of the track.

"Alex!" Each letter was drawn out, and she wiggled out of her uncle's arms and took off toward me. It was not a clear path, and G was tiny, but it was like she parted the damn sea. People smiled at her, moving out of the way as her little legs carried her across the track and she launched herself into my arms right as I crouched down to meet her.

"I knew you'd beat Zio," she whispered to me with an evil smile. I shook my head and laughed, squeezing her. In the chaos I did not notice who was around us. While Matteo and Lucia had been tucked in the corner, keeping Lucia and Gia slightly out of sight from the photographers, we were now in the middle of it all. I suddenly felt hyperaware. There were so many people around me as I looked around, all eyes on us, all cameras pointed at us. That same pressure reappeared, squeezing around my heart, gripping like a vice. I couldn't even see Lucia through the crowd that had assembled. But I knew she didn't want Gianna surrounded by photographers; it was overwhelming as an adult, I couldn't imagine for a child.

I pulled Gia closer, shielding her face. It all happened so fast, cameras and people surrounding us, lenses being pushed way too close to Gia's face. *Fuck this.*

"Okay, back up, back the bloody hell up," I shouted at them as they closed in on me. Some looked slightly bewildered at my harsh tone, the others ignored me and pressed closer. Lenses of cameras felt like they were everywhere, and while I didn't care about that on the track, knowing that it could affect Gia made bile rise in my throat and my heart pick up and thunder in my chest.

"She is a child, back the fuck up." I seethed. The photographers paused and Anna pushed her way through the crowd, her hair slightly tousled, unlike her usual perfectionist lifestyle. She looked just as flustered as I felt.

"Back up, you do not have permission to publish a single one of those, delete them right now or you will be sued till your last goddamn penny." She commanded the space, and the photographers froze, all looking down and pressing buttons, muttering apologies. I took the moment to see a clear path and get us the fuck out of there. I could hear Anna in the background, demanding each person show her proof they deleted the photos.

"Gianna DeLuca, you can't run away from me like that!" Lucia's voice was thick with worry as she ran up to us. We were tucked away in the Moretti area now.

"I'm sorry, Mama, I wanted to see Alex," she said, her bottom lip quivering, tears welling. Lucia's eyes softened, her own eyes looking like she could start crying too. I hated it. I wanted to make every worry disappear—pluck them out of this situation and keep them both safe. I shook my head, refocusing on Gia.

"I know, baby, but you can't do that again, okay? It's not safe, there are too many people here. If you want to see Alexander far away, you ask me, and we go together, okay?" Lucia asked her gently, her hand on her daughter's cheek as Gia stayed in my arms.

Gia sniffed, tears escaping her eyes. She turned her head and buried it into my chest with a sniffle.

"I'm sorry!" She cried and my heart just about broke in half.

"It's okay, G. We just want to keep you safe." I soothed her as she buried her face into my shoulder. We stood like that for a moment, the room was quiet, the outside noise muffled. Gia was holding onto me with a fierce grip, Lucia was rubbing circles on her back, her brow creased. It was rare she cried, but her eyes glistening gave her away. I let out a sigh.

"Anna took care of it and had the photos deleted," I whispered to Lucia. She met my eyes and nodded. I reached out my extra arm, motioning for her to come closer. She wiped at her eyes and leaned into me.

"I just don't want her hounded, or scared, if we are going to be around the circuit a lot. I know it's hard and she'll be in photos sometimes and that's fine. But here, inside the paddocks and around the circuit, I thought maybe some separation would be good? I don't know if that even makes sense." I understood. Being in the spotlight was hard, controlling the narrative was near impossible, and all of it was overwhelming. But wanting the place we worked in to feel safe shouldn't be a hard ask.

I would make sure it felt safe for her.

The door swung open and Matteo walked through.

"Luce, I am so sorry. We had them all sign NDAs days ago, they knew better." Lucia only nodded. Matteo came over to us, and his gaze reached Gia, who was still hiding her face, smooshed against my race suit.

"G, you okay?" Matteo asked, the worry thick in his voice. Matteo was a fierce protector of his niece. He had once said he would burn down the world for her. We were drunk, but honestly, I believed him, because, as protective as I felt over her, I knew Matteo's was tenfold.

"I didn't mean to run away," Gianna mumbled as she brought her head away from hiding. Her eyes were rimmed red and I wanted to fucking kill those asshole photographers. Gia reached out for her uncle, who took her from me. I took the moment to step away from them, letting Lucia and Matteo talk. I pulled out my phone, texting Dante.

ALEXANDER

We were surrounded by paps, me with G. Get rid of them.

DANTE

On it

ALEXANDER

Don't let it happen again on circuit.

DANTE

Understood.

My fingers buzzed with the need to fix it. I knew Dante would make sure it never happened again on circuit, but we would need to be careful when we went out too. Matteo could fly under the radar as a newer driver. But the paps followed me everywhere. Maybe I should give them their space, they didn't need me there anyway. I was a magnet for the paparazzi, even since I had cooled down on the partying. Anna had fixed it all, shielded me from the pissed-off managers and made my PR image sparkly clean. But the paparazzi were always trying to catch me in the act of something they could spin into drama.

Alexander on a date with a model!
Alexander Wright dating a new actress?
Is she knocked up?
New model, new week!

They were just friends, but the magazines and tabloids didn't care. Needed to sell a story. And I would not involve Lucia or Gia in that. The press could be vile, I didn't want them to experience that.

"It's taken care of," Anna said with a big sigh, breaking me out of my thoughts. The door slammed shut behind her. She sunk into the chair, looking defeated. I genuinely don't think I had ever seen her like that. It made me pause.

"Are you okay?" I asked. Lucia and Matteo all looked at Anna. Lucia scurried over to her, sitting next to her and reaching out a hand. Anna nodded to me and then talked with Lucia in quieter voices. Lucia's arm wrapped around Anna, making me admire how easily Lucia loved and took care of people, despite her past, despite everything that had happened, she loved so fully. Matteo walked to me with Gia still in his arms.

"I don't think I have ever seen her look..." He paused. "Defeated?" He glanced back to her, then to me again.

"What the fuck is going on?" I shook my head, running a palm over my face. Today was a fucking day. Suddenly the exhaustion seemed to hit me like a battering ram. My body felt heavy, my eyes felt sore, and was that a headache starting? Fuck, I needed to get it together.

"We were going to go out tonight, but I think we might just chill at the hotel," Matteo said, bouncing Gia up and down. "Wanna build forts?" he asked. Gia beamed.

"Yes, yes, yes!" she chanted.

7

LUCIA

When the day started, I did not expect it to end with rearranging the hotel suite's living room furniture and being inside a blanket fort. But here we were. Gia was knocked out in a bundle of blankets and pillows. A princess movie was on the TV, which we had built the fort around, because obviously. Alex had ordered pizza delivery right to the room, and boxes were strewn on the floor. Matteo had brought the wine. Nicola and Anna stopped by for a bit before going out together. Anna received some bad news today about her family. I didn't know much of the details but she needed a friend, and I was there. From what I gathered, she had been expected to take over or be a part of the family business, but she carved her own way into the world through motorsports, much to her family's dismay.

With everyone together, we had giggled and laughed, the boys recounting our summer on the vineyards to the group. How we would sneak out wine bottles from the fancy vintages and bring them to the lake, jumping into the freezing water under the moon. I missed home, I really did. But this was new and exciting and I was trying to be brave and do hard things. But going outside your comfort zone and in a new country with your toddler was fucking hard. Gianna running out of sight today had shaken me. It was so unlike her, she just slipped away so fast, then weaved her way to Alexander, and I felt like my heart had left my body. On top of that, something was going on with Anna. She was off tonight, and when I pulled her aside to ask her, she only told me it was a family complication. I sent a text out to Nicola telling her what happened with Gia and how Anna seemed disheveled. Nicola promised to do some recon and check in with Anna tonight, making my heart relax a little. Them stopping by before going out was a welcome surprise. I was new here but I already felt so attached to this little group we had made together. Anna and Nicola were like little guardian angels for Gianna, and if something was wrong, I wanted to help fix it.

"All right, I'm gonna go crash," Matteo announced. "Gotta beat this idiot tomorrow." He poked at Alexander, who smirked in reply.

"Good luck with that, mate, you're the one who ate the pizza and got wine drunk before a race."

"You brought the pizza, how was I not supposed to eat it!" Matteo whined. "I take full responsibility for the wine. Great idea." I laughed at them.

"The pizza and wine were great, thank you for tonight," I said, pulling the blankets around Gianna.

"My steak dinner was also great." Alexander smirked.

"Pizza was better." Matteo shrugged and pulled himself up. "Want me to put her to bed?" he said, nodding at my sleeping daughter.

"It's okay, I'll clean up first. Go to sleep though, you both need to rest before tomorrow, and your managers would kill me if they knew you were up late and ate banned food."

"I've done nothing wrong." Alexander threw his hands up. "My bedtime is eleven."

"Leo threatened me with my life last time I stayed out past

ten," Matteo grumbled, mentioning his own race engineer, and waved goodbye before leaving.

"I'll help clean up," Alexander said quietly, getting up slowly to not wake up Gianna.

"Thank you." I smiled. Alexander was always this person, extremely thoughtful with his actions. It was crazy to think of him before I knew him—the playboy, the serial dater. I mean, that's what the tabloids said, but the Alexander I knew was reading a book on the porch of my family's home in Italy. Sketching on any scrap of paper he could find and helping my mom do the dishes even though Matteo and Dad would be drinking and playing darts in the backyard.

We cleaned in silence. The stars were out tonight, the moon was full. We had turned off all the lights, letting only the television light our fort. Gia was still fast asleep as we cleaned. Once that girl went to sleep for the night, she was out. It was kind of amazing. I wish I had that superpower. I knew I would lie awake for at least an hour before I finally fell asleep. I had been that way since I had Gia—a restless mind at night, thinking about what I needed to do the next day, what to prepare, what activities we might do, and whether I needed to go into the city for new shoes for Gia who was growing like a weed.

"I think tomorrow it might be best if I stay on my own," Alexander said, breaking the silence.

"What do you mean?" I asked, trying to keep the shock off my face. Did he not want us around the Belen garage?

"I just—" He ran a palm over his neck. "The paparazzi have this fascination with trying to get me caught in drama." His eyes were sad, he looked overwhelmed if I had to pin it. It made my own heart crack and shoulders deflate. "I don't want to bring you into it, especially not Gia. I know you don't want her face in the media and you want to protect her. And I get it, I want the same. But I'm not a good person to be around."

I shook my head. "Alexander, no," I whispered. He was not

putting all the burden of today on his own shoulders. "You are family. You have the two of us cheering you on all race long, and if you aren't around it will break that girl's heart. She loves you so much," I said, reaching out my hand and resting it on his arm. "Don't do that." I shook my head. "Don't blame yourself for today. You can't control other people, only yourself, and you are the one who told them to stop and removed Gia from the environment. I don't think I even took a moment to thank you for"—I took a breath—"so thank you. For protecting her like she's family." An expression passed his face I couldn't place, but it was quickly replaced with his smile.

"Anytime." He shrugged, like it was no big deal. He busied himself with grabbing all the trash, and soon the room was clean from our night. I began pulling the blankets down, before reaching down and getting Gia. She snuggled closer to me, making my heart burst. I loved this kid.

"Night," Alexander whispered to us. I walked him out, holding onto Gia.

"See you tomorrow?" I whispered back, hopeful.

"Are you sure?"

"Of course. Plus, Anna threatened them within an inch of their life, she promised we would be good inside the circuit."

"My team is on it too," he said and I paused.

"Like who?" I asked hesitantly.

"Dante." I paused again, *oh*. He was *serious* serious. Dante scared the crap out of me. I still didn't know how he had connections to everything—I mean, I had an idea, but I was not about to ask questions. Scary-looking Italian man who could make anything happen and on Alexander's payroll? I don't need to know.

"Sleep tight." A tired smile formed as he looked down at Gianna, then looked up to me. "Night."

"Night."

Nothing could have prepared me for race day as a VIP. The lanyard was right there around my neck. I had changed my outfit like forty times before settling on this one. A black dress, tights, boots, and a leather jacket. It was safe, sure, but I had no idea what to expect, how dressed up the guests were.

I was terrified.

It was halfway through the race. I was on the edge of my seat. Gia was coloring while wearing her custom Moretti noise-canceling headphones. The race was a long time for her to pay attention. At home when we watched them from the comfort of our couch with a hundred blankets surrounding us, she would stay in the room but play with her toys and ask how Zio was doing every ten minutes.

"Who is this little one!" A kindly woman approached us. I peered up at her, trying to place the face.

"This is Gianna." She returned my smile in kind and held out her hand to me.

"I am Carlos's mother, Maria." While I had yet to meet the other Moretti driver, I had heard a lot about Carlos Torres. Matteo had mentioned they got on but were not close friends, that many were not actually close with their teammates, regardless of how the PR made them seem. In truth, Carlos was Matteo's biggest competitor.

Maria's dark hair curled under into a bob, pearl earrings adorned her ears, and on the outreached hand, an impressive diamond was on display, catching on the lights of the garage.

"Lucia, Matteo's sister."

"Have you been to a race before?" she asked.

"This is the first one down here." I motioned to all that was around us in the garage.

"Oh, how exciting. Do you live here?"

"No, but Gia and I are joining Matteo for the rest of the season."

"On the road with a little one, what an undertaking!" Her eyes widened but settled back into a pleasant smile. "My Carlos was the same. His late father was a driver as well, so he begged to go to every race he could."

"Oh wow!" I hadn't really read up on anyone, a fact that was becoming quite apparent; maybe I should familiarize myself with the drivers. A legacy and a rookie for the Moretti team. I knew my brother had been lucky. He worked his way up, racing in lower levels and dedicating his whole life to motorsport.

"Matteo is doing really well." Maria smiled warmly. I couldn't help but fill with pride. Moretti had taken a chance on Matteo as a rookie. He had done well in his first year and he was scoring high points for himself in both the Drivers' and Constructors' Championships.

The race continued, and I watched on the small screens for the live feed. Alexander was holding second and Matteo had dropped to fifth, fighting for fourth place with another team. It was invigorating to watch live, the sounds and bustle of the garage while the race was going. I felt a nudge before I realized Nicola appeared next to us.

Wanna escape? she mouthed. I nodded quickly. I could tell Gia could use a break from the constant noise, and honestly, I could too. She waved us to follow her. Once in our room, I let out an audible sigh of relief.

"It's so loud down there," I said, wide-eyed and overstimulated.

"Yep!" she said, popping the *P*. "You will get used to it, but the first day can be overwhelming for sure. I wanted to cry at the end of my first day."

"I'm sure Gia will have a meltdown, this is a lot."

"Okay, so don't be mad…" Nicola starts.

"What?" I ask, my mind blank at what it could even be.

"I talked to my dad."

"About?"

"You…" she said, looking stressed.

My heartbeat quickened. "About what?" I shouted, slightly shocked.

"Well, that to make his star driver happy, means his sister and niece are here the entire rest of the season, which means you need help, and I can help 'cause I am just floating around anyway. I also talked with Anna and we're going to switch off so that you can enjoy yourself too!"

"Nicola…" I said, tears pricking my eyes. "That is seriously so kind." I pull her into a hug. She's stiff and awkward and pats my back in response, and I can't help but laugh inwardly. Nicola was so aware of her surroundings and others' emotions, so empathetic, but she seemed to stray away from anyone showing her love back. I understood it; I was of a similar strain, accepting love in return felt overwhelming, like I could give it in endless waves, but accepting it felt like too much, like I didn't want to be a burden.

"We take care of our own here, and you are a part of the Moretti family, whether you expected it or not." She nudged me with her shoulder. "So get used to it." I could feel the emotions rattling around in front of me. Overwhelmed at the idea of anyone thinking about what I could need, I was so used to taking care of myself. I had felt so alone for years. While my parents had been wonderful the last three years, being a single mother in the countryside could be lonely. More often than not I just wanted to be home with Gianna. We loved our routine, our slow mornings, playing in the pastures and by the lake when the weather was warm.

"You made it so cozy in here too. It's perfect." Gia had pulled a pink fuzzy blanket onto the ground with her, huddled under the huge blanket, and waved a wand around Monty's head, who was sleeping in a fluffy dog bed on the ground. It made her feel safe, probably reminded her of home. Our favorite spot was in the living room on the overly large sofa my mom had imported from who knows where, because coziness was a requirement in the DeLuca family.

We sat on the couch, watching the middle of the race from our quiet room. The entire race I was clutching the blanket, on the edge of my seat, but the last half was something else. Matteo had secured fourth place, too far from the third place driver to catch up, and Alexander was neck and neck with Carlos for first.

It was five laps to go when Anna appeared, three cups in her hand. Hot cocoa for me and Gia, coffee for Nicola. We walked out to the garage, sitting with the other crew members. Everyone was cheering for Carlos, but I was biting at my nails, hoping for a pink and blue finish instead of a red one.

"Is Alex going to win?" Gia asked me, she was watching the screen, her attention more focused than it had been most of the race. "That's his car!" She pointed to the electric blue striped car on the screen. Less than a second in front of him was a red one.

"Let's go red!" someone shouted, and I swear Gianna glared.

"I hope Alex wins," she said, crossing her little arms over her chest. I smiled at her and leaned in.

"Me too," I whispered. On the third to last lap, Alexander went ahead of Carlos at the apex, the shiny black car shooting forward, electric blue blurring across the screen. It was the last moment for him to overtake, now all Alexander needed to do was hold the position.

The room erupted in frustrated groans, but my heart lurched with excitement. Alexander was first. The next two laps passed quickly, and soon it was his car that crossed the finish line. The room was clapping for the second place podium finish of Carlos, and Matteo scoring good points in fourth. I was cheering alongside, but my eyes glued to the screen where the cameras zoomed in on Alex. His fist was in the sky, pumping into the air, he touched his heart then pointed to the sky, and I knew the familiar smile was beaming under his helmet.

8

ALEXANDER

We did it. We fucking did it.

My cooldown lap was a blur, tears were in my eyes. It had been six races since I had stood on the top step at the podium. After some changes to the car, FIA penalties, and growing pains, the car had been giving me hell. I had managed to scrap by a third place and second place, a few times not placing at all in the top three. The weight of it all was heavy. I needed the points to secure my next championship, and this win was exactly what we needed today.

"Congrats, mate, a good run, a real good run," my engineer said over the radio.

"Thank you to the team. Good work today! Let's keep 'em coming!" I replied. Pulling behind the first-place marker, I got out of the car and stepped onto the front, raising my hands in the air for a cheer. I could hear my team's loud screams of victory. I closed my eyes to soak it all in. When I opened them, there was a sea of black, blue, and pink. I jumped down, walking over to Carlos and shaking his hand.

"Nice job." He congratulated me.

In third was my own teammate, James, and we ran to each other and collided in a hug.

"Let's fucking go!" he cheered.

The cameras clicked off rapidly around us. They loved our bromance. It was rare to be close to a teammate, since they were, in a sense, your biggest competitor. He had a long way to go, but I was in his corner nonetheless. He would be one of the legends, I felt it in my bones. Plus, the barely twenty-year-old was one of the youngest drivers on the circuit. He was already cementing his status.

After congratulating James, I ran to my team, throwing myself over the barrier and into their arms. The cheers and shouts took over my senses, a few were chanting my name, and I was on cloud fucking nine. Someone came over, pleading with me to get down, to finish my weigh-in before celebrating. But I took the moment to soak it in. I needed this, needed this win. These winning points would get me within arm's reach of Theo Bauer, who was sitting in first for the Drivers' Championship.

Over by weigh-in, Matteo was grinning like an idiot. "Proud of you, mate," he said, knocking me with his shoulder.

"Did you expect anything else?" I shrugged, stepping off the scale.

"Was waiting for you to get your head out of your ass." He laughed. It was a true Matteo laugh, a deep belly laugh. He was like his sister, sunshine incarnate. Lucia filtered into my mind and I couldn't stop myself from looking around, hoping to see a familiar blonde and a mini version in her arms. I knew they were out of the way, out of the center of attention, but I still found myself looking forward to seeing Lucia, getting an excuse to have her in my arms. *Fuck, snap out of it, Wright.* The thought sent me into a state of shock as I walked to the cooldown room. I had always enjoyed spending time with the DeLucas. I loved Gia like she was my own family and would do anything for that girl, but the whole wanting to have Lucia in my arms thing? *What the fuck was that.*

My mind was occupied during the post-race interviews. I smiled and answered the questions, PR training was no joke, and we were all threatened with bodily harm from the Belen PR team. Anna had cleaned up my reputation for sure, but it was also a big push from Belen Racing. They were over me getting into messes. I had been with Belen for five years now, won the championship in all five of them. Year one and two were an actual blur. I remembered little of it. Parties and high-end lifestyle, I was the first to admit that the money alone went straight to my head. It was life changing; for the first time in my life, I was in control. I could do what I wanted when I wanted. But it caught up to me fast—the drinking, partying, and the high-adrenaline lifestyle. But when Matteo was brought up as a reserve driver for his rookie year, I accidentally became somewhat of a mentor to him, which helped slow me down. We had known each other in F2 and karting back in the day. Once he was pulled up, he just kind of appeared like a lost puppy and began following me around. It was annoying as hell in the beginning, but Anna had liked him, and while she wouldn't admit it, she definitely had a hand in me unceremoniously becoming his mentor. Mentorship turned to friends, after he invited me to the DeLuca Vineyards, the whole brother-for-life thing kind of cemented itself. I was damn lucky to have him and his incessantly positive attitude. It had been a long time since anyone felt like family, until Matteo came around.

I finished getting my things and went to find the DeLucas.

9

LUCIA

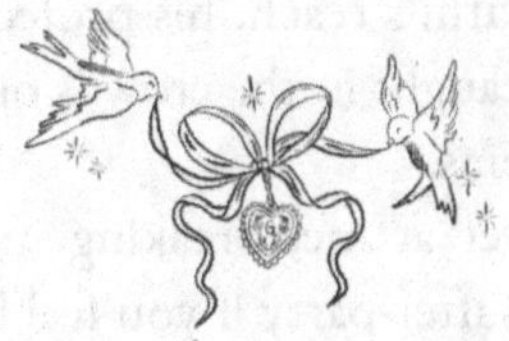

The roar of the engines still echoed in my ears, even though the race was over and the crowd had long since started to thin out. Standing by the barriers with my daughter perched on my hip, I felt the cool wind of the evening sweeping in. Gia was clinging to me, her big eyes wide as they tracked the colorful blur of chaos along the tracks. She might not know much about Formula One yet, but her Uncle Matteo was already her hero, and Alexander was a close second.

Matteo strode toward us, still in his racing suit half folded down, helmet under one arm and a grin breaking across his face when he spotted us. His hair was a mess of loose, chocolate curls, the perfect match to our father's, all espresso eyed and olive skin. Gia's little hands clapped with excitement, and I couldn't help but smile as he lifted her out of my arms, spinning her around in a moment that made the long hours, the travel, and the noise worth it.

"So, what did you think of your first race, G?" he asked, settling her on his hip. She rambled about her day, filled with jittery excitement and joy. Matteo nodded along, the way he always did, like she was speaking the most important words in the world, giving her his undivided attention. I loved that about my brother, how he gave everyone his full attention, made you feel loved and important.

As he did, I glanced around, wondering if Alexander would join us here for the little post-race gathering. Ever since Matteo convinced me to travel with them, Alexander had seemed...around. Hovering just within arm's reach, his protective stance made sure Gia and I were never caught in the crowds or left vulnerable to the endless flashes of cameras.

Matteo looked over at me, breaking me from my thoughts. "You know, there's an after-party if you feel like mingling," he said with a wink. "I talked with Anna and she can take Gia tonight." He lowered his voice. "And I wanted to surprise Alex and take him out after his big win. This one was really important to him."

I bit back a smile, he knew he would get me with that. One of my favorite traits about my brother was how intentional he was with his time. I wasn't sure why this was a big race for Alex, or if there was more going on behind the scenes, like pressure from the team. Matteo had mentioned how his points holding him in first for the Drivers' Championship were affected by the last few races, that Alex hadn't secured first in a few races. Last year, and the year before, and the one before that, Alexander had dominated.

I glanced down at my feet. "Matteo, I wasn't exactly planning on a night out," I replied, shifting my weight as I looked toward the sleek, lively tents filled with people celebrating the end of the race.

"Oh, please," he said, laughing. "I know for a fact you were planning on staying in, but this is why you came, to try new things, find your spark again!"

Just as his words left his mouth, I felt a presence behind me. Turning, I found Alexander, fresh from the win, his racing suit pulled down around his hips, a black undershirt hugging his form that looked anything but ordinary. I had seen the outfit on plenty of others, but the whole rippling pectorals and abs that were basically like a shining sign that said *look at me* was doing something to my brain chemistry. He had changed his hair before race season; gone were the braids, and now a clean-cut fade. The sun makes his dark skin glow. Alexander stood out as the only Black racer on the Formula One circuit; he had fought through unimaginable battles to get here, championed young Black drivers daily, starting programs for them around the globe. Everything about him was attractive, his heart, his new hairstyle, his eyes, his damned godlike body that was basically on display, the rose tattoo on his hand, and the black ink that covered his arms. I shook my head, trying to shake off the rumble of butterflies in my stomach as he walked toward us. His eyes sparkled with something like amusement when he saw my hesitation.

"You'll come, won't you?" he asked, his voice low, smooth, and persuasive. He glanced at Matteo and back to me. "It'll be good for you. I know this isn't exactly your world, but we'll keep you company."

"Did you two plan this?" I ask, mouth agape at Alexander simply entering the conversation, cool as a cucumber, as if he didn't just win a Formula One race and stand on a podium with a giant golden award.

"I don't know," I said, glancing at my daughter and lowering my voice. "Leaving her..." I sighed. "It just feels like a lot."

"How about we go for an hour then reassess? We can even leave after Gia goes down so you can put her to bed, Anna will just hang out in the living room and call us if she needs anything." Matteo offered a rather compelling option.

"All right, but only if you promise me I can leave if I hate it."

He held out his arm, mock-formal. "You have my word."

I rolled my eyes but agreed anyway. Matteo gave me a playful salute, already retreating with Gia. She waved from his arms, her tiny fingers grasping at the air as we followed behind them.

Gia went down easily that night, as if the whole world was screaming at me to go out and have fun. It felt so odd to get dressed up to go clubbing. I felt so far from that phase of life, but here I was smoothing down my black dress, the boys on either side of me.

As they guided me toward the celebratory tent, the atmosphere shifted. The pulsing lights and upbeat music hit me, but Alexander's steady presence kept me grounded, even as Matteo was quickly pulled aside by other drivers, already having his attention split a million ways. Alexander, however, he stayed close by, always one step ahead to ensure I wasn't swept up in the bustling crowd or that I didn't feel out of place.

Inside, there was an electric excitement, a mix of race crew, VIPs, and fans clinking glasses and toasting the day's events. Matteo's eyes found me from across the way, still managing to keep me within his sight and nodding at me occasionally to check in.

When he finally made his way back to me, he offered me a glass. "Not too overwhelming, is it?" Alexander appeared beside me, his cologne wafted over my senses. He smelled like a cozy cabin during Christmas, or like some candle labeled *Leather and Brandy*. I wanted to wrap myself up inside it.

Woah, calm down, Luc, this is Alexander. Brother's best friend, the one the tabloids are obsessed with? The most eligible bachelor on the Formula One circuit. Not the person to have a crush on, get it together.

"Honestly, it's a lot." I laughed, but the admission made me feel lighter. "But I'm glad I came."

"Good," Alexander replied, his gaze warm as he watched me. "You deserve a little fun, plus this is just the first stop."

I looked away, trying to keep the blush from creeping up my

cheeks at his tone, it was so soft and doing things to my insides. "What do you mean?"

"This is the fake party, where we show up for the sponsors and the reporters while they take their posed pictures. The fun part is after." He looked on, as if surveying the crowd. "Honestly, we could leave now, no one would notice."

"You literally won the race, Alexander," I said, nudging his shoulder. The small touch seemed to jolt him, and his eyes collided with mine. Sharp and observant.

"I win a lot of races." He shrugged as if it was nothing, but the playful smirk was playing at his lips all the same.

"Let's get out of here." Matteo reached out, taking my drink from my hand and placing it on the bar next to us.

"Hey!" I protested.

"Relax, I'll buy you whatever you want." Matteo rolled his eyes at me, as a brother does. "Literally anywhere but here." The boys were both surveying the crowd, as if waiting or watching for something. I followed their glances, noticing a bunch of the drivers were seemingly silently communicating through looks. Soon we were shuffling out of the back and into a black town car being escorted to a new location.

I smoothed down my dress for what felt like the hundredth time, tugging the hem nervously. The after-party was buzzing with the energy of the race and the excitement of Alexander's victory, and while I was proud and thrilled, I also felt like a fish out of water. This was the real party, the dark room, the loud music. Matteo and Alexander were right at home among the flashing lights and lively crowd, while I clung to my drink, already on edge from the attention swirling around them. They were engulfed in conversations, being pulled into other groups, and being congratulated. I had migrated to a corner for a small breather, giving myself a mental pep talk.

Matteo noticed from across the room and began weaving his way through the crowd to reach me. "Lucia, come on, loosen up! You're here to celebrate, not stand in the corner looking like a deer in headlights," he teased, nudging my shoulder, then his expression softened. "You're with us—you're safe."

I rolled my eyes, trying to hide my nerves. "Easy for you to say, Matteo. You've been doing this for years. I'm not exactly used to being in clubs." I glanced toward Alexander, who was surrounded by other drivers.

Matteo gave me a reassuring smile. "You'll be fine. And don't worry, I've seen Alexander keeping an eye on you all night," he said, nodding toward the crowd where Alexander was excusing himself and heading our way. "It's like he's got a radar for you or something."

My cheeks warmed as Alexander approached, his eyes finding mine with that familiar, steady gaze. He looked relaxed, but as soon as he got close, I could see the hint of concern in his expression.

"You okay?" he asked, his voice low so only I could hear.

I managed a smile, feeling my nerves ebb slightly. "I'm fine, really. Just...still getting used to this scene."

He chuckled softly, eyes glinting with humor. "Well, we can't have you hiding all night." Alexander reached for my hand, giving it a comforting squeeze, making a zing run through my fingers. "Let's dance, Lucia."

Before I could respond, he was already pulling me toward the dance floor, our fingers intertwined. I threw a helpless look over my shoulder at Matteo, who grinned and gave me an encouraging thumbs-up.

As Alexander led me into the middle of the dance floor, he kept his hand on the small of my back, guiding me with a gentle firmness that eased my nerves. His gaze softened, a hint of warmth beyond the usual calm exterior he wore around the cameras.

"You're really good at this," I murmured, letting myself relax in his arms.

He leaned in close, his voice a low rumble that sent shivers down my spine. "At winning or at dancing?"

"Both, apparently," I teased, laughing softly. "But mostly the dancing. I didn't know that was in the skill set of a five-time champion."

There was a playful glint in his eye. "I've been known to have a few surprises up my sleeve."

We swayed in comfortable silence for a moment, and I felt myself forget about the crowd and the flashing lights as I focused on him. There was something grounding about Alexander, something steady and unwavering.

After a while, he murmured, "As much as we want you to try new things, you don't have to do anything you're uncomfortable with, you know. If it's too much, I can get you out of here."

I shook my head, giving him a grateful smile. "No, I'm okay. As long as you guys don't leave me alone again, that was awful."

He looked at me, his gaze filled with something deeper, a quiet promise that melted any last traces of tension. "You're not getting rid of me that easily, Lucia."

The bass thumped through my chest, and for a second, I let myself get lost in the beat, feeling a tiny pulse of excitement under all my nerves. I glanced at the bar where Matteo was deep in conversation with people, looking like they'd walked straight out of some high-fashion ad with their suits and easy smiles. How was I the one overthinking every move while they just blended right in?

Enough of that, Lucia, I told myself, determined to shake the anxious thoughts. If I was going to be here, I might as well *be here*. I reached out my hand, pulling Alexander behind me, taking both me and him by surprise. I marched us over to the bar and to my brother, feeling the music push me forward, and raised my voice just enough to get his attention.

"How about some shots?" I said, trying to channel a boldness I didn't quite feel. "One round, just to...you know, help me get out of my own head."

Matteo's face lit up instantly, clearly thrilled at the idea. "Now that's the spirit! Little sis wants shots? We're doing shots." He was already motioning at the bartender, ordering some top-shelf, way-too-expensive tequila.

Alexander's eyebrows lifted, a slow grin spreading across his face as he looked at me. There was that familiar spark of amusement, but something else too—something that felt like he understood exactly why I was doing this. "Here you go." He grabbed the shot glass as soon as it touched the sleek metal bar surface, and held it out for me. I didn't let myself overthink it, I grabbed it quickly and threw back the liquid. It burned down my throat, but before I could even acknowledge it, I dropped the glass onto the counter with a clank and swiped the shot glass out of my brother's unsuspecting hand. With one breath, I tipped it back, feeling the sharp burn of the liquor slide down my throat, igniting a warmth in my chest. I made a face as the aftertaste hit, but as soon as I opened my eyes, I felt lighter, like I'd broken some invisible barrier.

Matteo slung his arm over my shoulder, pulling me close. "I am *so* proud of you right now," he said with an exaggeratedly solemn tone, as if I'd just solved world hunger. "First time you've ever suggested shots in your life, probably. Alexander's a good influence, huh?"

I rolled my eyes but couldn't hide my smile. "Yeah, yeah, don't get too excited. It's just one round." But it felt like something. A step away from my usual careful, too-aware self.

"All right," Alexander said, raising his own shot glass and handing one to my brother. "Here's to...getting out of our heads?"

I laughed, nodding. "Exactly."

Matteo held up his glass, and Alexander followed suit. "To Lucia, who's finally learning to let loose," Matteo said with a smirk.

They clinked their glasses.

"You okay there?" Alexander asked, his eyes twinkling with amusement as he watched my expression shift from surprise to amusement.

I laughed, a little too loud, a little too free, but it felt amazing. "Better than okay," I said, giving him a grin.

"Then let's go for another!" Matteo said, already waving to the bartender. Before I could think about it, another shot appeared in my hand, and the three of us were clinking glasses again. By the time I took that third shot, a buzzing warmth had settled in, spreading through me like confidence.

Someone pulled Matteo onto the dance floor, and I was left with Alexander, who watched me with that steady gaze, his smile softening as he took in my slightly tipsy grin. "Having fun?" he asked, leaning in close to be heard over the music.

"Yeah," I admitted, feeling the words slip out without hesitation. "A lot more than I thought I would."

"Well, let's keep it that way," he said, holding his hand out to me. "What do you say? Dance with me again?"

I took his hand without thinking twice, letting him guide me into the crowd, the bass thumping, the lights flashing all around us. And for the first time in as long as I could remember, I didn't feel the need to look over my shoulder or worry about what anyone else thought. I was just...here. With him, in the middle of it all, and for once, I felt like I belonged in this moment.

10

ALEXANDER

I stopped drinking about four hours ago, but the DeLuca siblings were still going strong. To put it mildly, they were absolutely trashed. Matteo, I was used to. The guy's always a friendly idiot when he's had a drink—or three—but Lucia? Drunk Lucia? That was a whole new ball game.

She was a slippery little troublemaker when she was drunk, darting in and out of sight faster than I could keep up. I'd just turned my attention to Matteo for a second, trying to stop him from ordering yet another drink. Instead, I slipped some water into his glass, convincing him it was a vodka soda, a little tactic I had perfected over the years. That's when I was going to do the same with Lucia.

But when I turned around, she was gone. My heart dropped, a dull thud in my chest. The music felt too loud all of a sudden, the bass like it was pulsing straight through my ribs. Every neon light seemed too bright. My senses were overloaded, and in the chaos of the club, all I could think was: *Where the hell is she? And why the hell was she so damn small?*

I shook it off, trying to focus, but Matteo's voice broke through the fog, still going on and on about the time he'd jumped off a double-decker yacht in his birthday suit. He was laughing, recounting every embarrassing detail, and of course, he failed to remember that I was the one who'd dared him to do it in the first place.

"Mate, I need you to stay here, okay? I have to find your sister." I grabbed his shoulder, forcing him to focus.

Drunk Matteo went completely still. Too still.

"Oh fuck, did we lose her? She doesn't do well alone, or drunk, or drunk and alone. This is bad. This is really bad," he started rambling, the panic creeping into his words.

I took a deep breath, trying to calm him down. "It's okay, mate. Stay here. I'll find her, and then we'll head to the hotel. Sound good?"

Matteo blinked at me like I had just spoken a different language. Then, in true Matteo fashion, he grinned like a fool and changed the subject. "There were these cheesy chips in the minibar area. I'm gonna fuck those up when we get there."

I rolled my eyes, running my hand through my hair. Drunk, idiotic, rambling best friend. I pointed at him. "Stay. I'm going to find your sister."

Then I was off, weaving through the crowd.

Lucia was small, and this club? It was huge. The dark lights and thick haze of smoke didn't help either. Everything felt like it was closing in. The floor seemed sticky, the music louder than ever. *Had it always been this dark in here? Where the hell was she?*

My heart was hammering now, and I tried to stay calm. But the whole night felt like it was slipping through my fingers, and I wasn't going to let anything—anyone—slip away tonight.

I pushed through the crowd, my eyes scanning every corner, every face. My heart was racing, like I was on a clock, and time was slipping faster than I could catch it. The club was a mess of flashing lights, pounding beats, and the chaos of bodies moving, grinding, lost in the night. But there was no sign of her. No small blonde head bobbing in the sea of people. I could feel the tension building in my chest, that gnawing sense of worry I tried to ignore, but it was clawing at me now.

I turned, my gaze darting between faces, hoping I'd catch a glimpse of Lucia's sharp, searching eyes, her laughter in the mix. *Nothing.*

And then, just as I was about to give in to the panic creeping up on me, I saw her.

She was standing near the back of the club, by the exit, looking like she was trying to slip past unnoticed. She had her arms crossed tightly, like she was hiding from something—or someone. She hadn't seen me yet, but I could see the way her eyes flicked nervously around, like she was too aware of everything around her but not enough to be fully present.

Lucia.

I moved toward her in a flash, dodging people, my legs pushing faster as my pulse thudded in my ears. When I finally reached her, I grabbed her arm gently but firmly.

"Hey," I said, my voice a little rougher than I meant it to be. "What the hell are you doing?"

Her eyes met mine, and there was this instant recognition, followed by a flash of irritation. She gave me a lazy half smile, but it was more mischievous than anything else. "Trying to find you," she said, her words slurring just a little. "Too many tall people."

I sighed, relief mixed with annoyance. "Well, I'm right here now."

She gave me a wobbly shrug, but her face softened, the edge of her defiance flickering out, replaced with that vulnerable look I hated seeing on her. "I wanted to dance, but then it was like the people swallowed me up and I couldn't find you or Matteo." Her voice was quieter now, almost lost in the thrum of the club.

I stepped closer, lowering my voice. "It's all right, I've got you." I reached out, taking her elbow and gently steering her away from the crowd.

Lucia let me guide her, her steps unsteady, toes catching on the sticky floor. "I don't want to go back yet," she mumbled, her voice soft but laced with determination. Her eyes darted over my shoulder, like she was already plotting an escape route. Then she looked up at me, her bottom lip jutting out in a pout.

"I want to dance," she whined, her tone petulant, fists balled at her sides like she was on the verge of stomping her foot. It was so ridiculously endearing that I almost laughed. She looked exactly like Gia when she wasn't getting her way—the same scrunched-up expression, the same wide, pleading eyes. Damn it, she even had the same pout.

I sighed, knowing I didn't stand a chance against that look. If I said no, she'd wriggle out of my grasp and head straight for the dance floor anyway, and I was not about to lose her again.

"Fine," I said, caving with a shake of my head. "One dance."

Her face lit up, her eyes catching the neon lights and sparkling like she'd just won the lottery. A soft smile tugged at her lips, entrancing me. She knew she won.

The music shifted to a slower, sultry beat as we moved onto the edge of the dance floor. I wasn't even sure why I'd agreed to this. Lucia was drunk, light on her feet, swaying like the music was stitched into her bones. She grabbed my hand and pulled me into the rhythm before I had time to think, her touch soft but insistent.

"See?" she said, laughing as she spun herself around, her hair catching the lights like gold. "Not so bad, is it?"

I didn't answer. I couldn't. All I could do was watch as she let go of herself, her movements fluid, carefree. This was a side of her I'd never seen before—uninhibited and glowing with joy, like nothing else in the world mattered except this moment. Her arms lifted above her head, her hips swaying as she stepped closer to me.

Too close.

"Come on, Alexander," she teased, her voice light, her eyes locking on mine. "You can't just stand there like a statue."

She reached for my other hand, and without thinking, I let her take it. She guided me into the rhythm, our movements clumsy at first, but then something shifted. I found myself falling into step with her, the music weaving us together. The small touches of her fingers grazing mine, her shoulder brushing against my chest, sent sparks racing up my spine. I wanted more, I wanted my hands to outline the curve of her waist, to pull her closer.

Her laugh bubbled up again as she stepped even closer, as if hearing my thoughts, the faint scent of her perfume wrapping around me. It was intoxicating, and I hated how much I noticed. Hated how the heat of her skin so near mine made my pulse race. Hated how beautiful she looked, her cheeks flushed and eyes shimmering under the club's flashing lights.

This wasn't supposed to happen. Not with her.

"Admit it," she said, tilting her head up at me, her voice teasing but soft. "You're having fun."

I swallowed hard, forcing my expression into something neutral. "It's the music," I replied, my voice gruff, trying to put some distance between us even as she closed the gap. "Hard not to move."

"Sure," she said, grinning, her fingers sliding down my arm like a featherlight trail of fire. "It's just the music."

Her touch lingered, and I felt my control slipping, the invisible line I'd drawn in my mind starting to blur. I couldn't stop looking at her, couldn't ignore the way her lips curved, or the way her hair framed her face like a damn halo.

She leaned in, her voice barely audible over the music. "I think you like this."

I huffed out a breath, a dry laugh escaping before I could stop it. "You're drunk, Lucia."

"And you're avoiding the question," she countered, her hand now resting lightly on my chest.

I should've stepped back, should've pulled away from the heat of her touch, the way her fingers splayed against the fabric of my shirt. But I didn't. I couldn't. Instead, I found myself leaning in, just enough to catch the faintest glint in her eyes.

"Lucia," I said, my voice low, a warning that didn't sound nearly as firm as it should have.

"What?" she asked, grinning like she'd won something. Her voice was playful, but there was something else in her gaze. Something softer, deeper, that made my chest tighten.

I shook my head, a small laugh slipping out despite myself. "You're impossible."

But the song ended, reality crashing back into me.

"All right, one song is done," I said, my voice firmer than before. "Let's go get your brother and head back to the hotel."

Lucia stopped mid-spin, turning to face me, her hair falling in loose waves over her shoulders. She pouted again, and I braced myself. The pout was dangerous—almost as bad as her smile.

"One song?" she said, her voice soft, teasing. "You're no fun, Alexander."

I sighed, raking a hand through my hair. "You're drunk, Lucia."

She tilted her head, her grin widening. "Exactly. Which means I'm having fun for once. You could try it, too, you know."

"I'm having plenty of fun," I muttered, though it was a lie. Fun wasn't the word for this. This was...something else. Something that felt too close, too dangerous.

She stepped closer, her hands finding my arm again. "One more dance," she pleaded, her eyes wide and sparkling under the neon lights. "Just one."

And there it was again—the way she looked at me. It made something twist in my chest, something I didn't want to name.

She's off limits.

She's off limits.

She's off limits.

If I repeated it enough in my own head, maybe my body would actually start to listen.

"I can't keep saying yes to you, Lucia," I said quietly, trying to sound stern, though I wasn't sure if I was convincing either of us.

"Why not?" she asked, her voice softer now. Her fingers curled slightly, a small, almost hesitant touch. "I think you like saying yes to me."

I swallowed hard, her words hitting too close to truths I didn't want to face. "Because I know where it leads."

She blinked, her smile faltering for just a second before it came back, this time with a different edge. "And where does it lead, Alexander?"

"Nowhere good," I said, my voice barely audible over the music, but she heard me. I saw it in the way her eyes flickered, her expression shifting into something more unreadable.

"Maybe you don't give yourself enough credit," she murmured, stepping back just a little. "Or maybe you're scared."

I stiffened, her words digging deeper than they should have. She didn't know—couldn't know—how close she was to the truth. That I had been pushing feelings down for too long, for years. But she was off limits, and I was losing any semblance of control around her. She was too close, her body lining up with mine, in a dark and loud room. I could just lean down and kiss her; no one would even see. But she was drunk, and damn it all to hell, if I was going to kiss her, she was going to be fully present and know full well it wasn't just some drunken decision.

"Let's go," I said, my voice sharper than intended as I broke the spell, stepping back from her touch.

For a moment, she didn't move, her gaze locked on mine. Then, with a small, resigned shrug, she nodded. "Fine."

I ignored the flicker of disappointment in her tone as I reached for her hand, leading her toward the exit. The warmth of her fingers in mine sent an electric hum through my body, one I tried desperately to ignore.

I needed to get her back to the hotel. Away from this place. Away from me. Because if I let myself stay in this moment any longer, I wasn't sure I'd want it to end.

The ride back to the hotel was pure chaos. Matteo was

sprawled out in the private car, alternating between belting out snippets of songs he didn't know the words to and recounting wildly exaggerated stories from their childhood, switching from Italian to English a hundred times. "Did I ever tell you about the time Lucia tried to sell lemonade but drank it all before anyone could buy any?" he slurred, grinning like it was the funniest thing in the world.

Lucia, curled up on my other side, just groaned. "That was when I was *seven*, Matteo," she muttered, her voice thick with exhaustion.

"Yeah, but it was entrepreneurial, or an attempt anyway," he shot back, pointing a triumphant finger at her.

I couldn't help but smirk, shaking my head at the two of them. Matteo might've been loud and obnoxious, but Lucia had gone quiet, leaning heavily against me, her head lolling onto my shoulder.

When her breathing slowed, I realized she'd fallen asleep.

By the time we pulled up to the hotel, Matteo was still talking to no one in particular. "I'm gonna raid that minibar. Those chips are calling my name. You think they restock 'em every day? They should. I am an athlete, I need the fuel. Fuel in the form of cheesy chips." He stumbled out of the car with my help.

"Yeah, yeah, let's go, chip boy," I muttered, steadying him as we made our way inside. "Room's this way."

Lucia didn't stir as I carried her out of the car and through the lobby. Matteo, thankfully, managed to stagger to his own door without too much help, though not before declaring, "I think all chips should be cheesy, don't you?"

I nodded, humoring him, before steering him inside. "Go to bed, mate."

"Chips first," he mumbled before disappearing into his room.

Once Matteo was settled, I turned my attention back to Lucia. Her room was just down the hall, where Anna had been watching over Gia. When I unlocked the door and stepped inside, Anna greeted me with a tired smile. She glanced at a sleeping Lucia in my arms and smirked.

"She was an angel," Anna whispered, motioning toward the bedroom where Gia was sound asleep. "I'll head out now. Have a good night."

"Thanks, Anna," I murmured, grateful for her help. "Are you okay? The other day..." I trailed off. Her shoulders dropped a little, a tired smile that didn't reach her eyes,

"It'll be fine, don't you go worrying about me now," she whispered, waving a hand.

"Want me to call Dante?" I asked softly. I knew her family history was complicated, but Anna was private.

Her eyes went wide. "God, no."

As soon as she was gone, I carried Lucia over to the couch, trying not to wake her. When I set her down, her eyes fluttered open, and she blinked up at me, confused.

"Gia's asleep," I said softly.

Lucia sat up slowly, rubbing her eyes. "I'll sleep here, on the couch," she mumbled, her voice groggy. "I don't want to wake her."

"All right," I said, already moving toward the closet to grab extra pillows and blankets.

When I returned, Lucia was attempting to undo her hair, her fingers fumbling with the pins.

"Here," I offered, sitting beside her. She hesitated for a moment, then let her hands fall to her lap.

I worked quietly, sliding the pins free one by one until her hair fell loose around her shoulders. It was softer than I'd imagined, and the scent of her shampoo lingered faintly, like berries. I closed my own eyes.

Get it together, Wright.

When I opened them, she had turned to look at me, her dark eye makeup making her eyes seem brighter. I realized she might not want to sleep in that. So I walked to the bathroom, quietly rifling through a few bags on the countertop. I found a pack labeled *makeup remover* and brought it over to her. Her head was on the pillow, looking like she was fighting to stay awake.

"Close your eyes," I whispered, and I gently wiped away the remnants of her makeup, the cool cloth smoothing over her cheeks and forehead.

"Why are you being so nice?" she murmured, her voice barely audible.

I paused, then shrugged. "You take care of everyone, let me take care of you."

She let out a soft hum, her eyes still closed, and leaned back slightly as I worked.

When I was done, I helped her settle onto the couch, tucking the blankets around her and adding an extra pillow behind her head. "Comfortable?" I asked, standing back to make sure she had everything she needed.

She opened her eyes, meeting mine with a tired but grateful smile. "Yeah."

I nodded, stepping back toward the door, but her voice stopped me.

"Alexander," she said, her words slurring slightly with sleep.

I turned. "Yeah?"

Her eyes fluttered shut. Within seconds, her breathing evened out, and she was asleep.

I stayed there for a moment, watching her, my chest inexplicably tight. She looked peaceful, wrapped up in the cocoon of blankets, her hair fanning out across the pillow. Too peaceful for the chaos of the night we'd just had.

With a sigh, I turned off the lights, leaving just the soft glow of the lamp by the couch, and slipped out of the room, closing the door behind me.

11

LUCIA

The soft glow of morning light seeped through the curtains, warming my face as I stirred awake. My neck ached, a dull throb radiating down my back from sleeping on the couch. Blinking groggily, I pushed myself up on one elbow, my hand automatically going to my pounding head.

On the side table next to me was a glass of water and a small packet of ibuprofen. I stared at it for a moment, a faint smile tugging at my lips.

Alexander.

Of course.

I reached for the water and pills, swallowing them gratefully. As I sipped the last of the water, fragments of the night before began filtering through the fog in my brain. The pulsing music, Matteo's drunken antics, the warmth of Alexander's hands guiding me out of the club. And then...

Oh God.

I groaned, burying my face in my hands as flashes of memory surfaced. Dancing with Alexander, the way I'd practically dragged him onto the floor. The teasing comments, the way I'd touched his arm, his chest, flirting with him like some drunk, carefree version of myself I barely recognized. I was so close to kissing him, to pulling him down into my space and brushing my lips to his.

I cringed, the heat of embarrassment creeping up my neck. What was I thinking? This was *Alexander*—stoic, composed, ridiculously handsome, famous millionaire Alexander. Matteo's best friend. Gia's unofficial godfather. The man who'd been nothing but patient with me since this whirlwind of a trip began. He could have anyone he could ever want, why would he want me?

And I'd...what? Batted my lashes at him under neon lights and tried to pull him into my tipsy, reckless world? The memory of his low voice, his steady presence, flickered in my mind. The way he'd looked at me—not annoyed, not judgmental, but something else entirely. I was probably making it up in my head, I mean, I was drunk and the man was beautiful, I couldn't deny that. But he was my brother's best friend. Off limits. Beyond off limits, actually.

I pulled myself up, leaning over to glance into the bedroom, the curtains were shut, blocking out the morning light in that room despite the light in the living room side. I glanced toward Gia's crib, where she was still sound asleep, her tiny fists curled up near her face. The sight of her calmed me, grounding me in the present.

Sliding my feet to the floor, I wrapped the blanket Alexander must've tucked around me tighter, running a hand through my hair. He'd undone it for me, I realized. I expected my eyes to be groggy, with an unwashed face, but when I went into the bathroom, my face was clear and the makeup wipes were on the counter instead of in my travel bag.

I bit my lip, the weight of the night pressing down on me again. I owed him a thank-you, and maybe an apology.

The sudden dread of guilt crept into my mind as I remembered we had all agreed to meet in my room for breakfast. I glanced at the clock, way too little time to get myself together, but it would have to do. I pulled out my phone to text my brother.

I began hustling around the suite as quietly as I could, picking up discarded clothing and toys, trying to make the room look less like a chaotic mess.

As I moved around the suite, trying to restore some semblance of order, I couldn't stop my thoughts from drifting back to Alexander. The memories of his steady hands guiding me to the couch, his careful attention to the little details—like leaving water and ibuprofen—made my chest tighten.

I shook the thought away, focusing instead on the task at hand. I gathered Gia's favorite stuffed giraffe from under the coffee table and set it neatly on the couch. I folded the clothes that had been tossed over the back of a chair, stuffed a few stray toys into her travel bag, and wiped down the coffee table.

"Not bad," I muttered, stepping back to survey the room. It wasn't perfect, but it didn't scream *hurricane aftermath* anymore.

Gianna stirred in her crib, a soft coo escaping her lips. I crossed the room and peeked over the edge, her tiny face scrunching up as she began to wake.

"Good morning, sunshine," I whispered, reaching down to stroke her soft curls. She yawned, her little arms stretching above her head as she blinked up at me.

I scooped her up, holding her close as she nuzzled into my shoulder. The warmth of her small body in my arms was a reminder of why I was here, why I'd agreed to this crazy trip in the first place.

"Let's get you changed and ready for breakfast, hmm?" I said softly, carrying her over to the changing table.

Just as I finished getting Gianna dressed in a tiny floral romper, there was a knock at the door. My heart leapt, and I glanced at the clock. *Already?*

"Coming!" I called, quickly setting Gianna down with her toys before hurrying to the door.

When I opened it, Alexander stood on the other side, holding two steaming cups of coffee and looking far too composed for someone who had dealt with drunk Matteo and me the night before.

"Good morning," he said, his voice warm and even, like he hadn't spent the night carrying my drunk self back to the hotel.

"Morning," I replied, suddenly hyperaware of how disheveled I must look in my oversized sleep shirt and messy bun.

He held out one of the cups. "Thought you might need this."

I took it, my fingers brushing against his for a moment. "Thank you. And...thanks for last night. I know I wasn't exactly easy to handle."

A small smile tugged at the corner of his mouth. "You were fine. Matteo, on the other hand..."

I laughed, shaking my head. "I can only imagine."

He stepped inside, his gaze sweeping over the room before landing on Gia, who was happily playing with stuffies on the floor, her favorite bunny wearing a lopsided crown. His expression softened in that way it always did around her, and it made my chest ache.

"Did I come too early? Matteo texted he'll be late."

I glanced down at my sleep shirt and bare legs, heat creeping up my neck. I had stripped out of the dress I slept in and pulled on my favorite oversized, ratty T-shirt I always slept in. It was white with hot pink distressed lettering that said *surviving on spite and coffee.* It had seen its fair share of wear and I was suddenly very aware of the way I looked. "I was just about to get ready, actually."

"I'll keep an eye on Gia," he offered, already walking over to her to join her on the floor on her play mat.

I hesitated for a moment, watching as he picked up one of her toys and held it out to her. She squealed in delight, her little hands reaching for it. His attention was fully on her now, he was making voices to go with the stuffies she pointed out.

I sighed softly, before retreating to the bedroom to throw myself together as quickly as possible.

I closed the bedroom door behind me, letting out a breath I hadn't realized I'd been holding. My reflection in the mirror confirmed what I already knew: I looked like a complete disaster. My hair was a tangled mess, circles under my eyes, and in my favorite albeit very old oversized tee with nearly nothing underneath. I felt the blush creeping up my neck as I noticed how little the shirt seemed to cover.

I grabbed some fresh clothes and ducked into the shower. The hot water was a welcome relief, washing away the remnants of last night—the sweat, the embarrassment, and, maybe, the lingering thoughts of Alexander's steady hands and quiet smile.

Focus, Lucia, I told myself, scrubbing shampoo through my hair. *You have a brother who's probably still half drunk and a toddler who needs breakfast. You don't have time for whatever...this is.* I knew what this was, it was an infatuation, an ever-present crush I had on my brother's best friend. It needed to be shoved back down, down into a deep, deep small box in the back of my mind. *Again.*

After rinsing off, I stepped out, towel-drying my hair before twisting it into a loose braid down my back. A little concealer under my eyes and some tinted lip balm brought me back to life. I fixed my favorite butterfly and locket necklaces that never left my body and gave myself a stern look in the mirror.

You got this, I told myself. I loved affirmations; sure, they were cheesy, but it was something I had instilled in myself and Gianna. We did them together most mornings when I did her hair, looked straight into the mirror and hyped ourselves up. Gianna was a huge fan.

Feeling more like myself, I padded back into the main area of the suite, the soft thud of my socks against the floor barely audible. Alexander sat cross-legged on the rug beside Gia, holding her stuffed bunny aloft and making it fly in wide loops. Gia was giggling uncontrollably, her little hands reaching up to grab it, her face lit with pure joy.

The sight stopped me in my tracks, my chest tightening in a way I didn't expect. He looked so natural with her, so at ease, like he belonged there. *Dangerous*, I thought, quickly shaking the idea away. It wasn't like I hadn't seen him play with her before, so why was my brain short-circuiting now? Tequila shots were *definitely* a bad idea.

"All set," I said, pulling on a sweater and stepping over to scoop Gia into a hug. She squealed, her tiny hands pushing against my cheeks as I planted a loud kiss on hers.

"Mu-uhhh-mom," she groaned through a giggle, wriggling in my arms like she couldn't decide whether to escape or stay.

I let her go, turning to find Alexander watching us. His expression was unreadable, but there was something soft in his eyes, something that made my pulse flutter.

"You clean up well," he said, his tone light but sincere.

For a split second, I froze, sure my jaw was hanging open. *Nope*, not going there. But maybe that flirting last night wasn't only one sided?

A knock on the door jolted me out of my spiraling thoughts, and I scrambled to get it, grateful for the interruption. Matteo was on the other side, sunglasses perched over his bloodshot eyes, a scowl firmly in place, and a bottle of water clutched like a lifeline.

"How are either of you alive?" he grumbled, pushing past me and shutting the door with a lazy shove. "And where the fuck is the food?"

"You drank double what we drank," Alexander shot back.

"Stop screaming," Matteo growled, collapsing onto the couch like the dramatic fool he was.

"Food's on the way," Alexander replied, unfazed as he returned his attention to Gianna. She was now explaining, in great detail, why her stuffed unicorn was a princess and the bunny Alexander was holding was the fairy princess.

"Obviously," she concluded with a look of absolute authority, pointing a tiny finger at Alexander.

"Obviously," he echoed, nodding gravely, his lips twitching with a smile he was trying to suppress.

I watched them from the corner of the room, my heart doing a stupid little flip. It was just breakfast. Just another chaotic morning with Alexander and Matteo. My brother. My unknowing brother who was lying haphazardly on the couch, his hand falling dramatically over his eyes.

"I'm dying," he muttered, clearly convinced that mere exhaustion could kill him after all the *hard work* of drinking last night.

I raised an eyebrow, crossing my arms. "Oh, poor baby," I drawled.

Matteo peeked a bloodshot eye out from under his arm, eyeing me with mock suspicion. "Why do you look so...chipper?"

I smirked. "I slept like a baby."

"Ugh, the world is so cruel," Matteo muttered, flopping back down onto the couch like he had just been betrayed by the universe. "Just give me the food." Matteo groaned again from the couch, making it sound like I was the one causing his misery.

"Could you *be* any louder?" I asked, my tone sweet as honey.

"Don't tempt me," Matteo grumbled, and I had to stifle a laugh.

"Don't worry, food will fix everything," Alexander said, his voice still light but with a hint of sincerity beneath it. He held out his hand to Gia, letting her fly the stuffed bunny around in circles again.

I watched him for a moment longer, wondering why the

simplest things—like him sitting on the floor playing with my daughter—felt so *important*. And why, despite my best efforts to act like it didn't matter, my heart had the audacity to give a little jump whenever he smiled.

DRIVER CHAMPIONSHIP STANDINGS

1. Theo Bauer   215 pts
Kaz Energy Racing

2. Alexander Wright   203 pts
Belen Racing

3. Carlos Torres   140 pts
Moretti Racing

4. James Hansson   116 pts
Belen Racing

5. Matteo DeLuca   96 pts
Moretti Racing

12

LUCIA

The last two weeks had been a blur of roaring engines, pit stops, and hotel rooms. Life on the road with Matteo—and by extension, Alexander—was a whirlwind, but I was starting to find my rhythm.

Mornings started early, with Gia demanding breakfast long before I'd had my first sip of coffee. Afternoons were a mix of Matteo's training sessions, team meetings, and the occasional trackside stroll to stretch our legs. Evenings were quieter, spent in hotel suites or at low-key team dinners where Gia was quickly becoming everyone's favorite distraction.

It was...nice.

The one thing I couldn't quite get used to was the media attention. Matteo had warned me. Alexander had also, but I hadn't understood the scope of it until now. Cameras were always there, just out of sight but somehow always present. Paparazzi weren't the worst of it; no, it was the fans. The diehards. The ones who lived and breathed Formula One and wanted to dissect every second of every interaction their idols had.

And apparently, that now included me.

It started small. A few casual glances as I walked with Gia

through the paddock. A couple of harmless photos snapped as I stood beside Matteo's car. But it escalated after someone posted a photo online—one of those grainy, zoomed-in shots taken from across the paddock.

The caption read: *Alexander Wright seen chatting with a mystery woman! Could this be a new romance brewing?*

The "mystery woman" was me. Or, more accurately, the back of my head as I stood next to Alexander while he played peekaboo with Gianna. There had been some rumors, some gossip websites and articles about us dating only because we were around each other. But the media spun the narrative in ways that seemed unfathomable. It all felt so out of our control. My phone buzzed incessantly after that. Matteo forwarded me the post, laughing about how the fans were already spiraling into conspiracy theories. Alexander apologized for the attention, promising to shut it down if it got out of hand.

But it wasn't the post itself that bothered me. It was the comments.

Some were harmless, speculating about whether Alexander had a secret girlfriend. Some speculating it was me, others not. Others were...less kind. The usual mix of online toxicity: calling me a nobody, questioning why Alexander would even bother with someone like me. Then the personal ones, the truly mean ones.

I told myself it didn't matter. I wasn't dating Alexander. There was nothing to feed the rumors. And yet, as I scrolled through the comments late at night in my hotel room, I couldn't help but feel... exposed.

I was jolted out of my thoughts by a soft knock on the door.

"It's open," I called, setting my phone down as Matteo strolled in, dressed in his team's branded hoodie and sweatpants, his hair still damp from his post-training shower.

"You look like you've seen a ghost," he said, plopping down on the couch beside me. "What's up?"

"Nothing," I said too quickly, which of course made Matteo narrow his eyes suspiciously.

"Lucia," he said, drawing my name out like he used to when we were kids and I was caught sneaking extra cookies from the jar. "What's going on?"

I hesitated, then sighed, flipping my phone around to show him the post. "This."

Matteo stared at the screen for a second, then burst out laughing. "This is what's got you all worked up? Lucia, you can barely even tell it's you!"

"It doesn't matter," I muttered, crossing my arms. "People are...saying things."

Matteo's laughter faded, his expression softening. "Look, I get it. The attention sucks. But you've gotta let it roll off your back. They don't know you. And anyone who knows you wouldn't say a damn thing like that. It's hard to remember, but it's not real, what they say...none of it is real."

I bit my lip, his words offering some comfort but not enough to shake off the unease entirely. I knew he had gone through his own media scrutiny, all the drivers had.

"And for what it's worth," Matteo added, leaning back against the couch, "if anyone messes with you, they're messing with me. And you *know* I don't take that lightly."

I smiled despite myself. "Thanks, Teo."

"Anytime," he said, ruffling my hair like he used to when we were kids. "Now, c'mon. Gia's got Alexander wrapped around her little finger again, and you're gonna miss it if you stay cooped up in here."

I followed him out, letting the door click shut behind us.

Matteo and I made our way down to the hotel lounge, where the team had set up a makeshift family area. The soft hum of conversation mingled with the occasional burst of laughter, and I spotted Gia right away. She was sitting cross-legged on the floor, holding court like a tiny queen, her stuffed bunny tucked under one arm as she talked animatedly to Alexander and Anna.

Alexander sat with his legs stretched out, an easy smile on his face as he nodded along to whatever Gia was telling him. Anna stood nearby, her phone in hand, though she glanced up every so often with a fond smile at Gia's antics.

"Zio!" Gia squealed, spotting Matteo. She scrambled to her feet, running over to him with her arms outstretched.

"Principessa!" Matteo scooped her up, spinning her around dramatically before planting a loud kiss on her cheek. She giggled, and I couldn't help but smile at the sight.

Alexander's gaze flicked to me as I approached, and his easy smile faltered just slightly. He stood, brushing off his hands, and motioned for Anna to give us a moment. She nodded, slipping out of the room with a knowing look.

"You okay?" he asked quietly, stepping closer.

I hesitated, glancing at Gia, who was now thoroughly engrossed in Matteo's silly stories. "I'm fine," I said, though the tightness in my chest betrayed me.

Alexander's brow furrowed, and he stepped closer, lowering his voice. "I saw the post, it's down now, but I know comments can be awful, I'm sorry you had to experience that side of the fans."

"It's not a big deal," I said, trying to wave it off.

"It is to me." His voice was firm but gentle. "I don't like the idea of you being dragged into this mess because of me."

I blinked, caught off guard by the sincerity in his tone. "It's not your fault, Alexander. I knew what I was walking into when I came on this trip, you guys did so much to make me feel safe here, having anyone inside the circuits not take pictures of us, it's helped a ton. And I knew there would be photos here and there, you guys are all famous and handsome and rich, so..."

He smirked. "You calling me handsome?" I rolled my eyes. "That doesn't mean you should have to deal with it though, I know how much it can be and how they control the narrative." He sighed, running a hand through his short hair. We sat in silence for a moment, I felt the cloud coming back, the overwhelmingness of it all. I had worked hard to feel like myself again, to gain confidence again, but the comments felt like they were flashing before my eyes.

"What if we use it to our advantage?" he mused.

"What do you mean?" I asked, narrowing my eyes slightly.

He rubbed the back of his neck, a sheepish smile tugging at his lips. "I have an idea. Hear me out before you say no, okay?"

I crossed my arms, tilting my head. "I'm listening."

Alexander glanced around to make sure no one was within earshot, then leaned in. "Anna and I were talking...and we thought maybe we could spin this. So the pitch is, we date."

I blinked again. "Excuse me?"

"Look," he said, speaking quickly now, "the media's already speculating, right? If we lean into it, it could take the heat off you. They'll lose interest once they see we're not sneaking around or giving them drama to chew on, we can control the narrative instead of letting them run with rumors. And for me..." He trailed off, his jaw tightening.

"What about you?" I pressed.

His gaze flicked away briefly before meeting mine again. "Belen's been on my case about my image. They think I'm too much of a playboy, not serious enough. It's bad PR for the team. Anna's been working overtime to fix it, but..." he hesitated, then added, "a 'committed relationship' would go a long way in shutting them up."

I stared at him, my mind racing. "You want us to pretend to date?"

"Yes." His tone was steady, his expression earnest. "It doesn't have to be complicated. We set some ground rules, keep it simple. Just for the cameras, Lucia. Nothing more."

I bit my lip, glancing back at Gianna, who was now attempting to put a stuffed crown on Matteo's head. It would take the pressure off me, sure. And if it helped Alexander with his PR...

But fake dating Alexander Wright? That felt like walking a tightrope with no safety net.

"I don't know." My heart was racing. "Gianna..." I trailed off.

"I think if we feed them enough, give into the beast, they'll leave us alone more," he said softly, drawing my attention back to him. "You'd be doing me a favor. I swear, I'll make sure this doesn't come back to bite you. Gia included. Also means more for your yes year, I'll take you wherever you want to go. Movie premiers, fancy parties, fashion shows."

I studied his face, searching for any hint of hesitation or ulterior motive, but all I saw was sincerity.

"I don't know, Alexander," I said finally, my voice uncertain. "This feels...risky."

"It's just for a while," he promised. "Until the hype dies down or Belen backs off. Then we go back to normal."

Normal. Like anything about this situation had been normal since the moment I stepped into it.

I sighed, running a hand through my hair. "Okay," I said, my voice barely above a whisper. "But we need to set some serious ground rules."

His smile was soft but triumphant. "Of course. Whatever you need."

The moment we sat Matteo down in Alexander's suite to explain the plan, I regretted agreeing to it. My brother leaned back in one of the oversized chairs, arms crossed, a skeptical scowl plastered across his face as he listened.

Alexander was calm, composed, like he was briefing a

teammate on strategy. Me? I was squirming in my seat, dreading Matteo's reaction.

"So let me get this straight," Matteo said, his tone dripping with disbelief. "You two are going to *pretend* to date. To throw the media off, control the narrative or whatever, and help Alex's PR image?"

"Exactly," Alexander said smoothly, his voice steady and confident. "It's temporary. Just until the noise dies down."

Matteo snorted, shaking his head. "And you think this is a good idea?" His gaze darted to me, and I could see the mix of concern and protectiveness bubbling just beneath the surface.

"It's not like we're getting married," I said, attempting to inject a little humor to lighten the mood. "It's just for the cameras. Nothing more."

Matteo's eyes narrowed, his scowl deepening. "Nothing more, huh?"

"Nothing," Alexander confirmed. His voice was resolute, but there was a subtle edge to it, a seriousness that even Matteo couldn't dismiss. "I would never hurt her, Matteo."

My brother's gaze locked onto Alexander, the moment felt like it lasted forever. "Good," Matteo said finally, leaning forward with a sharp edge in his voice. "Because if you do, I don't care how many championships you've won or how good of a friend you've been—I'll make you regret it."

Alexander didn't flinch. "Understood."

"Matteo," I interjected, my voice firm. "This isn't some grand scheme. It's practical. We control the narrative, and Alex gets to clean up his image, which will help with management. It's a win-win."

"Yeah, sure, win-win," Matteo muttered, slumping back into the chair. "Except for the part where my baby sister is fake dating one of the most gossiped-about athletes on the planet. That part feels like a loss."

I rolled my eyes. "I'm a year younger than you."

"Not the point," he shot back. "You're my sister. My *little* sister. And Alex..." He glanced at his best friend, sighing heavily. "You're...Alex."

Alexander raised an eyebrow. "I'll take that as a compliment."

"Don't." Matteo pointed a glare at him, but there was less heat behind it now. "Look, I get it. It's not the worst idea. I mean, the media's been circling like vultures since you got here, Lucia, and Alex's playboy reputation could use a break."

"Gee, thanks," Alexander said dryly.

"You know it's true." A smirk tugged at the corner of Matteo's lips.

I glanced between the two of them, the tension in my chest easing slightly. Matteo might not love the idea, but he wasn't completely against it either.

"So, you're okay with this?" I asked hesitantly.

Matteo sighed again, scrubbing a hand through his hair. "I'm okay with it as long as *you* are. But," he added, pointing at Alexander again, "if this goes sideways in any way, I'm holding you responsible."

"Fair enough," Alexander said with a nod, his expression serious.

Matteo leaned back, finally cracking a small smile. "Well, this should be fun to watch."

"Oh, shut up," I muttered, but I couldn't help the smile creeping onto my own face.

Matteo might be a protective pain, but at least he was on board.

Sort of.

13

ALEXANDER

I can't believe I suggested fake dating *Lucia DeLuca*, and she agreed. Even more shocking, Matteo is on board. Well, *reluctantly* on board, but I'd count that as a victory.

As the door to my suite clicked shut behind Matteo, I let out a breath I hadn't realized I was holding. My best friend's halfhearted threat was still ringing in my ears. Not that I blamed him.

I glanced over at Lucia, who was perched on the edge of the couch, her arms crossed and her brows furrowed like she was deep in thought. Her lips were slightly pursed, and it hit me that I was staring way too long at them.

"This is insane, isn't it?" she asked, pulling me out of whatever trance I'd slipped into.

"It's not *insane*," I said, trying to sound more confident than I felt. "It's...strategic."

She snorted, giving me a look that said she didn't buy it for a second. "Strategic. Right."

"Look, it'll work. The media will move on once they realize there's no scandal here. No drama. And you'll get to live your life without worrying about being involved in some scandal they make up."

Her expression softened a little, and she sighed, leaning back into the couch cushions. "I guess it does make sense. But I still can't believe Matteo didn't completely lose it."

"Trust me," I said, rubbing the back of my neck, "he almost did. But he would go along with anything you wanted, it's you."

That earned me a smile—a soft one, but still. I found myself grinning like an idiot.

"So," she said, looking at me with that sharp, curious gaze of hers. "How exactly is this going to work? Are we going to hold hands in public? Pose for selfies? Declare our undying love in front of the paddock?"

She was teasing, but her words still made something twist in my chest. "Nothing over the top," I replied, forcing myself to keep it casual. "Public appearances together at races and events. A little PDA to sell it."

Her eyebrow shot up. "Define 'a little PDA.'"

I shrugged, trying to ignore the way my pulse kicked up. "Holding hands, an arm around your shoulder. Stuff that looks natural."

She gave me a look that said she was clearly imagining how unnatural that would feel. I couldn't exactly blame her.

"And how long is this supposed to last?" she asked, her tone all business now.

"The rest of the season?" I said. "Or long enough to convince the media and keep Belen Racing off my back, whatever comes first."

"Right." She nodded, chewing on her bottom lip like she was still trying to process everything. I didn't let myself dwell on how distracting that was.

"You okay with this?" I asked, my voice softer than I intended.

She looked up at me, her eyes meeting mine. For a second, I thought I saw something flicker there, something unsure and vulnerable, but it was gone as quickly as it appeared.

"Yeah," she said with a small smile. "I'm okay with it."

I nodded, trying to ignore the wave of relief that washed over me. "Good. Because if this is going to work, we need to look convincing."

"Convincing?" She tilted her head, her smile turning sly. "You mean like *this*?"

Before I could react, she had crossed the space and was next to me, a hand sliding down my arm, making my body react before my mind could. My own hand wrapped around her waist and kept her against me. She leaned in and my entire body went on high alert. Was she about to kiss me? She paused, looking up with glittering eyes.

"Oh, Alex," she said in an exaggerated, too-high, breathy voice, batting her lashes dramatically. "You're just so dreamy."

"That's terrible. If that's what you're bringing to the table, we're doomed."

"Hey, I'm just getting into character," she shot back, her grin widening.

"Maybe leave the acting to me." She rolled her eyes but didn't argue. And for a brief moment, it felt...easy. Natural, even.

This was going to work.

At least, that's what I kept telling myself.

But as I watched her get up and head toward the door, the playful smile still lingering on her lips, I couldn't shake the feeling that this whole plan might be more dangerous than I'd realized.

Time passed in a blur when we were in season. The fast-paced lifestyle of Formula One seeped back into my bones, adrenaline coursing through me. I loved it, loved the pressure and high stakes. With the last win under my belt, I felt the adrenaline racing through my bones already. I was sitting in first place in the Drivers'

World Championship standings, but only ten points behind was Theo Bauer, I couldn't afford any mistakes.

The Italian Grand Prix was its own kind of chaos. Monza wasn't just another race, it was a cathedral of speed, where mistakes were unforgiving and victories immortalized. Even now, as the morning sun poured golden light over the paddock, the atmosphere thrummed with energy. Fans already chanted in the grandstands, their cheers rising like waves crashing against the walls of my concentration.

I made my way to the garage, helmet in hand, sidestepping the cameras that tried to catch every flicker of emotion on my face. Today, there was no room for emotion. Not for nerves. Not for doubt. And definitely not for the thoughts of Lucia DeLuca that had crept into my head at the worst possible times this weekend.

I tightened my grip on the helmet as I crossed into the calm, orderly chaos of the garage. The mechanics were already at work, checking tire pressure, monitoring telemetry, and preparing for the grueling hours ahead. They didn't look up; they didn't have to. We all knew what was at stake.

"Morning, Wright," came the clipped voice of my race engineer, Simon. He handed me the day's strategy sheet.

"Morning." I skimmed the paper, I needed it etched into my instincts.

"Feeling good about the setup?" Simon asked, his sharp eyes scanning me like I was another component of the car.

"Car's strong. It'll be all about the start and managing the tires in sector two." My voice was even, but my brain itched to get on track and feel the balance under me. Words only went so far in a sport where the difference between glory and disaster came down to fractions of a second.

But as I tried to picture turn one, the braking point at Variante del Rettifilo, my thoughts veered off-course. To her. To Lucia.

She'd come to the paddock yesterday, a little wide-eyed but trying to hide it under her usual quiet composure. When I'd stepped in to stand by her side, the tension in her shoulders had eased, and damn it, if that hadn't felt like a win. Gianna was with her grandparents, who were in town for the race, and Lucia looked a little lost without her. I nodded at Anna and she seemed to understand my silent plea. *Make sure Lucia isn't alone.*

The fake-dating arrangement was supposed to make everything *simpler*. A barrier for the media, a shield against the inevitable questions about why she was here. Instead, it felt like the start of a slow, impossible spiral. We had decided to start the charade after this race since her parents were in town. When we last talked about it, she had pressed her body up to mine, batted her lashes, and been silly, but having her that close, breaking past that invisible line of personal space. Between that and the night at the club, I was one step away from losing restraint. I wanted her there. I wanted to breathe in her berry-scented perfume, or hair product, or whatever it was. *Fuck, I sound like a lovesick fool.* I'll admit the extra time with Lucia was nice. I loved seeing Gianna and having them here in the circuit. Enjoying the company of someone is fine, that is totally fine. But breathing in their scent, Jesus. *Get it together, Wright.*

I shook my head, forcing the memory away.

"Something wrong?" Simon asked.

"Nothing." I handed the strategy sheet back to him. "Just ready to get out there." The pre-race routines came next: the engineering brief, the driver's meeting, a final stretch to shake out the nerves. I stayed quiet through most of it, letting myself get in the zone. This morning I had already started to zone out the world, getting race ready. Matteo carried the conversation when we saw each other at the hotel this morning; his parents were getting in soon, but not before we needed to be on the track. His easy charm kept the conversation light as we traveled to the circuit together, but I knew him well enough to spot the slight edge in his voice. Racing at home always did that to him, to anyone, really. Home races were another level entirely.

Out on the grid, the crowd was deafening. Italian flags whipped in the breeze, and fans called Morretti's name louder than anyone else's. The Italian team was a powerhouse, and Matteo had been buzzing with the same energy as we partied this morning. As I walked down past each team's lounges and club rooms, I tried to visualize the team strategies on the track, where everyone would be starting, and how to implement the plans based on final formation.

Until, a familiar laugh cut through the noise. I glanced up, and there she was, standing with Matteo near the barrier of the Moretti team space. I had walked the length of the area to get my mind refocused before I was needed in the garage, but here I was, sucked in by the voice I had come to search out.

Lucia's parents were beside her, I could see how she fit in this world that felt so foreign to her. The same warm smile as her mother, the same fierce light in her eyes as Matteo. She caught me looking, and instead of shying away, she gave me a small, almost mischievous wave.

There goes my focus.

I send an easy smile their way, waving to her and her parents, before turning back toward the Belen area. I worked through my mental routine, headphones in as I waited for go time. After a few final checks with the engineers, it was time.

I climbed into the cockpit, pulling the helmet down to seal myself in. The roar of the crowd dulled, replaced by the steady thrum of my heartbeat.

"Radio check," Simon's voice crackled in my ear.

"Loud and clear," I replied, gripping the steering wheel. The formation lap was a blur of instinct and preparation, each corner a reminder of what was coming. As we lined up on the grid, the world seemed to hold its breath.

I flexed my fingers, eyes locked on the lights above. This was my arena, my battlefield. I focused on the car, my sanctuary, and the world narrowed. It was just me and the machine now.

Five red lights.

This was it.

They went out, and I launched forward, every thought, every doubt burned away in the white-hot clarity of the race.

The race ended in a blur of heat, sweat, and raw adrenaline. As I crossed the finish line, the checkered flag waving wildly, the roar of the crowd hit me like a wave. Second place. Not the top step, but damn close, and Matteo wasn't far behind.

"P2, Alex. Hell of a drive," Simon's voice crackled through the radio, calm but brimming with satisfaction.

"Thanks, team. Good work today," I said, my voice tight with exhaustion and relief.

My muscles ached, and the cockpit felt stifling as I rolled behind the marker indicating second place. Cameras swarmed the area, their lenses hungry for reactions, but all I could think about was getting out of the car and catching my breath. It was a lower-ranked driver that snagged first today, they drove damn well too. Theo was knocked back by a small crash on the twelfth lap, finishing in fifth. That gap in points would hopefully help my standing in the weeks to come.

I climbed out, greeted by the cheers of the team and the familiar claps on the back from engineers and crew. Matteo pulled in behind me moments later, his grin as wide as the Monza track itself as he got out of his car.

"Not bad, huh?" he said, his helmet tucked under his arm.

"Third place in front of your home crowd? I'd say more than *not bad*, mate," I replied, clapping him on the shoulder.

Together, we made our way to the podium ceremony. The champagne was sticky on my skin, and the trophy felt solid and heavy in my hands. But it wasn't until I stepped off the stage that the real celebration began. As soon as Matteo and I walked back toward the paddocks, his family was there waiting. His parents, beaming with pride, engulfed him in hugs, while his mother fussed over his sweaty hair and his father laughed, shaking his head. They pulled me in with them, not letting me retreat back to my own team's paddock.

And then there was Lucia.

She hung back at first, her gaze flicking from Matteo to me. When I caught her eye, she hesitated for a fraction of a second before stepping forward, her smile shy but warm, as if the internal war of whether to greet me in the public eye was the right decision. I let her make the move, not wanting to push her until she was ready.

"Congratulations," she said, her voice soft but sincere as she grew nearer.

"Thanks," I replied just as quietly, as if we were in our own little world. Our bubble was popped by a tiny version of her jumping up and down and chanting my name.

"Hey, kiddo!" I said, bending down and pulling her up to sit on my hip.

"You're all sticky!" she said, poking at my race suit that was rolled down but drenched in champagne.

"Nonno and Nonna are here!" Gianna announced, and I turned to face them, a genuine smile bright on my features as I took them in. Matteo's mother turned to me with an almost maternal concern that caught me off guard.

"You were brilliant, Alexander. Absolutely brilliant." Her Italian accent wrapped around her words like a comforting blanket. "Do you have anyone here with you? Family?"

The question hit harder than I expected. The answer, of course, was no. I hadn't had a family waiting for me after a race in years. A pang of sadness shot through me, wishing my dad could be here, that he had his memory and could see me now. My team was incredible, their cheers and pats on the back weren't the same as this—this warm, chaotic bubble of love that Matteo and his family carried with them.

"No, just the team," I said with a shrug, trying to play it off.

She frowned, her gaze softening, and before I could protest, she pulled me into a hug, Gianna giggled as she was squished alongside us.

"Well, you have us today," she said firmly.

The words stuck in my chest, choking me up in a way I hadn't felt in years.

Matteo's dad clapped me on the back, a gesture that almost knocked the air out of me. "You're practically part of the family, anyway. You'll join us for dinner tonight."

Lucia looked up to me, "you really can't say no,"

14

LUCIA

Dinner with my family after the race felt like just what I needed—comforting, chaotic, and full of the kind of noise that made my heart feel full. I had missed the constant companionship of my parents, their bond with Gia, and their ability to make everyone feel important, the same superpower my brother had. The restaurant Matteo had chosen was nestled on a quiet street just outside Monza, with stone walls and flickering candlelight that made everything feel intimate and special. The air smelled like rosemary and garlic, and the low hum of conversation blended with the occasional clink of glasses.

I was wedged between my mother and Alexander, which felt like a particularly cruel setup orchestrated by Matteo since my mother was bound to want to talk to Alex all evening. My brother, sitting across from me, smirked every time our mother talked animatedly over me to Alexander. I shot my brother a glare, stabbing at the roasted potatoes on my plate with unnecessary force.

Alexander chuckled, the sound low and warm at something my mother said, and I couldn't help but glance at him. Gianna had moved into his lap, refusing to sit on her own. She was eating right off his plate now as he continued to talk to my mother. He was relaxed in a way I hadn't seen often, his usual sharp focus softened by the glow of the evening. He caught my gaze and gave me a quick wink, his eyes holding something that made my stomach twist.

"And how are you liking it, being on the road with Matteo and his circus of a sport?" my father asked, his booming voice cutting through the chatter.

"It's...different," I said, choosing my words carefully. "But it's good. Gianna loves all the excitement, and I think it's been good for me too. A change of pace."

"She's made friends with like every crew member already," Matteo said, mouth full of food.

"I am a delight, that's why," I shot back at him with a winning smile. He rolled his eyes in response.

My mother patted my hand, laughing softly. "You are, *cara mia*. I must say, you seem lighter these days, happier. It's been a long time since I've seen you like this."

Her words caught me off guard, the noise of the table faded into the background. I looked at her, trying to read the expression in her eyes. There was no judgment, no probing, just quiet, unconditional love.

"I am happy," I said, settling into the thought. I had met more people and traveled more in the last couple of weeks than I had in years. It was fun and new and exciting and I felt like that dormant spark inside was starting to glow again.

Matteo raised his glass. "To Lucia surviving life on the circuit."

"And to Matteo and Alexander," my mother added, lifting her glass as well, "for their amazing finishes today. We're so proud of both of you." I glanced to Alexander, whose eyes held a soft look. They shifted to meet mine, and he covered it with an easy smile, raising his own glass.

"To Matteo and Alexander," the table echoed.

I clinked my glass against Alexander's, and when our fingers brushed, it sent a jolt through me that I felt all the way to my core.

I quickly pulled back, trying to ignore the way my pulse quickened.

The evening stretched on with laughter and stories, the kind of night that wrapped around you like a warm blanket. Eventually, I excused myself to head to the restroom, needing a moment to collect my thoughts.

As I stepped out into the quiet hallway near the restrooms, I nearly collided with Alexander. He was leaning casually against the wall, waiting.

"Fancy meeting you here," he said, his voice low and playful.

I crossed my arms, tilting my head. "Are you following me, Wright?"

"Maybe." He grinned, and it was the kind of grin that made it impossible to be annoyed. "Or maybe I just wanted a break from Matteo's endless monologue about his overtaking move in the third sector."

I laughed despite myself, shaking my head. "He'll be talking about that for days."

Alexander's gaze softened, the teasing fell away. "You look really beautiful tonight, you know."

I blinked, caught off guard by the compliment. "Are you practicing already?"

"Hmm." He stepped closer, his voice dropping just enough to send a shiver down my spine.

"Careful, Alexander," I said, my voice lighter than I felt. "People might think you're flirting with me."

"Isn't that the idea," he replied, his fingers brushing mine as if testing the waters. The touch was barely there, but it sent heat coursing through me.

For a moment, I couldn't breathe. The world narrowed to just the two of us, the space between us charged.

But then I took a step back, forcing myself to break the spell. "We should get back."

His eyes lingered on me for a moment before he nodded, a small smile tugging at his lips. "Lead the way."

As I walked back to the table, I tried to shake off the feeling of his touch, the way my skin still buzzed where his fingers had brushed mine. But no matter how hard I tried, I couldn't stop myself from craving more.

By the time we landed in Azerbaijan, all I wanted was sleep. Gianna had been fussy the entire flight, which meant hours of trying to comfort her while she cried inconsolably. Matteo and Alexander had flown ahead on an ungodly early flight, leaving me to manage Gia alone. But it also meant Alex let me take his private jet. Thankfully, Nicola had offered to come with me so I wouldn't have to face the ordeal by myself. Between that and not having to deal with a commercial flight and other people, it was a godsend.

As we stepped off the plane, Gia was finally asleep in my arms, her little head tucked against my shoulder, her cheeks still damp from earlier tears. Nicola trailed behind us, juggling our bags with careful precision. The last thing either of us wanted was to wake Gia now that the storm had passed.

As we made our way through the quiet airport terminal, Nicola glanced over at me, her expression calm despite the whirlwind of the last few hours. "You're doing amazing, Lucia," she said softly, her voice a steady presence in the haze of my exhaustion.

I gave her a weary smile. "I don't feel amazing. I feel like I've been put through a blender. Thank you for coming with me, though. I don't know what I would've done on my own."

Nicola shrugged as if it were nothing, though the kindness in her eyes said otherwise. "It's no trouble. Gia's a sweetheart, even when she's having a rough time. And you? You're stronger than you think."

I let out a tired laugh, careful not to jostle Gia. "Strong doesn't feel like the right word. I feel more like...duct tape. Holding it all together by sheer force and praying nothing falls apart."

Nicola stopped walking for a moment and placed a gentle hand on my shoulder. "Lucia, listen to me. You're an incredible mother. You're doing everything you can for Gia, and it shows. She's happy and loved, even when she's cranky. You're not just holding it together; you're thriving in the chaos. And you're not alone. You've got me, Matteo, Alexander—everyone who cares about you."

Her words hit hard, I felt the sting of tears behind my eyes. The weight of everything—the flight, Gia's crying, the constant balancing act of being a mom—felt just a little lighter.

"Thanks, Nicola," I said, my voice soft. "I mean it. You didn't have to do this, but I'm really glad you're here."

She smiled, stepping back to pick up the bags again. "Of course I'm here. What kind of friend would I be if I let you handle all this alone? Now, let's get you and Gia to the hotel. You both need some rest, and I'm pretty sure I saw Matteo order extra snacks to your room. He's predictable like that."

A small laugh slipped out despite my exhaustion. Nicola always had a way of diffusing the tension, of making things feel manageable even when they weren't. As we stepped into the car waiting outside, Gia still asleep in my arms, I finally allowed myself to exhale. For the first time in hours, I felt a semblance of calm.

Once we got to the hotel, things finally settled. Gia had a snack, we played for a little while, and then she went down for a much-needed nap. As soon as I shut the bedroom door, I wandered into the smaller living space and collapsed onto the couch, letting out a sigh of pure exhaustion.

My phone pinged with a message from Nicola that read, *Open the door.*

Dragging myself up, I shuffled over and pulled it open to find her standing there, looking refreshed and far too energetic for someone who'd just survived the same trip I had.

"Hey," I greeted, my voice tired but grateful.

"Hey," she replied, stepping inside. "I took a nap, unpacked all my clothes, and now I'm here to hang out with G while she sleeps. You, on the other hand, are going to take a break. Go to the café downstairs, get a coffee, sit in silence for a bit—whatever you need. But go."

Her tone left no room for argument, and honestly, I didn't have the energy to resist even if I wanted to.

"You're a lifesaver," I mumbled, grabbing my bag.

"Yes, I am. Now go before Gia wakes up and I change my mind."

I laughed lightly, already feeling a weight lifting off my shoulders as I stepped out the door. I hadn't had the chance to shower or freshen up after the flight, but honestly, I didn't have the energy to care; sometimes not feeling trapped in a room was just what I needed. I walked until I found a couch with a little lamp and side table, and I decided that was good enough. A large bay window looked out and I pulled out my Kindle from my purse and I sat like that for an hour.

"Luce?" a familiar voice cut through the silent hallway.

"Hey!" I said, seeing Alexander. He was dressed to the nines, a baby blue knitted sweater and cargo pants that I swear no one except Alexander Wright could pull off. I realized I might have been ogling him a little too long once he cleared his throat.

"Sorry, um, tough day," I explained, coming back to reality.

A crease at his eyebrow appeared. "You okay?"

"Yeah, I'm fine!" I said, my voice pitching at the end, and I could tell by the way he looked at me that he was not buying it at all.

"You hungry?" he asked.

"I could eat."

"Come on." He held out a hand. I went to reach for it and was stopped by a big yawn taking over me. After the pause, I took his hand and he pulled it into the crook of his arm. Alexander led me through the maze of hallways until we reached a dimly lit lounge tucked away from the rest of the hotel. The space was stunning—candles flickered atop dark oak tables, and warm, ambient lighting glowed against the paneled walls. The soft hum of conversation mixed with the gentle clink of silverware and the smooth notes of jazz playing in the background. It felt like stepping into another world.

A host guided us to a booth in the far back corner, a cozy little nook perfect for two. As I slid into the plush seat, Alexander followed, his presence filling the space beside me. The intimacy of the setting wasn't lost on me—the low light, the quiet buzz of the room—it felt both magical and charged.

He picked up the menu, scanning it with ease, while I stared blankly at mine. The exhaustion from the day hit me like a wave, and the jumble of foreign words on the page was impossible to decipher. My expression must have given me away because Alexander glanced over and gently slid the menu out of my hands.

"Sweet or savory?" he asked, his voice low and calm.

"Uh...savory," I replied, too tired to argue.

He nodded, signaling for a server and placing the order in a language I didn't recognize. I blinked at him, surprised yet again by the layers of Alexander Wright. There was always more to him than met the eye.

When the server left, he turned toward me, leaning slightly against the backrest. "So," he said softly, his eyes meeting mine, "what happened today?"

Something about the way he asked—his voice steady, his expression open—made it impossible to brush him off. Instead of the usual, *I'm fine,* the words spilled out before I could stop them.

"Everything that could have gone wrong, went wrong," I admitted, pressing a finger to my temple. I recounted the disastrous morning: Gia's meltdown, the chaos at the airport, the overwhelming exhaustion.

When I finally stopped, Alexander tilted his head slightly. "I like Nicola," he said simply, a small smile tugging at his lips.

I smiled back, warmth filling my chest. "So do I. I'm lucky she came into my life when she did. It feels like I've known her forever, not just a few weeks."

"She's good for you," he said, his voice laced with quiet approval. Then, with that easy, devastating smile of his, he added, "Well, I can't fix today, but I can feed you. We'll start there."

His smile was disarming, bright enough to erase the lingering frustration from the day. It wasn't just a smile; it was *him*. Pure Alexander—effortless, charming, and unexpectedly kind.

"Also," he continued, a hint of uncertainty creeping into his tone, "I was thinking we should start the plan ahead of this race. Maybe post something? Get people talking before we show up together."

I perked up at the shift in conversation, happy for a distraction. "Totally! We could do a soft launch."

Alexander blinked at me, confused. "What the hell is a soft launch?"

"It's like a teaser," I explained, holding back a laugh. "You post something ambiguous, like a hand or the back of someone's head —just enough to hint that you're in a relationship but without showing everything. It's mysterious."

His brow furrowed, amusement flickering in his eyes. "How is it mysterious?"

"It draws people in!"

He rubbed a hand over his face.

"This will stir the pot, intrigue the media." Honestly, Anna would be proud of me for thinking of this.

He chuckled, shaking his head. "Fine. Whatever you think is best."

I leaned in, resting a hand on his arm. "This is going to be fun.

Something different to focus on. Honestly, I'm excited to have an identity outside of 'Mom' for a bit."

"You're an amazing mum," Alexander said, his voice soft with sincerity.

"I know," I replied with a small smile. "But it's consuming, you know? After I found out I was pregnant, my whole world shifted. It stopped being about me—it was all about Gia. And I wouldn't trade that for anything, but sometimes...it's a lot. Being responsible for an entire little human, knowing everything I do affects her."

He nodded, his gaze unwavering. Then, under the table, his hand brushed against my thigh and rested there. It was meant to be comforting, I knew that, but the jolt of electricity it sent through me made my breath hitch.

I pulled myself together quickly. "Anyway, come here," I said, grabbing his phone. I leaned into him, angling it to hide my face behind my hair as I snapped a photo. The image showed Alexander looking down at me, his face only partially visible, while my own stayed out of view.

"Perfect," I said, showing him the screen. "Post it before tomorrow, and we're set, we can take one for mine in one of the mirrors in the lobby, the pretty, big ones."

He stared at the picture for a moment, then back at me, a smile tugging at the corners of his lips. "You're something else, you know that?"

I handed him the phone with a grin. "You have no idea."

15

LUCIA

I had spent the entire night tossing and turning, only to wake up with dark circles under my eyes and the kind of exhaustion that no amount of coffee could fix. Today was qualifying day for Azerbaijan, and Alexander and I were making our first appearance as a *couple*. Nicola was staying back at the hotel with Gia, giving me the freedom to dive headfirst into this ridiculous, over-the-top plan of ours.

Naturally, I had spent most of the night overanalyzing everything and talking Nicola's ear off about it. She had listened with an amused smile before breaking into laughter and waggling her eyebrows.

Good luck not falling in love, she had teased, her tone dripping with smugness.

Sure, I liked Alexander—who wouldn't? He was devastatingly handsome, endlessly kind, and carried himself with the effortless charm of someone who always knew exactly what to say. Plus, he was a five-time world champion, for crying out loud. But just because I could appreciate all of that didn't mean I was about to fall head over heels for him. I didn't have time for love. My plate was already overflowing with reinventing myself, being a mother, and figuring out the rest of my life.

Still, Nicola had planted the tiniest seed of doubt in my mind, and it sprouted into full-blown panic right as I was about to leave.

"Are you going to have to kiss him?" she asked before I left, her eyebrows raised almost to her hairline.

The question hit me like a truck. *Kissing. Right.* That would definitely be part of the fake relationship package. Why hadn't that crossed my mind before?

As I walked out of the hotel lobby to meet Alexander, the thought looped in my brain on repeat: *I have to kiss Alexander Wright.*

By the time I slid into the back of the town car beside him, I was barely holding it together. He looked unfairly good, as always, wearing a street-style-adjacent suit that somehow managed to make him look polished and effortlessly cool all at once. My brain was officially mush.

"Hey, pretty girl." He smirked, laying on the act already.

I was vaguely aware that he said something to me as the car started moving, but I couldn't process it.

"Hmm?" I asked, blinking at him like an idiot.

"I was saying that—"

"We need to kiss," I blurted.

The words hung in the air between us, heavy and unrelenting.

"Um..."

I waved my hands in front of me, as if that would somehow help me reel in my spiraling thoughts. "I mean, they're going to expect us to kiss, right? At some point. And I didn't think about it until now, but if you kiss me for the first time out there, in front of cameras, I might panic. And then I'll flinch, or move weirdly, or you'll miss, and we'll end up on some *Most Awkward Celebrity Kisses* list."

His eyebrows lifted, but his lips twitched like he was fighting a smile.

"So," I continued, barely stopping for breath, "we should probably, you know, practice. For the cameras. For professionalism."

"Professionalism," he repeated, his voice laced with amusement.

"Yes." I nodded so hard I might've gotten whiplash. "Exactly."

Alexander's gaze locked onto mine, his expression softening. Then, without a word, he leaned toward me, his hand reaching out to cup my chin.

And then he kissed me.

His lips met mine in a way that was both deliberate and gentle, sending a jolt of warmth through my entire body. Soft, easy, and utterly disarming. I forgot how to breathe, how to think. All I could focus on was the feeling of his mouth on mine and the way my stomach was now home to an entire swarm of butterflies.

When he finally pulled away, a lopsided smile tugged at his lips.

"Figured we should get the first one out of the way," he said, leaning back in his seat like it was the most normal thing in the world.

I stared at him, utterly speechless.

"You're welcome, by the way," he added, smirking.

"For what?" I managed to croak.

"Saving you from the *Most Awkward Celebrity Kisses* list," he teased.

I rolled my eyes, doing my best to act unfazed despite the fact that my heart was still doing flips.

"Right," I muttered, crossing my arms and staring out the window. But my reflection in the glass betrayed me, showing the stupid grin I couldn't quite suppress.

Alexander just chuckled softly beside me. I was either in a trance, or we were closer to the racetrack than I had previously thought, but soon the car pulled up and I looked outside, seeing the front entrance, the grand signs, and where we scanned our passes. I also saw the sheer amount of photographers present.

Anna must have worked her magic, making sure our appearance would be well documented. She had sent us a message earlier wishing us good luck and that she would be in the Belen garage when we got in.

"Hey." Alexander's voice was low, his accent curling around the word like velvet. His hand brushed my exposed thigh as he leaned closer, his touch featherlight but electric, sending a ripple of chills up my spine.

"We got this," he murmured, his thumb grazing the edge of my knee now, grounding me in the moment. "I'll get out first and open your door. Then we walk in together, nice and easy."

He smiled, a real one, the kind that could light up an entire room, or in this case, calm the onslaught of chaos in my brain. It was maddening how effortlessly he could make the storm in my chest quiet with one look.

I exhaled slowly, nodding as I met his steady gaze. "All right," I said, my voice steadier than I expected.

His lips quirked in a teasing grin as his eyes roved over me for the briefest moment. "Plus," he added, his tone dropping slightly, "you look stunning."

And just like that, he slipped out of the car, leaving me to sit there like a deer caught in headlights, my cheeks heating faster than a Formula One engine.

The door swung open moments later, and the sounds of the outside world hit me all at once, fans shouting, cameras flashing, voices calling out Alexander's name.

"Alexander! Who's this?"

"Alexander, over here!"

"Alexander, is that Matteo DeLuca's sister?"

That last one sent the crowd into overdrive, and I swore my stomach dropped somewhere near my knees. Alexander didn't falter. He bent slightly, his hand extended toward me, his signature smile firmly in place. "Ready?" he asked, the word just loud enough for me to hear over the din.

I nodded, taking his hand as if it were a lifeline. His palm was warm and steady, his grip firm but not overwhelming, and the moment our skin touched, some of the tension in my shoulders eased.

The crowd roared louder as I stepped out, but I focused on him. *Just him.*

He kept his gaze forward, waving casually with his free hand while his other stayed wrapped protectively around mine. Then he dipped his head down to me, his breath warm against my ear, sending another wave of goose bumps across my skin.

"You're doing great," he murmured.

The words were like a balm, and I let them sink in. I forced a wide smile, tipping my head up toward him as if he'd just told me the funniest joke in the world. My laugh was soft but deliberate, a signal to the cameras. He pulled back just enough to meet my eyes, his expression soft and encouraging, and I knew I could do this.

We walked hand in hand through the crowd, the questions and camera flashes fading into white noise. I kept my grip on him firm, matching his pace as we passed through the security checkpoint. Even then, he didn't let go, his hand staying intertwined with mine like it was the most natural thing in the world.

As we moved deeper into the circuit, past the teams' lounges and toward the Belen Racing tent, the chaos of the crowd gave way to a more controlled buzz. But Alexander's hand? It stayed with me, his thumb occasionally brushing against mine in a way that felt deliberate. Comforting.

I couldn't help but glance up at him. He was calm and collected, a walking portrait of confidence and charm, but there was something grounding in the way he stayed connected to me, in how he made it feel like we were in this together. I felt steady.

The energy in the Belen Racing tent was electric, a buzzing mix of adrenaline, nerves, and excitement. Alexander stood in front of me, his arms crossed, but his expression was soft, his lips pulled into a small, teasing smile.

"So," he began, his voice casual but with a curious edge. "Do you want to stay here or head over to the Moretti tent with Matteo?"

I knew he was giving me an out, an escape to be with my brother, my safe zone, to start easy and not dive in head first. But I was ready to dive. I squared my shoulders and tilted my head at him.

"I think," I said, dragging the words out as if giving it serious consideration, "that if I'm going to be your fake girlfriend, I should probably stay and, you know, support my fake boyfriend. Commitment to the bit and all."

Alexander chuckled, the sound warm and low. "That's very selfless of you."

"I'm nothing if not dedicated."

He leaned in slightly, his expression shifting to something more serious, though his eyes still danced with humor. "And here I thought you just wanted better snacks. We have the good espresso machine, after all."

I feigned shock, placing a hand on my chest. "How dare you? As if I would be bribed by snacks and non-Italian coffee."

He smirked. "Not even a little?"

"Fine," I admitted with a dramatic sigh. "Just the snacks though."

His laugh was soft, almost too quiet to hear over the chaos of the team preparing for the race. I glanced around at the engineers, the mechanics, the monitors showing the track, and then back at him.

"Good luck out there," I said softly, my voice cutting through the noise like a secret meant just for him.

"Thanks." His voice was equally quiet, his gaze steady.

Before I could overthink it, I leaned up on my toes and pressed a quick kiss to his cheek. The touch was brief, but the heat that climbed up my neck as I pulled back was anything but.

"For luck," I added quickly, stepping back and trying to act like my heart wasn't pounding.

His smile widened, his eyes crinkling at the corners. "I'll take it."

With that, he turned and headed toward the pit lane, leaving me standing there feeling like my feet weren't quite touching the ground. We would do it all again tomorrow, with an even bigger crowd.

From my spot in the Belen garage, I could see everything; the mechanics working tirelessly, the monitors showing every angle of the track, and the sea of fans in the grandstands. It was a surreal experience, being so close to the action yet so removed from it at the same time.

The race began, and the tension was immediate. Alexander's car shot forward, holding steady in the top positions. My heart raced with every turn, every pit stop, every daring overtake. I found myself gripping the edge of my seat, holding my breath whenever the camera lingered on his car.

When a particularly intense battle for first unfolded between him and another driver, I couldn't help but gasp aloud. The crew around me cheered and groaned with every move, their energy infectious.

In a moment of distraction, I pulled out my phone. With the hum of the race in the background, I snapped a selfie, the Belen Racing logo in clear view behind me. I added a simple pink heart emoji to the caption and hit Post, feeling a strange mix of nerves and satisfaction. The soft launch of our "relationship" was officially underway.

When Alexander crossed the finish line securing his first-place position for tomorrow, the entire garage erupted in cheers. I found myself swept up in the excitement, running out with the crew to celebrate.

⸺⸺

The finish was chaos. Alexander's car rolled to a stop, and he was out in an instant, throwing his arms around the crew members gathered at the barriers. His helmet was off in seconds, his hair a mess, his grin brighter than the sun overhead.

And then his eyes found mine.

I froze as he broke away from the crew and strode toward me, his expression a mix of exhilaration and something else— something that made my breath hitch.

Before I could process what was happening, his arms were around me, pulling me into a tight hug. The world seemed to blur for a moment, the noise fading as I felt the solid warmth of him against me.

Our faces were close, so close that his forehead brushed mine. His breath mingled with mine, and I swore the earth tilted slightly on its axis.

In a flash of a decision, his lips met mine. It was soft, chaste even, but it sent a rush of warmth through me that left me feeling weightless.

When he pulled back, his gaze searched mine, a question lingering in his eyes. I couldn't find the words to answer, but the smile tugging at my lips must have said enough because his grin returned, just as dazzling as before.

The crew's cheers pulled us back to reality, but I couldn't shake the buzz of my skin, my heart racing, or the tingling on my lips.

DRIVER CHAMPIONSHIP STANDINGS

1. **Alexander Wright** — 265 pts
   Belen Racing

2. **Theo Bauer** — 240 pts
   Kaz Energy Racing

3. **Carlos Torres** — 186 pts
   Moretti Racing

4. **James Hansson** — 140 pts
   Belen Racing

5. **Matteo DeLuca** — 116 pts
   Moretti Racing

16

ALEXANDER

The checkered flag waved, and I crossed the finish line.

First place in Azerbaijan.

I exhaled a sharp breath, gripping the wheel so tight my knuckles ached. My radio burst to life with the sound of my engineer shouting my name, cheers and congratulations pouring into my helmet. The car still hummed beneath me, the vibration of the engine coursing through my body like electricity.

I'd done it.

The race had been brutal, a constant push and pull, wheel-to-wheel battles that demanded every ounce of focus I had. My rival had been relentless, cutting me off at corners, challenging me at every straight. But I'd stayed calm, waiting for my moment. And when it came, when I'd seen the perfect gap in the final laps, I'd taken it without hesitation.

Now, the world was an explosion of sound. The crowd roared, their cheers blending with the team's celebration over the radio. I pulled the car into the pit lane, my heart thundering in my chest.

As soon as I climbed out, after standing on my car and throwing a fist into the air, I climbed down and ran to my crew, pulling me into hugs, shouting in my ear, their joy infectious. I laughed, unable to stop smiling. This was what I lived for—the thrill, the triumph, the shared victory with the people who'd worked just as hard as I had to make it happen.

But then I saw *her*.

Lucia stood at the edge of the chaos, a small smile on her lips, her eyes wide and bright as she watched. She looked slightly out of place in the sea of team uniforms and machinery, but somehow, she belonged.

Something shifted inside me. Without thinking, I broke away from the team and headed straight for her, like a magnetic pull. I couldn't stop it even if I tried. Her expression changed as I approached, her smile growing, her eyes softening. I didn't stop moving until she was in my arms, her body warm and solid against mine. Our faces were close, so close I could see the faint freckles on her nose, the way her lips parted in surprise. My forehead rested against hers for a moment, the noise around us fading into a distant hum.

And then, I kissed her.

It wasn't planned. Hell, it wasn't even logical. But in that moment, it felt like the most natural thing in the world. Her lips were soft, her breath warm against mine, and for a few seconds, the world stopped spinning.

When I pulled back, her eyes searched mine, and I couldn't help but grin. She looked stunned, maybe even a little dazed, but she didn't pull away.

The cheers around us grew louder, pulling me back to reality. I gave her hand a quick squeeze before the team tugged me toward the podium, their shouts of celebration ringing in my ears.

Standing on the top step of the podium, champagne dripping from my hair and my suit, I felt alive in a way I hadn't in months.

The crowd was a blur of faces, their cheers vibrating in the air around me. I raised the trophy high, the weight of it grounding me. Cameras flashed, capturing every angle, but my mind kept drifting back to Lucia.

That kiss.

It hadn't been part of the plan. Hell, I wasn't sure what it meant. But it had felt right. More than right. I glanced out over the crowd, wondering if she was watching.

The adrenaline still hadn't worn off by the time I was back in the motorhome. My skin buzzed with the memory of the race, of the kiss, of standing on the podium with my team.

I ran a towel over my face, glancing at my reflection in the small mirror. My grin was still there, impossible to shake. As I pulled on a fresh shirt, my eyes scanned the room. Where was she? I hadn't seen Lucia since the podium. She'd been there one moment, and then the next, she was gone, lost in the sea of faces.

The sound of footsteps outside the door made my pulse quicken. It opened, and there she was, standing in the doorway with a hesitant smile.

"Looking for me?" she asked, her voice teasing but soft.

"Always," I replied, the word slipping out before I could stop it. Her eyes widened slightly, but she didn't look away.

I leaned against the counter, crossing my arms as I took her in. "So," I said, my voice low, "about that kiss..."

She raised a brow, her smile turning playful. "Which one? The car, before or after the race?"

I laughed, shaking my head. "All, I guess."

Lucia stepped farther into the room, her confidence growing. "Well, you did say we had to sell it."

"Did we sell it?"

"Oh, definitely." She smirked, pulling out her phone and showing me her social post. A selfie, her in the garage, the Belen logo in the background, and a single pink heart emoji.

"Subtle," I said, grinning, knowing my own socials would be blowing up.

Her cheeks flushed, but her gaze stayed steady. "Seemed effective."

"More than effective," I murmured, my voice dipping as I took a step closer to her.

Her breath hitched, and for a moment, the space between us felt electric again. But before I could close it, she cleared her throat, breaking the spell.

"Congratulations on the win." Her voice was light, but her eyes revealed more than she probably realized, always wearing her emotions on her sleeve.

"Thanks," I replied, my smile softening. "But I think you might be the real victory today."

Lucia rolled her eyes, but the blush on her cheeks gave her away. "Laying it on real thick, Wright."

My grin widened as I watched her fight back a smile of her own.

Lucia's blush was becoming one of my favorite things. It crept up her cheeks like a sunrise—soft, warm, and utterly captivating. She crossed her arms, clearly trying to brush off my teasing, but the way her lips twitched betrayed her.

I couldn't help myself. "You know, you make it way too easy," I said, my voice low enough for only her to hear. Her eyes darted to mine.

"You're insufferable," she muttered, but her cheeks darkened even more.

I laughed, unable to resist the urge to keep her on her toes. "Hold still," I said, pulling my phone from my pocket.

"What are you doing?" She narrowed her eyes at me.

"Might as well confirm it properly," I said, tilting the phone to frame both of us. She started to protest, but I slid an arm around her waist, pulling her closer. "Smile, Lucia. You have to look like you like me a little."

She rolled her eyes but gave a soft smile as I snapped the picture. I glanced at the screen, satisfied with the image. Her eyes were bright, her hair slightly tousled from the race-day chaos, and she looked stunning.

"Perfect," I murmured.

Lucia glanced at me, raising a brow. "You're really posting that?"

"Absolutely." I grinned, already opening the app. I typed out a caption, something simple and understated: *Big win, big day, and lucky to share it with her.* Adding a heart emoji for good measure, I hit Post.

"You're ridiculous," she said, but there was a hint of something softer in her voice.

"Maybe," I replied, pocketing my phone. "But it's confirmed from me first."

Her expression softened. "That's...thoughtful."

I shrugged, though her words warmed me more than I wanted to admit. "Just making sure you're seen in the best light. And, honestly, showering you with fake love online isn't exactly a hardship."

Her lips twitched like she was fighting a smile, but she didn't say anything. I found myself lingering, admiring the way her eyes shone under the fluorescent lights of the motorhome.

"You coming with me to media?" I asked suddenly. I hadn't planned on asking her, but I found myself wanting her with me, needed her with me, someone to see through the crowd, and keep me grounded. I had been doing this by myself for so damn long, but here I was already attached to my mate's sister.

She blinked. "Media?"

"Yeah. Post-race press stuff. I'll be surrounded by reporters for the next hour, and I'd rather not do it without my fake girlfriend nearby."

Her lips parted, like she was about to argue, but then she sighed. "Fine. But only because Anna will be there."

Hand in hand, we walked into the media center. The energy shifted the moment we entered, the usual hum of reporters giving way to a buzz of interest. Cameras flashed, and I felt Lucia's fingers tighten around mine.

"You're doing great," I murmured, giving her hand a reassuring squeeze.

Anna intercepted us, guiding Lucia toward the back of the room, where she could observe in relative peace. But even standing behind the sea of reporters, Lucia was impossible to miss.

The questions began, directed at the three of us on the podium. They covered the usual topics—strategy, the car, the race itself. I answered easily, the routine familiar after years in the sport. But then, inevitably, the questions turned personal.

"Alexander," one reporter started, her tone sly. "You looked especially jubilant today after the win. Is there someone special who might have contributed to that?"

The room chuckled, and I leaned into the microphone with a practiced smirk. "You know," I began, my voice smooth, "I am very lucky. It's not every day you get to win a race and have someone amazing waiting for you at the finish line."

The crowd murmured, clearly enjoying the comment. I didn't miss the way a few reporters glanced toward the back of the room, where Lucia stood with Anna.

Another reporter piped up, "Can we expect to see more of her at the races?"

"That depends," I said, a glint of mischief in my eye. "You'll have to ask her."

The room laughed, but I caught sight of Lucia shaking her head, a small smile playing on her lips.

As the session wrapped up, I made my way back toward her. She was talking quietly with Anna, her expression relaxed despite the attention she'd received.

"Ready to head out?"

Lucia turned to me, her eyes searching mine. "You handled that well."

"Comes with the territory," I said with a shrug. "But it helps when I have good material to work with."

She rolled her eyes, but her smile lingered.

"Come on," I said, holding out my hand. "Let's get out of here, I miss the mini version of you." Her fingers slipped into mine, and I couldn't ignore the way my chest tightened at the simple gesture.

"Me too." She nodded. I wasn't sure what was happening between us, or if it was just me, but for now, it was oddly comforting to have her with me. I mean, she had always been a comfort, had always made me feel as loved and welcomed as all the DeLucas, but this...her hand in mine. It was different. And it felt like a damn good different, I didn't want it to end.

17

LUCIA

Fake dating a five-time world champion race car driver was surprisingly easy. Fancy dates, amazing food, traveling the world, and having literally everything I needed delivered to me. I was quickly descending into spoiled territory. Gianna was having the best time, we explored on off days, cheered on the boys during practices and race days. Gianna was now telling everyone she would be a driver when she grew up. Matteo was thrilled. Alexander had been busy helping with the F1 Academy Driver & Youth Development programs. He played a big part in the driver program, mentoring young drivers on their racing journeys, and was a passionate advocate for increasing women's involvement in motorsports.. Nicola has been volunteering as well to help get them more exposure and funding.

It was two months into this journey, one month of fake dating Alexander Wright. I was beginning to feel like I had a front-row seat to a version of myself I hadn't seen in years. Like I was finding myself again, the part that was buried, or lost along the way. The part my past relationship had stomped out, then everything needed to be focused on having a baby, then raising said baby. But here, out in the world doing things for me, I was enjoying this new, fast-paced life. And Matteo, Alexander, Anna, and Nicola were the village to help me along the way, making sure I was participating in all the fun parts. I had now been to enough parties that they didn't feel overwhelming because I had my people. And slowly I could feel my walls breaking down, feel my old self reemerging, newer and braver, ready to take on the world.

Maybe it was the quiet assurance in the way Alexander always looked at me, like I belonged exactly where I was. Or the way he touched my hand in crowded rooms, steadying me when I felt overwhelmed. Or the ridiculous amount of wine he insisted I try on our not-so-real dates.

Whatever it was, I couldn't deny it anymore—I was starting to feel alive.

We were on a break before the next race in Texas, taking a rare moment to enjoy the lull in the relentless Formula One schedule. The five of us went to Spain. Nicola was ecstatic. She had literally shopped till we dropped the first day we arrived. Gianna was decked out in a new matching set, new shoes, and the cutest mini leather jacket you've ever seen. Matteo was his normal happy-go-lucky self, pulling us along on planned outings to see the sights.

Nicola and Matteo, ever the planners, had finally reached exhaustion and said they would stay in with Gianna for the night. Alexander had insisted we go out for dinner at a little place he swore had "the best paella you'll ever eat."

He wasn't wrong. The meal was divine—a medley of saffron, seafood, and rice cooked to perfection—and the wine flowed as freely as Alexander's easy charm. The restaurant itself felt like stepping into a postcard. The space was cozy and warm, with low, golden lighting casting a romantic glow over every surface. The walls were adorned with endless frames, each holding black-and-white photographs, colorful sketches, or vintage posters that told stories of the past. Strings of dried peppers and garlic hung along the beams, and shelves lined with wine bottles filled the space above the bar.

Soft Spanish guitar music played in the background, just audible over the happy murmur of people talking and laughing. Waiters glided between the tables with plates piled high, their voices warm as they greeted regulars. The smell of garlic, herbs, and fresh bread filled the air. Across the small table, Alexander was in rare form, teasing and playful, looking truly relaxed. His smirk was a weapon he wielded with ease.

"You've got sauce," he said suddenly, gesturing to the corner of my mouth.

I frowned, reaching for my napkin, but he shook his head, a mischievous glint in his eye.

"No, here." Leaning forward, he brushed his thumb gently across my lips, his touch lingering just a second too long.

It was such a simple gesture, but it left me frozen, my heart skipping a beat as heat crept up my neck. He leaned back, the smirk deepening, as if he knew exactly what he was doing. He nodded slyly to a paparazzo across the street. I sighed, trying to keep the butterflies in check. Alexander would flirt without cameras around, he would take me out to dinner with the prose of fake dates but then not take out his phone once and order everything on the menu and make me laugh all evening. It was so easy to be around him; he made me feel things that were creeping out of the box where I had long since shoved my crush.

After dinner, we decided to walk off the meal. The city was alive in the way only European cities could be at night, cobblestone streets glinting under the glow of lanterns, couples strolling hand in hand, and the faint hum of life around every corner.

The wine had left me warm and a little giddy, and Alexander

seemed perfectly content to match my leisurely pace, his hand occasionally brushing against mine as we walked.

"What do you mean no one has ever bought you flowers for no reason?" he asked.

"Well, I've been given flowers, but they were always for something—'I'm sorry' flowers, birthday flowers, but never 'just because' flowers. I feel like those are the ones that count, you know? There's something so romantic about your person being out, seeing flowers, and thinking of you, and then getting them for you."

"If it was any flower, which one?" he asked.

"Happy flowers, bright and full of life," I responded easily.

Somewhere along the way, we heard it: a soft, hauntingly beautiful melody drifting through the cool night air. We followed the sound to a small square, where a group of street musicians played under the glow of a single lamppost. The music was slow, romantic, and utterly enchanting.

Alexander stopped, turning to face me. "Dance with me," he said, his voice low. I blinked, glancing around at the small crowd of people scattered across the square. "Here? In the middle of the street?"

He grinned, his eyes sparkling in the dim light. "Why not?"

Before I could protest, he grabbed my hand and pulled me toward him, his arm sliding around my waist as if it belonged there.

"I'm a terrible dancer," I warned, my cheeks already heating.

"Good thing I'm not," he replied, his grin turning into a soft smile as he began to sway us to the music.

The world around us seemed to dissolve, fading into the soft glow of the streetlamp and the lilting notes of the street musicians' melody. The cool night air kissed my skin, but all I could feel was the warmth of his hand on my back, steady and sure. My heart pounded, but not from nerves. It was something deeper, something unnamed but undeniably real, spreading through me like wildfire.

"Lucia," Alexander murmured, his voice barely louder than a breath, yet it cut through the music as if it were meant only for me.

I tilted my head up to meet his gaze, and the intensity in his eyes rooted me in place. They were a shade of brown that seemed endless under the dim light, and they looked at me as though I was the only thing that mattered in the world.

"You look beautiful," he said, his voice soft but weighted, each word spoken like it was a truth he could no longer hold back.

The words hung in the air, wrapping around me and pressing against my chest until I could hardly breathe. My heart clenched, an ache I couldn't ignore spreading through me. The sincerity in his voice unraveled something inside, loosening the careful threads of resistance I had clung to.

I tried to summon the reasons I'd told myself over and over why this couldn't happen—why I couldn't let myself fall for Alexander Wright. He was too charming, too perfect, too everything. This was supposed to be fake. Carefully controlled. Safe.

But here I was, standing in his arms under a pool of moonlight, and I could feel it happening. Inexplicably, unavoidably, I was falling for this man.

The next morning, there was a bouquet of bright flowers on my hotel doorstep. A small handwritten note peeking out of the top petals:

Pretty flowers for a pretty girl xx-A

18

ALEXANDER

I was screwed. Completely, utterly, and irrevocably screwed.

It had been a full day since Lucia and I went out, leaving Matteo and Nicola to enjoy a quiet night in with Gia. And yet, I couldn't stop replaying the way the light had danced across her face, catching the warmth in her green eyes. It was maddening. I was acting like the leading man in one of those rom-coms Lucia seemed to love so much—head in the clouds, heart racing at the mere memory of her laugh.

This whole fake-dating idea had been practical. It made sense at the time. I needed a PR miracle to salvage my reputation with Belen Racing. The team wanted stability, proof that I could be more than a reckless bachelor. A committed relationship screamed responsibility, maturity, and growth. All the things my bosses wanted to see in me.

Lucia had been game. She didn't hesitate when I asked, offering to help without batting an eyelash. She said yes to fake dating like it was a casual favor, something she could do in her sleep.

So why didn't I see this coming?

The constant pull to touch her, to make her laugh, to kiss her —not for the cameras or the narrative, but because I wanted to. Desperately. I was in deep trouble because she was my best friend's sister, and I was supposed to be pretending.

Instead, I was thinking about her bows. Matching bows, for God's sake. Lucia and Gia had left for brunch earlier, wearing coordinated outfits, and Gia had spent ten solid minutes trying to convince me to join them. The kid even grabbed my hand and gave me that puppy-eyed pout I could never say no to.

And yet, I stayed behind because Matteo plopped on the couch beside me, beer in hand, ready to critique last week's race.

Now I wasn't sure if I should've gone to brunch, just to be near Lucia. The way she smiled when Gia tugged on her hand had my heart doing cartwheels.

I was losing my mind.

"Mate, are you even watching this?" Matteo grumbled, gesturing to the race highlights playing on the TV.

"Huh?" I blinked, realizing I'd zoned out completely. "Yeah, sure."

Matteo raised an eyebrow. "You're acting weird."

I ran a hand down my face. Great. Now Matteo was noticing.

"Just tired," I said, but my voice sounded unconvincing, even to me.

Matteo studied me for a second longer before shrugging. "Well, you should rest up. We're hitting the circuit hard next week."

I nodded, grateful for the out, but as Matteo turned back to the screen, I couldn't help but glance toward the door, wondering when Lucia would be back.

Matteo muted the TV, leaning back against the couch with an appraising look. "Tired, huh? You don't usually zone out like this unless something's up."

I forced a laugh, shaking my head. "I'm fine, Matteo. Just thinking about strategy for the next race."

His brow furrowed. "Strategy? You've been racing long enough to know you don't think about strategy until you're sitting in the car. What's actually going on?"

"Nothing," I said, a little too quickly.

Matteo's eyes narrowed, and he tilted his head. "You're a shit liar, Alex. Always have been. Spill it."

I hesitated, weighing my options. Matteo was my best friend, but I couldn't exactly confess. *Hey, your sister is all I think about, and I'm this close to kissing her every time we're in the same room, no cameras necessary.*

"Seriously, Alex. What's eating at you? Is it the team? Are they still not talking about renewal yet?"

I opened my mouth to deflect again, but Matteo's serious expression stopped me. He'd always had this uncanny ability to sniff out bullshit. I *was* stressed about a renewal, it just wasn't at the forefront of my mind at the moment.

"Yeah, mate, I know I could find another seat, but I want to stay with Belen."

"I'm sure it's just some backend bullshit. The media is eating up the whole fake relationship. Belen has to see that the media is taking you seriously again, even though they should have always taken you seriously, they just suck."

Matteo grabbed another round of beers and we got into it.

19

LUCIA

The boutique was bustling, full of chatter and the soft rustle of clothes being pulled from racks. Nicola was rifling through a rack of dresses, holding one up and then immediately putting it back with a dramatic eye roll. Meanwhile, Gia sat in her stroller, her little fingers wrapped around a stuffed giraffe, playing pretend with it.

As Nicola held up another dress for inspection, my phone buzzed in my pocket. I pulled it out, expecting a text from Matteo or Alexander, but my stomach dropped when I saw the message.

UNKNOWN NUMBER

I know what you're doing.

The words stared back at me, cold and accusatory. My heart skipped a beat, and a chill ran down my spine.

"Lucia? What's wrong?" Nicola's voice pulled me back to reality. She was looking at me with concern, her hand frozen mid-reach for another dress.

I handed her my phone without a word, unable to say it out loud.

Her eyes scanned the screen, and her expression darkened. "Oh, hell no."

"Do you think...?" I trailed off, my voice shaky.

Nicola's lips pressed into a thin line. "It's him, isn't it? Your ex?"

I swallowed hard, nodding. "I don't know who else it could be."

"That bastard," she hissed, gripping my phone tightly. "Lucia, you need to tell Matteo and Alexander. This isn't something you can handle on your own. Come on, we're going back to the hotel. You're telling them. No arguments."

Back at the hotel, Nicola wasted no time. She handed Gia her favorite book and a snack, then scooped her up. "I'll take her into the bedroom. You go talk to them. And, Lucia," she added, her voice softening, "they'll want to help you. You don't need to do everything yourself, let us take care of you now and then."

I nodded, my stomach twisting with nerves. I could hear the voices of Matteo and Alexander from the living area. Taking a deep breath, I stepped into the room. Matteo glanced over first, his easy smile fading when he saw my face.

"What's wrong?" he asked immediately, sitting up straighter.

It had been so long, I hadn't heard from Josh since I left. Nothing, now this. Maybe he saw me on some magazine or online? I should have been more careful.

Alexander turned his attention to me, too, his brow furrowing in concern. "Luce?"

I held up my phone, my hand trembling slightly as I handed it to Matteo. "I got this text."

Matteo read it, his jaw tightening with every word. By the time he finished, his expression was pure fury. "That son of a—" He stood abruptly, pacing the room. "He thinks he can threaten you? After everything?"

Alexander stayed seated, but his calm demeanor was deceiving. His eyes were stormy, his jaw clenched. "You're sure it's him?"

"Who else would it be?" I said quietly, wrapping my arms around myself.

Matteo stopped pacing, his hands fisted at his sides. "We'll get extra security. I'll make sure someone's with you and Gia at all times."

Alexander stood, crossing the room to stand in front of me. "Lucia," he said gently, his voice low but firm. "If he ever shows his face, he'll regret it. I'll make sure of that."

I looked between the two of them, overwhelmed by their protectiveness. "I don't want to cause trouble. I just...I don't want him anywhere near Gia."

"He won't get near her. Or you," Matteo said firmly. "I'll make some calls."

Alexander reached out, brushing a hand over my arm in a reassuring gesture. "You're not alone in this, Lucia. We'll handle it."

Their words were comforting, but the knot in my chest remained.

20

ALEXANDER

The race was in a few hours, and here I was, sitting in one of the side rooms, feeling like I couldn't breathe. I had this strange tightness in my chest, like something was suffocating me from the inside out. I wasn't sure how to describe it, but it felt...wrong. Like I was on the edge of a cliff, just waiting for everything to fall apart.

I wasn't usually like this. I was Alexander Wright, five-time World Champion, the guy who could shake off a crash like it was nothing. But this...this was different. It was about Lucia, about Gianna, about the text from her ex, the ever present missing my dad. I couldn't shake the feeling that something was about to go terribly wrong. I had called Dante right away, asked him to track the bastard and get a tail on him immediately. When Lucia had moved home, when she found out she was pregnant, I had gone into overdrive. Dante had sent someone to get the asshole to sign over full custody. The papers were delivered right to her family's vineyard as soon as they could be. It was one small thing, one small thing I hadn't told anyone I was involved in, but it was something I could do, something I could help with.

I felt like I needed to control everything today, but I couldn't.

The team was counting on me. Belen Racing was counting on me. What if I couldn't pull it off?

I glanced at my hands, which were gripping the sides of the couch as though I could hold on to something, anything, that would steady me. I rubbed my face. I didn't even know what I was feeling. Was it just stress, or was it something else entirely? Why wouldn't my brain shut up and my heart calm down?

No one ever warned me that racing would involve this kind of mental gymnastics. Or that I'd care so damn much about someone other than myself. I mean, this thing with Lucia—it had started out as a fake-dating gig, right? Help her out, look good for the cameras, smooth over some of the media drama. But now? Now it felt like I was keeping her and her daughter in a safe bubble, and my head was spinning with the need to protect them. Especially from that bastard of an ex who thought he could mess with their lives again. I wasn't going to let that happen.

But I couldn't control everything. That much was clear.

The door to the room opened quietly, and I didn't even look up at first. My hands were shaking now, my breath coming in shallow, uneven bursts. I could feel the haze creeping in, and I had no idea how to make it stop.

"Alex?"

I blinked, and there she was—Lucia. Her brow furrowed as she took a couple of quick steps toward me. Her eyes were sharp, assessing. She must've known something was wrong because the moment she saw me, her face shifted from concern to urgency.

"Hey, hey, what's going on?" Her voice was calm, but I could hear the worry in it.

I tried to speak, to tell her that it was fine, that I was fine, but nothing came out. My mouth was dry, and my chest tightened even more.

"I can't..." I stammered, running a hand through my hair, feeling a wave of dizziness. "I don't know what's wrong. I just...feel like I can't breathe."

"Okay," she said softly but firmly, kneeling in front of me. "Just breathe, Alex. Focus on me. Let's slow it down."

I closed my eyes for a second, trying to focus on her voice, on her presence.

"Can you hear the hum of the lights above us?" she asked, gently placing her hand on my knee.

I nodded, trying to tune in to anything that would help me ground myself.

"Good," she encouraged. "Now look around. What do you see?"

I glanced up, trying to focus. "A couple of chairs...a table...the door...the clock."

"Great," she said, keeping her voice steady. "Now, can you smell anything?"

"Uh...the cleaner in the hallway. And...coffee. Maybe? From the other room?"

She nodded, her calmness settling over me like a warm blanket. "Okay. You're doing great. We're just focusing on the little things. You're safe. You're okay."

It took a few more seconds, but slowly, I started to feel the pressure lift. My breathing slowed, and the dizziness started to fade.

"I—I don't know what happened," I muttered, running a hand over my face. "I just...everything's...it's not in my control. I hate it."

Lucia reached out and cupped my face gently, her thumb brushing over my cheek. "It's okay. You're doing your best, Alex. You're going to do great out there today. You're scoring high, I can feel it. And Belen Racing? They're going to see just how important you are. They'll come through for you. I know it."

I swallowed hard, trying to steady myself. She was right, of course. I knew what I was capable of. I focused one her, on my sunshine girl, the one who showed up for me, who showed up for everyone when they needed it.

"Just breathe with me. I know it seems silly, but focus on my breath and try to match it, okay?" she said gently. So I focused on her, on the soft rise and fall of her chest. I matched her breath for breath. I leaned into her touch, feeling a little calmer, more grounded than I had in the last few minutes.

"Thanks," I whispered, my voice hoarse. "How do you know how to do that?"

She smiled softly, brushing her thumb across my lips. "I've had my fair share of panic attacks."

"A panic attack?" My eyes widened and she nodded.

"Feeling like you can't breathe, feeling out of body and out of control?" Her voice was soft as she asked, and it all resonated; it was exactly how I was feeling. So I nodded, feeling the weight on my chest ease. Slowly, I stood, my legs a little shaky, but the haze had passed.

"Right," I said, pulling myself together.

Lucia stood, her hand slipping into mine, and I felt a small rush of gratitude. It wasn't just about the race, not anymore. It was about her, about Gianna, and about the weird, inexplicable way they'd become the most important part of my life. I wanted to do it for them, to make Gianna proud.

My head was still cloudy. Even as the race began, I felt...off. The sensation hadn't completely worn off—the tightness in my chest was still there, and my grip on the steering wheel felt wrong, loose. It wasn't how I was used to feeling on the track. Normally, everything was precise, controlled. But today, it felt like I was trying to keep a hundred different things from slipping through my fingers at once. I hadn't had a panic attack before, or maybe I didn't know I was having them. It felt like this whole new thing I now had to figure out.

The lights went out, and I pushed forward with every intention to get ahead, to make up for lost time. I tried to focus, tried to shake off the fog that clung to me like a shadow. But it wasn't just the car—it was everything. My mind wouldn't settle, my body wasn't responding right, and the track...the track felt like it was moving too fast.

I took the first turn too aggressively, my grip still off. The car slid, and I barely corrected it in time. It wasn't pretty. I was already trying to claw my way up, but the sharp turns and tight corners made it harder. I wasn't doing enough, I knew it.

"Come on, come on..." I muttered to myself, pushing harder than I should have.

"Push, push," my engineer's voice crackled through the radio, tight with concern. My teeth gritted, but I didn't ease off. Not yet. I needed to get ahead.

Another turn came, this time a sharp left, and I didn't adjust quickly enough. I misjudged the angle and felt the back end of the car slip. I tried to correct, but the steering didn't feel responsive. There was a sickening moment where the tires lost grip entirely, and before I could react, the car veered off track.

"Shit—no!" I cursed, the tires screeching as I tried to regain control. My vision blurred as I felt the car fishtail, sliding uncontrollably.

The impact was jarring. The world tilted sideways. My body jerked with the force, my neck snapping as the car crumpled against the barriers, and I felt a sickening crunch of metal. I gripped the steering wheel harder, but it didn't matter. The car was out of control.

The world around me felt like it was moving in slow motion. My heart raced in my chest, pounding with adrenaline, and a sharp, searing pain shot through my body. Panic clawed at me, but I forced myself to stay calm.

"Alex, do you copy? Alex, are you okay?"

The voice came through my radio, but it felt distant. The haze was creeping in.

"I'm okay," I grunted, though my words didn't feel convincing, even to me. The adrenaline was rushing through my veins, but I knew something wasn't right. The pain in my neck, the dizziness, the headache...I had to focus, had to make sure everything was still working.

The aid car arrived quickly, and the medics rushed to check on me. Their faces were blank, but I could tell they were worried. I forced myself to sit still as they checked my vitals, making sure nothing was broken. I wanted to be angry, to get back out there, but the fog in my mind made it hard to concentrate. The dizziness lingered, and the pain in my neck felt like a dull throb. I had to close my eyes for a second, just to breathe. I focused on the sounds, the smells like Lucia had done with me earlier, and the haze began to lift.

"Everything's going to be okay, Alex," the medic said, though I could tell he wasn't entirely sure. They helped me into the aid car, and I let myself be driven back to the garage, the low hum of the engine doing little to calm my racing thoughts.

As the car pulled into the garage, my mind still felt like it was underwater. My focus was blurry, but I couldn't shake the thought of what I'd just done—or how stupid I'd been to push that hard. The team was going to be pissed.

But then, I saw her.

Lucia.

She was standing at the edge of the garage, her eyes wide with worry, her face pale. And as soon as the aid car came to a stop, she was running toward me.

I could barely make sense of the scene. My body was stiff as I climbed out of the car, but all I could focus on was her—her hands reaching for me, her face full of concern.

"Alex!" she cried, her voice shaking.

She reached me in an instant, her hands gripping my face with such urgency, such tenderness, that it felt like a shock to my system. She looked me over, her eyes searching for any sign of injury, her fingers brushing against my jaw.

"You're okay?" she asked, her voice breaking as she searched my face, her touch gentle but firm.

"Yeah, I'm fine," I muttered. I could see the worry in her eyes, and it hit me harder than I thought possible.

But what really knocked me sideways was the realization that, in that moment, it wasn't just concern. It was something deeper, something that went beyond the surface.

No one had ever cared for me this way. Not like this.

Her hands were still on my face, holding me steady. I just let myself feel the weight of it—the connection between us, raw and real.

"I'm fine," I said again, quieter this time, my voice softer.

"Please, don't ever do that again," she whispered, her voice thick with emotion. Her hands lingered, tracing my features gently, her touch a lifeline in the chaos of everything.

I could see the worry, the fear in her eyes, and I hated that I had put her through it.

"I'm okay," I promised, my voice thick, the words harder to get out than they should have been. I couldn't help but pull her closer, needing to be near her. I didn't want to lose her. I didn't feel invincible, not when I had someone waiting for me at the end of the track.

21

LUCIA

The crash rattled me. The moment Alexander's car hit the barrier, my stomach dropped, and I barely registered anything else until I was sprinting toward the garage. Now, sitting beside him on the couch, my hand gripping his, I was struggling to steady my breathing. His face was pale, a small bruise already forming near his temple, but he was here—alive, unbroken. That was enough.

We stayed there as the race continued, watching the screens in the garage. Matteo was putting in a stellar performance, and as the final laps counted down, we cheered when he crossed the finish line, taking second place. Alexander grinned, clapping along with the team, but his grip on my hand stayed firm, as if he wasn't ready to let go just yet.

Then my phone pinged. I pulled it from my bag, a chill creeping up my spine as I read the message.

UNKNOWN NUMBER

Seems like your new man ain't that great anyway.

You can't hide from me.

My stomach churned. I swallowed hard, willing the panic to stay at bay.

Alexander noticed immediately. "What's wrong?"

I tried to brush it off, but my shaking hand betrayed me. He didn't wait for an answer. He took the phone from me, his eyes narrowing as he read the text.

His expression darkened. "This him?" he growled, his voice low and dangerous.

I nodded, unable to speak.

Alexander's jaw tightened, his knuckles whitening as he gripped my phone. Without a word, he pulled out his own, tapping a contact. "Dante," he said as soon as the line connected, his voice sharp. "We have a problem."

I couldn't hear what Dante said, but Alexander's terse reply sent a shiver down my spine. "Find out where he is. Now."

By the time we were leaving, I was exhausted, walking out of the security entrance toward the parking garage with Anna while Alexander handled post-race interviews.

That's when I saw him.

A man in a hoodie stepped out from the shadows, his posture tense and angry. My heart stopped as recognition hit. *Josh.*

"Well, look who it is." He sneered, his voice dripping with venom. "Didn't think you'd get away from me forever, did you? Just followed another man around with more money?"

I froze, fear coursing through me. "What are you doing here?" I managed to choke out.

"What am I doing here?" he spat, his voice rising. "You took my daughter, Lucia. You ran off to play house with some fucking race car driver while I'm left with nothing. Wondering where the hell my family is."

"She's not your family," I shot back, my voice trembling. "You lost that right when you—"

"Don't," he interrupted, stepping closer, his face twisted with rage. "Don't act like you're some saint. You're just a dumb whore, running off the first chance you get. Sending someone to get custody papers signed over to you, having someone threaten *me*."

"Hey!" Anna's voice cut through, sharp and angry. She stepped forward, her petite frame trembling with fury as his words sunk in. "Back off, or I'll call security."

Josh's lip curled. "Oh, the nanny's got a mouth on her. Cute."

Then he turned back to me, his voice lowering into a menacing growl. "You think you're safe with him? That fancy driver of yours won't keep you for long. And when he's done, you'll come crawling back."

When he raised his hand, I flinched.

But he never got the chance to strike.

Out of nowhere, Alexander was there, his fist connecting with Josh's jaw with a sickening crack. Josh staggered back, falling to the ground, and Alexander didn't hesitate, landing another punch.

"You don't fucking touch her," Alexander roared, his voice echoing in the parking garage.

"Alex, stop!" I cried, but my voice barely registered.

Josh tried to scramble up, spitting curses, but Alexander was relentless.

"Enough!" Matteo's voice thundered as he arrived with security. He pulled Alexander off Josh, his grip firm. "He's not worth it."

Security swarmed, pinning Josh to the ground. Matteo turned to him, his face cold with fury. "If you ever come near her again, you won't just deal with him—you'll deal with me. And trust me, you don't want that."

Alex had guided me to a car. I was numb—silent and still. It wasn't until he slid in next to me. The doors locked and the car began to move. That was when the dam broke, when the walls I had so carefully placed brick by brick crumbled. It was like years of trauma, the shit that awful man had put me through, all crashed into me. Alexander pulled me into him. I was clutching Alexander's shirt as I sobbed into his chest, the walls had crashed down, the dam was broken. He held me, his arms strong and steady, stroking my hair and murmuring soft reassurances.

"You're safe," he whispered, his voice a soothing balm. "I promise you, Lucia. He won't hurt you again. Ever."

His words wrapped around me like a shield, but the fear still lingered. The memory of Josh's sneer, his voice—it clung to me like a shadow I couldn't shake. I knew he was full of shit. I had full custody of Gianna. He hadn't even fought me on it; papers just appeared three years ago. Josh's own words came back to me, *"sending someone to get custody papers signed over to you, having someone threaten me"*

⸻◦⸻

When we got back to the hotel, I felt like a hollow shell. But then, the door opened, and Gia's joyful squeal filled the air.

"Mommy!" she cried, running toward me, her tiny arms outstretched.

I dropped to my knees, pulling her into a tight hug, tears streaming down my face as I held her close.

"Mommy, are you okay?" she asked, her little hands brushing my cheeks, her brow furrowed with concern.

"Yes, baby," I whispered, my voice breaking. "Mommy's okay. I promise."

I held her tighter, breathing in her scent, letting her warmth chase away the lingering fear. In that moment, I knew I would do whatever it took to keep her safe. Whatever it took.

I wasn't alone that evening. No one went out and celebrated, no parties were attended. For the first time in a while, all six of us stayed together. Nicola and Anna ordered food—bought every comfort snack they could think of. Matteo had extra security posted around the hotel, and Alexander had already had a restraining order in the works through Dante. Not only would none of them let that piece of shit near us again, but they would make sure he would be arrested, no matter the country, if he even tried to get close.

Matteo and Nicola had been talking in hushed tones. They entertained Gianna when I needed a moment, but I wanted her near me, just like I wanted them all with me. This was my family, mismatched and found, but mine all the same.

Gianna went down early that night. Nicola, Anna, and Matteo left after tight hugs and sad smiles. When it was just Alexander left, I turned to him. The room felt too big, I didn't want to be alone. So I didn't think, I just said what I needed.

"Stay," I asked in a whisper. He nodded, led me to the bathroom, and sat me down on a chair. He pulled out items from my bags and began taking care of me. I felt frozen, but I allowed it. Allowed someone to help, allowed myself to accept the help.

With gentle hands, Alexander moved around the room. He found the right skin-care products on the counter and knelt in front of me, softly dabbing away the remnants of my smeared makeup. His hands were steady, soothing in a way I didn't realize I needed.

When he handed me my toothbrush, I managed to handle that part myself, but the moment I finished and turned back around, he was pointing at the chair again.

"Sit," he said softly, but firmly.

I hesitated, but when I saw what was in his hand, a bright pink hairbrush, I couldn't help the faint smile that tugged at my lips.

"Where did you even get that?" I asked, my voice small but lighter than before.

He shrugged, a lopsided grin playing on his lips. "I think it's Gia's, but I figured you wouldn't mind."

I sank into the chair, exhaustion draping over me like a heavy blanket. When he began to gently glide the brush through my hair, a lump tightened in my throat. Each stroke was deliberate, tender, as if he knew exactly how to unravel the tension knotted deep inside me.

The tears came quietly, slipping down my cheeks before I could stop them. I didn't speak, and neither did he. He simply kept brushing, his fingers occasionally brushing my skin—a touch so small, yet somehow grounding.

"This is the second time you've done this," I said, my voice breaking. "Did you ever think you'd be brushing a crying woman's hair after a race?"

"For you, I would," he replied softly. I let my eyes close, let myself be taken care of.

With my eyes sealed shut, afraid of the real answer, I asked in barely a whisper, "Was it you...behind the custody being signed over?" A pause, a silent breath, hearing the wind outside breezing in through a cracked window.

"Yeah," his reply came, so softly it was barely audible. I turned and wrapped my arms around him, I heard the clatter of the brush on the counter and then I was enveloped into his arms.

By the time I shuffled into bed, clad in my softest pajamas, I could barely keep my eyes open. Alexander slid in beside me, pulling me into his arms. His warmth surrounded me, and I nestled into his chest, the sound of his heartbeat steady and calming.

And as I drifted off, three words were whispered, like a quiet mantra wrapping around me like a shield:

"I've got you."

22

ALEXANDER

If someone had told me I would wake up next to my best mate's little sister in a hotel room during the racing season, I wouldn't have believed them. But here I was.

I woke up to the soft sound of her breathing, it was a peaceful contrast to the whirlwind of yesterday. For a moment, I stayed still, not wanting to disturb the warmth of her body pressed against mine. My arms were wrapped around her, and her face was tucked into my chest, her light hair spilling everywhere in a mess of silk. I wanted to stay like this. Right here, being needed by someone. It was a new feeling. I cared for my people deeply, but it was like something took over my body yesterday. The thought of her ex—Josh, that vile excuse for a man—filled me with a quiet, simmering rage. I'd knock him down again without hesitation if he even so much as thought about coming near her or Gia. When I walked to find them and saw them from afar, I knew something was wrong, their body language off. When I got within earshot and heard the words, my blood boiled. When I saw his hand raise as I ran toward them, saw Lucia flinch, I saw pure red.

The room was still dim, the first rays of sunlight peeking through the curtains, casting a soft golden glow over everything.

My gaze drifted down to her, and I couldn't stop the faint smile tugging at my lips.

She looked so small curled up next to me, her face relaxed and free of the tension that had gripped her last night. My thumb brushed lightly over the back of her hand resting on my chest, and I couldn't help but marvel at how delicate she seemed—and yet how fiercely strong I knew she was.

God, she'd been through so much. More than anyone should have to handle. She stirred slightly, her nose scrunching up as she nestled closer to me, and I froze.

For all the people I've been with, this—this feeling of simply holding someone, protecting them while they slept—was unfamiliar.

I shifted slightly to adjust the blanket over her shoulders, and her eyes fluttered open. They were still heavy with sleep, a soft, mossy green that blinked up at me with lazy confusion before recognition set in.

"Morning," I murmured, my voice low.

At first her brows scrunched together in confusion, but as she blinked in her surroundings, her lips curved into a faint smile. "Morning," she whispered back, her voice raspy and warm, like honey dripping from a spoon.

We stayed like that for a beat, neither of us moving, neither of us rushing to shatter the fragile peace that had settled over us.

"How'd you sleep?" I asked, brushing a stray strand of hair from her face.

"Honestly, better than I have in a long time," she admitted, her voice barely above a murmur. I kept my own voice low so as not to wake Gianna. Her words settled in my chest, heavy and warm. The thought that I could give her even a sliver of peace made something inside me tighten.

"I'm glad," I said softly.

Her stomach growled, loud and insistent, breaking the moment. She groaned, hiding her face in my chest.

"Guess I should feed you," I teased, chuckling as I pressed a kiss to the top of her head.

She tilted her head up, her cheeks pink. "Guess so," she said with a smirk.

"Stay here. I'll grab something." I gently untangled myself from her, the loss of her warmth immediate and noticeable.

As I got out of bed, I couldn't help glancing back at her. She was sitting up now, the blanket pooled around her waist, her hair a wild, beautiful mess. Her eyes met mine, it felt like the world narrowed to just the two of us.

"Thank you," she said softly, her voice carrying more weight than the words themselves.

I just nodded, not trusting myself to speak. Because in that moment, I realized something dangerous, something I wasn't sure I could ignore anymore.

I didn't want to let her go.

Dragging myself out of bed with a groan, I immediately noticed the dull throb in my hands. When I glanced down, angry purples and blues painted my knuckles like a warning.

Great.

I tiptoed past a sleeping Gianna, her tiny form peaceful in the crib, and slipped into the adjoining room. My phone was abandoned on the couch where I'd left it, blinking incessantly.

Hundreds of notifications lit up the screen. Missed calls, texts —most from Matteo.

MATTEO

Someone published photos of you knocking Josh out.

My stomach sank. Attached was a link. I tapped it, and there it was —a picture of me mid-swing, fists bloodied, with Josh crumpled beneath me. His nose was clearly broken. Not exactly my finest moment.

I swiped out of the article and checked my missed calls.

> Anna (3 missed calls)
>
> Belen Management Office (1 missed calls)
>
> Belen Management Office (1 voicemail)
>
> Matteo (25 missed calls)

I ran a hand over my face and grabbed my jacket. Sliding my phone into my pocket, I eased the door shut behind me, careful not to wake Gianna, and headed down the hall. Matteo's door opened before I even knocked.

"Where the *hell* have you been?" Anna's voice pierced the air, sharp enough to make my headache ten times worse. Her usual composure was gone, replaced by a fury that radiated off her in waves.

"Nice to see you too," I quipped, though it barely came out as a mutter. Her glare could've set me on fire.

Behind her, Matteo lounged on the suite's couch, looking grim. "It doesn't look good, mate," he said simply.

"I assume you've talked to Dante?" I asked, turning back to Anna.

Her lips pressed into a thin line as she stepped aside to let me in. "Of course," she muttered, clearly irritated. Anna *hated* Dante. Their interactions were rare, but if she needed information and couldn't reach me, she had no choice.

"I'm charging you for emotional damages," she grumbled before flopping into a chair next to Matteo.

Once we were all settled, Anna launched into a furious lecture. "Do you have any idea how bad this is for Belen? For your career? The damage control alone—"

I tuned her out as she scrolled through her phone, probably

coordinating with every PR team in a fifty-mile radius. When she finally paused her tirade, she exhaled in frustration.

"The story dropped late last night, too late to suppress it properly. Every time I get it pulled from one outlet, it pops back up somewhere else. They're spinning it badly. Anger problems, reckless Alexander is back, and so on."

The tense atmosphere in Matteo's suite thickened, the room buzzing with unspoken worries. I was about to respond when a soft knock sounded at the door. Matteo raised a brow at me, but before either of us could move, the door creaked open.

Lucia stepped inside, holding a sleepy Gia against her chest, her eyes flashing with determination. Even in her pajamas and with her hair in a messy knot, she looked like a force to be reckoned with. She was wearing the same shirt she had so many mornings ago now when I had shown up early. Hot pink letters spelling *surviving on spite and coffee*. Gia blinked at us groggily, clutching her little stuffed bunny.

"I got the texts," Lucia said, her voice low but firm. Her gaze locked on mine, and I felt a jolt of something I couldn't quite place. "And I saw the news."

Her tone was steady, but there was a flicker of guilt in her expression, a shadow that told me she blamed herself for this.

"I'm so sorry, Alexander," she continued, adjusting Gia on her hip. "This whole thing, it's my fault. You shouldn't have been dragged into my mess, but I'm going to help fix it."

I opened my mouth to argue, but she didn't give me the chance.

"First," she said, stepping farther into the room, "we're doubling down on the fake-dating thing. We need to get ahead of this. Appear together more often, give them something to focus on other than the fight."

Anna, who had been furiously typing on her phone, paused and glanced up, eyebrows raised.

"And second," Lucia went on, her jaw tightening, "I'll go to

Belen Management myself. I'll explain the situation. They need to know this was my baggage, not yours."

"Lucia—" I started, but she cut me off again, her voice sharp.

"No, Alexander. You've done enough to protect me and Gia. This happened because of *me*. Because Josh wouldn't leave me alone, and I should've handled it before it got to this point." Her voice cracked slightly at the end, but she held her head high, her fiery resolve unshaken.

Gia stirred against her, and Lucia immediately softened, kissing the top of her daughter's head. For a moment, the room was silent.

"I appreciate the sentiment," Anna said finally, her voice measured, "but walking into Belen Management and claiming responsibility won't magically fix this. The optics are what matter now. If anything, making more public appearances *together* might help shift the narrative. Show unity, make people root for you two as a couple. Who doesn't love a man protecting his woman?"

Lucia met her gaze head-on. "Exactly. That's why I'm saying we lean into it. Hard. Give them a reason to talk about something else entirely. Pictures of us, interviews, red carpet appearances, whatever it takes."

"You're serious about this," Matteo said, speaking for the first time in a while. His tone was laced with both admiration and concern.

Lucia nodded, her grip tightening on Gia. "Dead serious. I'm not letting Alexander's career take a hit because of me."

I stepped closer, lowering my voice so only she could hear. "Lucia, you don't have to do this. None of this is your fault. Josh is—"

"Stop," she interrupted, looking up at me with a mix of guilt and fire. "You stood up for me. For *Gia*. The least I can do is stand by you now."

Her words hit me harder than I expected. She was fierce,

protective, and determined to shoulder the weight of this mess with me.

"All right," I said quietly, nodding. "We'll do it your way."

Lucia's shoulders relaxed, just slightly, and she gave me a small, grateful smile. Gia snuggled closer to her, unaware of the storm brewing around us.

Anna clapped her hands together, the sharp sound breaking the tension. "Then it's settled. We'll start crafting a plan. But Lucia, with regards to management, this has to be handled delicately. I'll deal with it. I'd rather you don't speak with them directly."

We all settled into our respective roles—Matteo offering quiet support, Anna orchestrating the PR angle, and Lucia fiercely taking charge.

For better or worse, I wasn't facing this alone.

23

LUCIA

Tonight was the night of my first red carpet event. As promised, we were in high gear trying to fix my shitty past coming up and messing with Alexander's entire future. I had been sitting in anxiety all morning. Even a calm day out with Nicola and Gianna exploring the city only distracted me for so long. The dress Anna had sent hung from the door frame like a silent challenge. Sleek, emerald green, with a neckline that plunged just enough to make me blush. The fabric shimmered faintly in the light, clinging to every curve and promising a kind of boldness I wasn't sure I could pull off.

Nicola sprawled across the armchair in the corner of my room, tossing grapes into the air and catching them with a precision that was both infuriating and impressive. "You, my dear, are looking drop-dead gorgeous," she declared, barely looking up from her phone.

I huffed, smoothing my hands down the dress again. "I feel like I look silly."

Nicola rolled her eyes dramatically. "Don't be ridiculous. You've got the curves, the confidence—you're gonna knock them dead. Alexander won't know what hit him."

I turned to her with a mock glare. "I'm not doing this for *Alexander*. This is about the PR disaster."

"Uh-huh. Sure it is." She waggled her brows, a teasing grin spreading across her face.

I tossed a pillow in her direction, and she dodged it effortlessly, laughing. "I'm serious, Nicola. This is just damage control."

"And if damage control happens to involve you looking like a goddess and making Alexander Wright drool a little, that's just a bonus."

I couldn't help the smile tugging at my lips, even as I turned back to the mirror. Nicola had been a godsend over the past few weeks—always ready with a joke, a sassy comeback, or a much-needed reality check. She'd swooped in like a whirlwind of energy, and unsurprisingly my daughter adorned her as much as I did.

"Okay," Nicola said, standing and dramatically dusting invisible lint from her jeans. "Let's get you zipped up and looking like a million bucks. Gia and I will be rooting for you from here."

"You're not going to make this a bigger deal than it already is, right?" I asked, stepping into the dress carefully.

"Absolutely not," she said solemnly, then winked. "I mean, I'll probably teach Gia how to cheer every time your face comes on TV, but that's it. Totally low-key."

I rolled my eyes, but a laugh slipped out. "Thanks, Nic. For everything."

"Always, babe," she said, giving me a firm pat on the shoulder. "Now get out there! The world isn't ready for you tonight."

After one last look in the mirror—where I barely recognized myself—I grabbed my clutch, kissed Gia's forehead, and headed out. Nicola gave me a loud wolf whistle as I left, and I shook my head, trying not to laugh.

The elevator ride down felt endless, my heart pounding with every floor. By the time I reached the lobby, the nerves had settled into a steady hum. I stepped outside, and there he was.

Alexander leaned casually against the sleek black car, but

there was nothing casual about the way his eyes met mine. His suit was tailored to perfection, the black-on-black ensemble making him look impossibly sharp. But it wasn't his suit that stole my breath. It was the way his expression shifted the moment he saw me.

For a second, I thought he might have forgotten to breathe. His jaw tightened, his lips parting slightly as his gaze swept over me—slowly, deliberately, like he was memorizing every inch.

"You..." he started, then stopped, swallowing hard before trying again. "You look incredible."

Heat rushed to my cheeks, and I ducked my head, wishing I could play it cool. "Thanks," I said softly, clutching my bag tighter.

When I looked up again, he was still staring, his eyes dark and filled with something I couldn't quite name. Admiration? Desire? Whatever it was, it made my pulse quicken.

"You ready for this?" he asked, his voice low, almost reverent.

I nodded, stepping closer. "Are you?"

His lips curved into a small, knowing smile, and he opened the car door for me. "With you? Always."

The car glided to a stop, and the world outside exploded into a dazzling chaos of lights, cameras, and the buzz of a crowd I wasn't prepared for. I'd seen red carpet events on TV before, sure. They always seemed so glamorous, so polished. But sitting here now, staring out at the flashing lights and the sea of people shouting names, I felt like an impostor in my borrowed dress and heels that pinched just a little too much.

Alexander leaned over, his hand brushing mine. "Ready?" His voice was low, steady, the kind of voice that made you believe you could walk into a lion's den unscathed.

I forced a smile, pushing my nerves deep down, and nodded in response. When the door opened, the noise surged. Alexander stepped out first, effortlessly commanding attention like he was born to live in this world of spectacle. Then he turned, his hand extended toward me. For a split second, I hesitated. This wasn't my world. This wasn't my life. But the way he looked at me, his eyes warm and unwavering, made me forget all that.

I placed my hand in his, and the moment I stepped out, the crowd erupted. Cameras snapped, flashes went off in every direction, and the shouts—my name mixed with his—felt like a surreal kind of dream.

"Lucia! Alexander! Over here!"

"Lucia, give us a smile!"

I felt his hand on the small of my back, grounding me as we began walking down the carpet. It stayed there, warm and steadying, as we walked. The red beneath my heels seemed endless, like we were walking toward some magical, glittering horizon. My pulse thrummed in my ears, and my breath caught when I spotted the enormous movie poster at the entrance. This wasn't just a premiere—it was *the* premiere. The kind people talked about for weeks afterward.

"Relax," Alexander whispered, his voice brushing against my ear like velvet. "You're doing great."

I nodded, too overwhelmed to speak as we stopped in front of the step-and-repeat. Cameras flanked every inch of the space, the flashes relentless as we posed. His hand stayed firm on my back, a subtle anchor that kept me from floating away in the sheer absurdity of the moment.

"Smile," he murmured, his lips curving into one of his devastating grins. So, I did. I smiled, and the cameras seemed to go wild, the crowd's shouting crescendoing like an orchestra hitting its peak.

And then, as if on cue, Anna appeared like a hurricane in heels. "This way," she said briskly, ushering us toward a woman with a microphone and a camera crew stationed a few steps away.

The interviewer greeted us warmly, her smile genuine as she gestured for us to join her. "Alexander Wright and Lucia DeLuca," she said into the microphone, her tone like honey. "You two are absolutely stealing the show tonight."

Alexander chuckled, his hand slipping from my back to take my hand instead, his fingers lacing with mine like it was the most natural thing in the world. "That's all Lucia," he said smoothly, his grin widening. "I'm just lucky to be here with her."

My cheeks burned, but I managed to nod politely, pretending this was no big deal even as my heart cartwheeled.

The interviewer turned to me. "Lucia, this is your first public appearance at an event like this, isn't it? How does it feel?"

How did it feel? Like I'd stumbled into a movie and couldn't find my way out. I swallowed hard, gripping Alexander's hand for dear life. "It's...surreal," I said honestly, hoping my voice didn't betray how overwhelmed I felt.

"She's a natural," Alexander said, his voice warm with pride. His gaze hit mine and I swear I felt myself melting under it.

I blinked up at him, caught completely off guard by the sincerity in his voice. He didn't even seem to realize what he was doing to me, how those words were slipping through the cracks in the armor I'd so carefully built.

This wasn't real. It couldn't be. Alexander was just playing his part, saying all the right things to keep the illusion intact.

But then he looked at me, really looked at me, and I couldn't shake the feeling that maybe, just maybe, some of it *was* real.

I was in trouble. Falling for my fake boyfriend was never part of the plan, but here I was, heart racing, wishing I could freeze this moment and live in it forever.

Alexander and I had spent the week attending fashion shows, strolling through staged public dates, and participating in carefully orchestrated PR stunts. But it wasn't the glamorous events that stuck in my mind. It was the quiet, unguarded moments in between that I found myself replaying late at night. The pastry bag left on my nightstand with Alexander's familiar scroll on it, *sugar for the sugar monster* it had read. Enough for myself and Gianna. He became rather fond of leaving notes everywhere, hiding them for me to find later. Little paper cranes he would make with hotel stationery for Gianna littered the rooms, making me smile every time I saw them.

It was a Tuesday morning, I was sitting at the kitchen table, texting Anna and trying—yet again—to convince her to let me speak to Belen's management directly about the PR strategy. Predictably, she shot me down.

That's when Alexander arrived, an actual wicker picnic basket in one hand and his signature smile on his face.

"Fancy a getaway?" he asked, leaning casually against the door frame. "No cameras, no fake smiles. Just us. Plus," he added with a lopsided grin, "I miss spending time with G."

My heart did a little flip.

"She's very jealous of all our time together lately," I managed, trying to sound casual.

That made him laugh—the real laugh, the one that crinkled the corners of his eyes and made him look devastatingly approachable.

Thump thump.

"Where's my girl at?" he asked, glancing past me into the room.

Thump thump.

My girl.

Somebody sedate me.

"Alex!" Gia's tiny, excited voice rang out from the living room, and suddenly she was bounding toward him, abandoning her princess movie without a second thought. She launched herself into his waiting arms, and he caught her easily, lifting her up like she weighed nothing. She clung to him like a little koala.

"I missed you!" she declared, her tiny brows furrowed in mock indignation. "Mama's been stealing you."

Alexander nodded solemnly, playing along. "I know. It's so unfair."

"She's right here, you know," I said, crossing my arms, but my grin betrayed me.

Gianna placed a hand on her hip, her tone exasperated. "Mama always wants Alex time."

I snorted, recognizing Nicola's sass in my toddler. Alexander, on the other hand, looked thoroughly delighted.

"I was thinking," he said, shifting Gia so she perched more comfortably on his hip, "how about a picnic? Maybe near a park?"

"Yes, yes, yes!" Gia chanted, squirming in his arms. "Mama! Park!"

I gave in immediately, not that there was any other choice. "Okay, baby. Let's go to the park."

Alexander smiled at me, soft and warm, like I'd given him more than just an afternoon plan. I let my eyes linger for a moment, taking in the rare sight of him dressed casually—a short-sleeve knit button-up that showed off the tattoos curling over his ebony skin, from the rose on his hands and up to the delicate wings on his neck.

I was not going to survive this day.

By the time we reached the top of the hill at the park, the sun was shining, and Gia was perched on Alexander's shoulders, giggling endlessly. She was pointing out trees and rating them based on their "prettiest colors." Alexander played along enthusiastically, giving each tree a dramatic flourish as if it were the most extraordinary sight in the world.

Meanwhile, I lagged behind, cursing my decision to wear heeled ankle boots on what turned out to be a grassy incline. But honestly, I couldn't even be mad. Alexander kept slowing down, waiting for me. My view? Alexander and Gia, laughing together in the sunlight, like they'd been doing this forever.

Alexander waved his free hand dramatically, apparently narrating something to Gia that sent her into peals of laughter. Whatever it was, I couldn't hear it from my spot a few paces back, but it didn't matter. Watching them was enough.

It hit me then, with a force that left me breathless.

This wasn't fake. This wasn't a PR stunt or an arrangement or a temporary illusion.

This was my daughter, my life, and this man who somehow made everything feel like it could be real.

I was in so much trouble.

The picnic blanket was spread out under a sprawling oak tree, the kind Gianna had deemed a "queen tree" on our walk up the hill. Alexander knelt by the basket, pulling out neatly packed sandwiches, fruit, and—of course—a bottle of sparkling water because, apparently, he couldn't even pretend to be low maintenance.

"Did you pack a three-course meal in there?" I teased, plopping down onto the blanket.

"I was going for four courses, but Anna stole my dessert," he quipped, flashing me a grin as he handed me a plate.

Gianna, having grown bored of sitting still, had already dashed off to the playground, her laughter ringing out as she climbed up the tiny rock wall attached to the play structure, her stuffed bunny in tow.

Alexander followed my gaze, his smile softening as he watched her. "She's fearless," he murmured.

"I don't know where she gets that, I wish I was that free," I said absently, then immediately regretted it. I glanced at Alexander, worried I'd soured the moment, but he didn't flinch.

Instead, he leaned back on one arm and let out a noncommittal "Hmm," his relaxed posture entirely too charming. "And the sass?" he asked, raising an eyebrow.

"Me, but also Nicola has been quite the influence," I admitted easily with a laugh.

"She's perfect, just like her mum."

Heat bloomed in my cheeks, and I busied myself with my sandwich, trying to ignore the way my heart had started its now-familiar fluttering. "You're laying it on thick today, Wright."

"Just being honest," he said, shrugging like it was the most natural thing in the world.

We ate in companionable silence for a while, the kind that felt easy and warm, punctuated only by the sound of Gia's laughter. I caught her out of the corner of my eye, spinning herself dizzy on a tire swing.

"I missed this," Alexander said suddenly, his voice low enough that I almost didn't hear him.

I looked over at him, confused. "Missed what?"

"This." He gestured vaguely, his hand sweeping over the scene in front of us. "Spending time together just because we want to. No cameras, no headlines, no Anna breathing down our necks." He paused, his gaze fixed on Gia as she waved enthusiastically at us from the monkey bars. "I want more days like this."

My stomach flipped, but I tried to play it cool. "You mean getting tackled by an almost three-year-old and carrying half her weight up a hill?"

He chuckled, shaking his head. "I mean *this*. Being with you. With her. Not because we're trying to sell some story, but just because...it feels right."

My throat tightened, and I took a sip of the sparkling water to give myself a moment to think. "It's not exactly part of the plan," I said lightly, though my voice came out quieter than I intended.

"Screw the plan," he said, and when I turned to look at him, his expression was entirely serious. "The plan is just something Anna cooked up to keep everyone happy. But this? This is what makes me happy."

I stared at him, completely disarmed. My brain scrambled to come up with something clever to say, but all I could think about was the way his eyes softened when he talked about Gia, the way he laughed when she teased him, and the way he looked at me now.

"Alex!" Gia's voice broke through the moment, and we both turned to see her standing triumphantly at the top of the slide. "Watch me!"

He grinned, standing up and cupping his hands around his mouth. "I'm watching, superstar!"

She slid down with a squeal, her arms in the air like she'd just conquered Mount Everest.

"She's the best part of my life," I said softly, surprising myself with the admission.

"I know," he replied, sitting back down beside me. "You're allowed to let someone else in too."

I glanced at him, the sincerity in his voice making my chest ache. Sometimes it was like he could see right through me, right down to my soul. Just casually bringing up my biggest issue. It was so hard to let others in fully. To lean on anyone. Somewhere down the line, after being let down too many times by too many people, I stopped. Why rely on others when I had myself.

"You know," Alexander said softly, "I see you." It was only three words. A simple sentence, really, but I knew what he meant —we were similar in that way; our walls were different, but we both relied on ourselves, focused on that, didn't want help or expect it.

"It's kind of annoying." I shook my head and let the silence settle as we watched my daughter playing and showing off tricks.

"Well, if you keep looking, you'll notice that I'm okay on my own."

"Of course you are," he replied easily. "But you don't have to be on your own all the time. There's a whole village of people who love you."

"Oh yeah?" I teased, trying to keep it casual, but he doubled down instead.

"I do the same, you know." He sighed.

"I know," I replied gently, turning to him. He looked angelic, the sunlight casting through the trees on his skin. The winged tattoo on his neck was on display.

"When did you get this one?" I asked, nodding at his neck. His hand went to it immediately.

"Sometime last year."

"It reminds me of a poem I read the summer I found out I was pregnant," I admitted. His eyes caught mine as I recalled part of the poem.

"'These wings are mine; I built, I grew. No chains can hold, no sky deny. For I am the storm, the boundless sky,'" Alexander recited, looking to the clouds. My heart stopped.

"You read it?" I asked, shock flooding me. I had a book of poems with me that I carried around like a security blanket when I was pregnant. It was filled with these gorgeous poems all about starting new and being brave.

"You brought it with you everywhere," he replied.

"Yeah, but I would have noticed if you were reading it!"

"It was a day by the lake, you and Matteo went swimming, your back was hurting, so you were floating. Remember that giant pink floatie your dad bought you? You were out there for an hour, sleeping under the sun, Matteo rigged a rope to it so you wouldn't float too far." He looked far away, as if recalling the day. "I read the whole thing."

"You—" I gasped in shock, at a loss for words.

"I liked that one best." He turned to me again with a soft smile. His brown eyes were so light today, like caramel and gold.

"Me too," I whispered, breaking eye contact with him and blinking back the tears. We sat like that for a time, side by side, watching Gia play before she ran back to us. We snacked on the food and she curled up in my lap. Alexander rifled through the basket, pulling out a picture book.

"One more surprise," he said to Gianna, who beamed in return.

"Is it a princess story?" she asked.

"You bet, your favorite one, if I am not mistaken." He turned the book over to reveal the front. And there was Gianna's favorite princess. A certain ice queen that every single toddler to ever exist was obsessed with. Though I couldn't be mad about it. Sisterly love winning the day? A badass ice queen who doesn't need a man? Yes please.

Alexander moved over and put a hand on my shoulder, gently tugging me back. Gia giggled as we leaned back and she snuggled in even closer. Alexander began reading and my daughter was transfixed.

I wished the day could go on forever. That every day could be like this.

24

ALEXANDER

I was in love with my best friend's little sister, my fake girlfriend, and the only woman who had ever captured so much of my attention. I didn't want to be with anyone else, or doing anything else. Honestly, all this PR bullshit would have been insufferable if not for her. I wasn't used to it, though—the whole *not being alone* thing. Not having to only rely on yourself.

When she had asked me about my angel wing tattoo, my heart felt like it might have thumped right out of my chest. Because it was from the poem, the dog-eared page, the underlined words. I had read every page of that book that day on the lake. I had committed it to memory. But that one hit me hardest. I was the first to admit that I was a sap for shit like that. Poems, songs, they just knew how to pull at the heartstrings.

"Well, Alexander," started Mark, his glasses perched low on his nose as he tapped his pen against the table. He was not my favorite person currently, holding my renewal contract over my head like the rest of the management team for Belen that sat in front of me. "We've had an interesting week, haven't we?"

The office had the kind of polished sterility that made me uncomfortable. Too clean, too controlled. The walls were a pale, uninspired gray, decorated with awards and framed photos of past victories. Nothing personal. Just the way Belen liked it. I sat in one of the sleek chairs across from the management team, three of them sitting like a jury on the other side of the long mahogany table.

"That's one way to put it," I replied, leaning back in my chair. My tone was calm, almost indifferent, but inside I was braced for the blow.

"We're not thrilled about the fight being plastered all over the news," chimed Claudia, head of corporate strategy. She folded her hands neatly in front of her. "It's...unprofessional. Not the image we want associated with Belen Racing, especially not from one of our champions. While Anna was in contact with us about the so-called reasoning, it did not sit well with upper management."

"I didn't start it," I said, meeting her gaze directly.

"Doesn't matter who started it," Mark interjected, his tone clipped. "What matters is that the world saw *you* involved in an altercation. It's not the kind of headline we want associated with Belen."

"Understood," I said, biting down on the words I really wanted to say.

"But," Claudia cut in, glancing down at a stack of papers in front of her, "there is...a silver lining." She looked up, her expression softening slightly. "Your relationship with Lucia."

Mark nodded, leaning forward. "The public response has been overwhelmingly positive. People see you as more relatable, grounded. The fight, surprisingly, hasn't overshadowed that narrative. If anything, it's framed you as fiercely protective—of Lucia, of Gia."

Claudia smiled faintly. "They like you, Alexander. The protective boyfriend, the father figure, it's a good look. You seem... committed. In love."

I didn't miss the way she emphasized the last word.

I kept my face neutral, though my chest tightened at the mention of Lucia. "And about the renewal?"

Mark leaned back in his chair, his fingers steepled. "The play is to keep doing what you're doing. Show that you're serious about this relationship. Corporate likes the image. You in love and all. You'll need to maintain that positive reputation if you want things to go smoothly."

"If I want things to go smoothly?" I repeated, my voice carrying an edge. It felt like a threat and I did not like it. I knew how much went down behind closed doors, all the pieces that needed to fall just right, but still not having a renewal this late in the season was nerve racking, to say the least. I had seen the articles, questioning if I would even have a seat next year. Obviously I would; I had been consistently high in the points week after week. But would it be in a Belen seat or someone else's?

"The renewal offer," Claudia clarified, her tone measured. "It's still in the works. There are...logistics to iron out."

I nodded, though the frustration simmered beneath the surface. They were holding my future over my head, as if my performance on the track hadn't already proven my worth a hundred times over.

"But," Claudia continued, "if you keep up the good press, if you stay out of trouble and show the world the Alexander Wright they love—the loyal partner, the champion, the team player—all will be well."

"Noted," I said, standing up before they could dismiss me like some rookie. "Anything else?"

Mark opened his mouth to speak, but I didn't wait for him to respond. Claudia stood up before I could leave, shook my hand, and said goodbye.

Anna immediately intercepted me as I left the management's office.

"So?" she asked expectantly, falling into step with me. I was walking at an unreasonably fast pace, too amped up to slow down. But she matched me, step for step.

"So?" Anna repeated, her voice sharp enough to cut through the haze of my frustration.

I didn't answer immediately, weaving past a group of junior staff who scrambled to get out of my way. Anna stayed on my heels, unfazed.

"They love the relationship angle," I said finally, my tone flat. "But they're not happy about the fight. Apparently, decking that guy didn't scream 'brand ambassador of the year.'"

Anna huffed, rolling her eyes. "Of course, they aren't happy about the fight. They're corporate robots—they'd prefer you to smile and shake hands, even with someone who deserved a punch to the face."

"Great advice," I said dryly, pushing open the door to the quieter hallway that led to my private suite.

Anna followed, undeterred. "What about the renewal? Did they give you anything concrete?"

"No." The word came out harsher than I intended. "It's still 'under discussion.'" I made air quotes with my fingers, my frustration finally bubbling to the surface. "But they made it pretty damn clear that my future depends on me keeping my 'good reputation' intact."

Anna frowned, her pace slowing as we neared the end of the hall. "So let's keep the relationship front and center, push on the family side with Gia too.

"I don't know," I said, running a hand through my hair. "I'm supposed to keep being the perfect boyfriend. Keep making them money, but the brand deals are up, money is rolling in, what else do they want?"

I paused outside my suite, the irony of the words hanging heavy in the air. Anna tilted her head, studying me like she was waiting for me to say something more.

"And what about you?" she asked suddenly, her voice softer now.

I turned to look at her, startled. "What about me?"

"Are you okay?"

The question hit me like a gut punch. Anna wasn't one to mince words, and she had a way of asking things that made you confront truths you weren't ready to face.

I opened my mouth to brush it off with a joke, but no words came out. Instead, I thought about Lucia—about her laugh, her fire, the way she held Gia like the world began and ended with her daughter. I thought about the way she'd smiled at me that morning, soft and hesitant, like she was still figuring out what to make of all this.

The answer was there, buried under layers of denial and complication, but I couldn't bring myself to say it out loud. Not yet.

Anna didn't press, just gave me a knowing look. "You might want to figure that out," she said, her tone brisk again. "Because how much you care for that girl, both of them, that's real. No matter how many times you try to tell yourself it's a part of the act. I would tell her before it's too late."

Before I could respond, she turned on her heel and walked away, leaving me alone in the hallway with her words echoing in my head.

I exhaled sharply, pulling open the door to my suite. The room was quiet, dimly lit by the afternoon sun streaming through the curtains. I tossed my keys onto the table and sank onto the couch, my head falling into my hands.

Anna's words wouldn't leave me alone, no matter how hard I tried to push them away. Because deep down, I knew the truth. I wasn't just playing a role anymore, hadn't been in some time. And that scared the hell out of me. I pulled out a notebook shoved into a bag, a sketchbook I tried to keep on me. I had always liked to sketch when I had free time, it helped clear my mind. As I opened the notebook, a folded piece of paper fell out. I opened it.

As long as I'm alive, you'll always have someone who's proud of you in everything.

She left me a note.

❦

It was the morning of the Mexico GP, and the paddock was alive with energy. Mechanics rushed between the garage and pit lane, finalizing setups while the engineers huddled over screens analyzing data. My team's signature black, blue, and pink gear blended into the chaos, a testament to how close-knit and efficient we were. I had secured pole position in qualifying yesterday, but the weight of today loomed heavy. With Carlos from Moretti breathing down my neck in the Drivers' Championship, today's points were pivotal. A win here could solidify my lead—or leave me vulnerable. I had woken up with a certain type of determination. I had thought about what Anna had said, that whatever this was between me and Lucia, it was real. And if I didn't want to lose her when this whole fake relationship was up, then I needed to man up. So I told myself when I woke up, if I win this race, then I'll tell Lucia how I feel, for real.

My pre-race ritual was designed to keep me centered. I'd woken before sunrise, the city's quiet broken only by my footsteps as I jogged around the track with my trainer. Afterward, I refueled with a perfectly portioned meal from my nutritionist—light, clean, nothing too heavy. Meditation followed, grounding me amid the pressure. Now, I was back in my private lounge, pacing the limited space like a caged animal, headphones in, playlist blaring. The bass thumped in my ears, syncing with my heartbeat as I tried to push away the nerves clawing at my insides.

Everyone on the team knew better than to disturb me during this sacred time. Even Anna, my PR manager, avoided me unless it was an emergency. The room was my sanctuary, and I intended to savor every minute of solitude before heading to the grid. At least, I thought I would. A knock broke my focus, cutting through the music and my thoughts like a sharp blade.

I tugged one earbud out. "Yeah?"

"It's me," Lucia's voice filtered through the door, soft and hesitant.

My hand moved on instinct, pulling the door open. She stood there, slightly out of breath, her cheeks flushed from what I assumed was chasing after Gianna or running an errand. Her hair was pulled back in a loose ponytail, and she held her purse against her chest.

"Hey," she said, her voice quiet but filled with an edge of urgency.

"Hi." My tone softened, her presence somehow settling the turmoil in my chest.

"I know you're getting ready," she started, eyes dropping to her hands, which she was twisting nervously. "I just...I wanted to make sure you were okay."

I tried for my usual dismissive response, the one that kept my nerves hidden. "Yeah, of course."

Her gaze lifted, cutting straight through me. Lucia always had this way of seeing the parts of me I tried to bury. I felt naked under her scrutiny, and it was clear she wasn't buying my brush-off. We had run into each other in the hallway of the hotel on our private floor at an ungodly hour. Gianna had kept Lucia up all night, and despite the lack of sleep, she had still noticed or caught on to me being off this morning.

"Okay," I sighed, rubbing the back of my neck. "I'm a little stressed. Today's points are huge. I need to win."

"You will," she said with a quiet conviction that knocked the air out of me. She spoke it as if it were a fact, not a possibility.

Before I could respond, she reached into her purse and pulled out a small bundle of notecards bound together with a thin ribbon. "This might be silly, but Gianna and I do affirmations every morning. They help us on hard days, and...well, I made some for you."

For a moment, I was speechless, staring at the cards she held out to me. The thoughtfulness of it, the effort she had put into this, hit me like a freight train. My throat tightened.

"Luce..." I murmured, taking the cards gingerly, as if they might break under my touch. "This is so nice."

Her lips quirked up in a small, self-conscious smile. "I know you're in prep mode, but maybe read them. It might help."

Before I could thank her properly, she stepped forward and wrapped her arms around my middle, surprising me. Her hug was firm, grounding, and it left me reeling. My arms found their way around her, pulling her closer. The fire in my veins, the one that usually came from adrenaline, shifted into something else entirely. Something more electric.

She pulled back after a moment, her cheeks pink. "Good luck, Alex," she said softly before disappearing down the hall, leaving me clutching the cards and feeling more alive than I had all morning.

By the time I lowered myself into the cockpit of my car, the affirmations were etched into my mind. Each one played in my head like a mantra, weaving through the noise of the crowd and the mechanics' chatter.

Radio checks crackled through my earpiece. "You good to go, Wright?" my race engineer asked.

I tightened my grip on the steering wheel, my pulse steady now, thinking of those affirmation cards from Lucia.

I am stronger than I know
I am as calm as the sea
I am prepared and aware

"Let's do this."

As the engines roared to life and the grid cleared, I couldn't see them, but I knew Lucia and Gianna were watching from the Belen garage today. Lucia had taken to switching between the Moretti garage to support her brother, and Belen's. Sure, it was to keep up the ruse, but it was also nice to have someone here for me, someone I knew in the crowd cheering me on.

My thoughts cleared as I watched the red lights go out.

And away we go.

25

LUCIA

The Belen Racing garage was alive with energy as the final lap of the race unfolded. Engineers and crew members leaned toward their screens, gripping headsets, their voices rising with excitement as Alexander maintained his lead. The roar of the crowd outside echoed into the space, a pulsating wave of sound that matched the pounding in my chest.

Gianna sat on my hip, her small hands clutching the team hat Alexander had given her that morning. Her tiny face was lit up with excitement, eyes glued to the screens as the cars sped through the last corner.

"Go, Alex!" she squealed, bouncing slightly in my arms.

I couldn't help but smile at her enthusiasm. The final stretch was a blur of speed and sound, but when Alexander crossed the finish line, securing first place, the garage erupted. Cheering, yelling, and laughter filled the space as the team celebrated. The sound was deafening, and Gianna clapped her hands, shouting, "He did it, Mommy! He won!"

"He did, baby," I said, my voice thick with pride and emotion. My heart swelled, watching the crew exchange hugs and high fives, pure elation rippling through them. An older man wearing a Belen

Racing shirt walked over to me with a wide smile. I tried to place him, he looked like Belen Management from his crisp white button up, Paul maybe?

"We're heading to the podium," he said, motioning toward the exit. "You and Gia should come too. He'll want to see you."

Before I could answer, Anna appeared beside me, her expression carefully neutral. "Lucia, just a heads-up—if you go out there, there's a good chance the cameras will catch you both. Are you okay with that?"

I hesitated, glancing at Gianna. The idea of us being photographed and broadcasted made me uncomfortable, but before I could decide, Gianna tugged at my shirt.

"Please, Mommy," she begged, her big green eyes full of excitement. "I want to see Alex and his trophy!"

My resolve crumbled instantly. I could never say no to her when she looked at me like that. I took a deep breath and nodded. "Okay. Let's go."

Paul gave a whoop of approval and led us out of the garage. The noise of the crowd hit us in full force as we moved toward the track. The podium loomed ahead, bright under the lights, and the cheers grew louder as Alexander climbed out of his car.

He stood on top of it, throwing a fist in the air, and the crowd went wild. Gianna clapped enthusiastically, shouting his name, while I stood frozen, watching him soak in the moment. His helmet came off, and everything seemed to slow. His hair was damp with sweat, his face flushed and shining with triumph, and his ecstatic smile made my chest tighten. He found me quickly.

The world fell away. In that moment, with the crowd screaming and the chaos of the team celebrating around me, it was just us. I saw him—truly saw him—and it hit me like a freight train. I loved this version of him. The one who was wild and free, the one who lived for these moments of pure joy.

Alexander turned his attention to the team, hugging his race engineer and managers as the reporters swarmed. He moved through the post-race motions quickly, his focus snapping back to us. I wasn't prepared for the way my heart leapt when he ran toward the barrier, his gaze locking on me again.

He reached the crowd of crew members, accepting their congratulations with quick hugs and pats on the back. Then his eyes landed on us—on me, holding Gianna close. A smile spread across his face, brighter than the lights above us.

"I knew you could do it," I said when he reached us, my voice barely carrying over the noise.

Gianna cheered, her little hands clapping furiously. "Yay, Alex!"

Alexander laughed, pulling us both into a hug. Gianna wrapped her arms around his neck, her giggles infectious. He squeezed us tightly, his forehead brushing against mine for the briefest moment before he leaned closer.

"I'm going to kiss you now," he murmured in my ear, his voice low and rough. "For me, not them. I am going to kiss you because there's nothing I'd rather be doing." My breath caught, and I nodded against him. He pulled away from the hug, cupping my face with one hand.

His lips found mine, and the world stopped. It wasn't like any of the staged kisses we'd shared before. This was raw, unfiltered, and all-consuming. His warmth, the taste of sweat and triumph, the electricity sparking between us—it was everything. My free hand clutched his arm, grounding me in the moment.

When he pulled back, the cheer of the crowd surged, and Gianna's giggles filled the air. Alexander grinned, pressing a quick kiss to Gianna's cheek before wrapping his arms around us both again. As he left us and made his way to the cooldown room, then the stage, I felt like I was still buzzing from that kiss.

ALEXANDER

On the podium, I could hear one voice standing out. When it quieted for the announcements, my favorite tiny was cheering my name.

"Alex!"

I looked down to see her, the miniature version of her mother. The biggest smile on her face I had ever seen. I wanted to win every race to earn that smile.

I wanted to stay in this moment forever.

27

ALEXANDER

The buzz of the post-race celebrations was still palpable as I stepped off the podium, the roar of the crowd and the taste of champagne lingering in my veins. My racing suit clung to me, sticky from the celebratory spray, but I didn't care. Every muscle in my body hummed with the high of the win, the championship lead solidified. The garage was a whirlwind of noise and movement as I ducked back inside, greeted by cheers, pats on the back, and the occasional shouted congratulations.

Paul was waiting near the edge of the chaos, his arms crossed and a knowing smile on his face. He stepped forward, clapping a hand on my shoulder with a firm grip.

"Better keep an eye on your inbox," he said, his voice low enough to be private. "A contract will be rolling through soon. I've had some words with the rest of management." He leaned in slightly, his tone dipping conspiratorially. "I'm in your corner, Wright."

The meeting he mentioned, the one where my future with Belen Racing had been thrown into question, felt like a distant memory amid the euphoria of today.

"Thank you," I said, meeting his gaze. "I really appreciate it."

Paul's expression softened, he nodded past me, toward the edge of the crowd where Lucia stood, Gianna perched on her hip.

"You and your girl," he said, his voice carrying a warmth that caught me off guard. "I had a love like that once. You hold onto it."

My chest tightened as I followed his gaze. Lucia was laughing at something one of the crew had said, her head tilting back slightly, the lights catching the loose strands of her hair. Gianna was chattering animatedly, her tiny hand clutching Lucia's necklace as she pointed at something. They stood out in the sea of red and black, like they didn't quite belong—and yet, they were the only thing that mattered in the room.

"She's—" I started to deflect, but the words caught in my throat. She *was* mine. Not in any official way, not yet, but in every way that counted, Lucia and Gianna were mine.

Paul gave me a knowing look and patted my shoulder before walking off, leaving me standing there, champagne-sticky and utterly undone. I let out a breath, running a hand through my damp hair, and turned back toward them.

The noise of the garage faded as I crossed the floor, weaving through the team until I reached them. Gianna spotted me first, her face lighting up like I'd brought the sun in with me.

"Alex!" she squealed, reaching out with both arms.

Lucia's smile was softer, but it carried the same warmth. Her eyes met mine, and the pride there was so palpable, it washed over me like a second victory.

"Hey," she said softly. "Congratulations."

As Gianna practically launched herself into my arms, and Lucia's hand brushed mine in the exchange, Paul's words echoed in my mind.

You hold onto that.

I wasn't letting go.

I wanted this.

For real.

But first I needed to talk to Matteo.

We headed back to the hotel to clean up after the race, and Matteo was practically vibrating with excitement. He was already talking about hitting the town, as if the energy from the track had followed him right to the elevator. Anna, bless her, had happily agreed to stay with Gianna so the three of us—Matteo, Lucia, and I—could go out tonight with Nicola and some of the other drivers. The anticipation was electric, even if part of me felt like I was walking a tightrope between exhilaration and something far more nerve racking.

I knocked on Matteo's door, and he yanked it open with a grin so wide I was momentarily blinded.

"Hey, man," he said, practically dragging me inside. "Help me with this outfit, would you? I can't decide, and you know I've gotta look sharp if I'm gonna be the life of the party. Which I obviously am."

I stepped into the chaos of his room, clothes flung over every available surface like a hurricane had passed through. Matteo was already rifling through a pile of jackets, half talking to himself and half ranting about the race. His sentences overlapped in a way that made no sense unless you were fluent in Matteo-ese.

"First of all," I said, holding up a pair of bright sneakers he'd apparently considered wearing, "what the fuck are those?"

Matteo rolled his eyes but tossed the offending shoes aside, letting me dig through his stuff to find something more presentable. Eventually, I found him an outfit suitable for a night out. "Here. You'll look like you've got your life together, even if we both know that's a lie."

"Thanks for the vote of confidence," he said dryly, sitting on the edge of the bed to lace up his, much better, shoes.

As he tied the last knot, he glanced up at me, tilting his head like a curious puppy. "What's up with you? You look...weird."

I snorted. "Weird how?"

"Weird like you've got something on your mind. Spill it, Wright. You know you can talk to me, right?"

I hesitated, my heart picking up speed. Then I decided to throw caution—and maybe a little bit of sanity—to the wind. "It's...complicated."

"Complicated how?" he pressed, his tone shifting from playful to cautious.

I avoided his gaze, suddenly finding the carpet way too interesting. "It's about Lucia."

Matteo's eyebrows shot up, and he froze mid-movement. "Lucia?"

"Yeah," I admitted, exhaling sharply. "This whole fake-dating thing—"

"Wait, wait, wait," Matteo cut me off, holding up both hands like a traffic cop. "You're not telling me it's going sideways, are you? Because if this blows up and my sister gets hurt—"

"It's not going sideways," I interrupted firmly. "She's amazing at this. Honestly, better at it than I am."

"Then what's the problem?" Matteo asked, his protectiveness melting into genuine curiosity.

I raked a hand through my hair, feeling the tension coiled in my chest. "The problem is...it doesn't feel fake anymore. At least not for me."

There was a beat of silence, and then Matteo let out a low whistle. "Oh, man. You are so screwed."

"Thanks for the support," I said dryly, glaring at him.

"Hey, I told you this might happen," he said, smirking now. "You're fake dating my sister, Alex. Did you think you'd come out of this unscathed?"

"I didn't expect this," I admitted, gesturing helplessly. "I can't stop thinking about her, Matteo. She's in my head, and it's...it's messing me up."

Matteo leaned back, crossing his arms as he studied me. "So, what are you going to do about it?"

"I don't know," I said honestly, the weight of it pressing on my chest. "This was supposed to be a PR stunt, not—"

"Not you catching feelings," Matteo finished, shaking his head in mock disbelief. "Look, Alex, I love you, man. But if you hurt her, I will kill you. And not in a *ha-ha, best friends forever* kind of way. I mean in the *they'll never find the body* kind of way."

I laughed nervously, but his expression didn't budge. "Noted."

"Good." Matteo's tone softened slightly. "For what it's worth, you two kinda work. Just don't screw it up."

"I don't plan to," I said quietly, the words carrying more weight than I expected.

Matteo clapped me on the shoulder, but his smirk returned. "So, what's the plan, loverboy?"

I hesitated, then shrugged. "I told myself if I won today, I'd tell her."

"Well, you won," Matteo said, crossing his arms and raising an eyebrow. "So?"

"So...now I tell her."

"What could go wrong?" Matteo threw his hands in the air with a laugh, but there was a flicker of seriousness behind it.

Everything. Everything could go wrong. But as her laugh echoed in my head and the memory of her smile burned bright, I knew I couldn't keep this to myself any longer.

We met the girls in the hotel lobby, and Matteo wasted no time diving into his usual antics. He immediately started flirting with

Nicola, who rolled her eyes and shot back a sarcastic remark about him only managing fifth place today.

Lucia glanced at her brother and Nicola, then back at me, her brows lifted in curiosity. "So…" she said, dragging the word out as she wagged her eyebrows. "That's new."

"I don't even want to know," I replied, shaking my head. "They give me whiplash. One minute they're bickering, the next Matteo's shamelessly flirting, and Nicola's roasting him like it's her favorite sport. Pretty sure it only makes him like her more, though." I shrugged. "Who knows where that's going."

Lucia's lips curved into a knowing smirk, but I couldn't focus on whatever she was about to say because—damn—she looked *incredible*. She was wearing a short, deep red, satin dress that melted against her curves and put her long legs on display, and I was definitely staring. But seriously, could anyone blame me? Lucia DeLuca was a knockout.

"You like?" she asked, spinning in a little circle with a playful grin.

"I love," I said without hesitation, a lazy smile tugging at my lips.

Her cheeks flushed pink as she gently nudged my shoulder. "You look nice too…I guess," she teased, her smirk softening the jab.

"Damn right," I shot back with a laugh, holding out my hand. When she took it, lacing her fingers with mine, my heart rate spiked like I'd just been called into the final lap of a race.

We were just stepping outside to the valet when Matteo piped up. "I, uh, accidentally called my own car. Guess we'll just meet you there," he announced, a little too casually, as two sleek black town cars pulled up.

"Accidentally?" I deadpanned.

He grinned like the cat that caught the canary, mouthing, *Good luck.*

Once we were alone in the backseat of the town car, I turned to

Lucia, feeling my pulse quicken again. "I was actually hoping to talk to you about something," I said, trying to keep my voice steady and not sound like a total idiot.

She looked at me with curious, open eyes, her lips parting slightly as she waited. And that's when I noticed her lips, glossy and red, glinting under the dim interior light. My train of thought completely derailed, leaving me sitting there like a guy who'd just forgotten how to form coherent words.

"Okay..." she prompted, her voice soft but tinged with amusement as she gave me an encouraging smile.

"The kiss," I blurted.

The second the words left my mouth, her cheeks turned pink, and she glanced down at her hands, fiddling with her fingers.

"It was—but I also wanted to check in, since we haven't kissed in front of Gianna before and..."

She met my eyes again, her expression unreadable but her cheeks still warm. My stomach flipped. This was my moment, my chance to say something—

The car jerked slightly as it pulled to an unexpected stop.

"What the hell?" I glanced out the window, confused.

"Apologies, sir," the driver called from the front seat. "We've got a flat. The other car is stopping to take you the rest of the way."

Of course.

Of course, this would happen.

I closed my eyes briefly, muttering a curse under my breath as Lucia bit back a laugh. "Guess we're carpooling," she said.

28

LUCIA

The town car jerked to a stop in front of us, and I barely had time to register the flat tire before Matteo and Nicola's car slowed to a halt right behind us. Alexander had seemed like he wanted to talk to me about something and I felt the pang of nervous energy. He mentioned kissing in front of Gianna, and it was the first time we had done that; we had been careful not to kiss in front of her so as not to confuse her. But she hadn't been fazed, had brushed it away when I asked her about it: *Mommy, you said you kiss people you love. We love Alex.* Then she returned to asking if we could watch a princess movie.

Alexander sighed beside me, muttering something that sounded suspiciously like a curse, as Matteo rolled down his window and leaned out.

"What'd you do this time, Wright?" Matteo called out with a grin, his elbow resting lazily on the window ledge.

"It's a flat tire, genius," Alexander shot back, opening his door. "Unless you think I went outside and slashed it for fun."

"I wouldn't put it past you," Matteo quipped, already opening his own door. "C'mon, get in. Plenty of room in our car for everyone."

Nicola groaned audibly. "Oh, *great*. Now we're playing sardines. Just what I wanted."

"Relax, Nic," Matteo said, smirking as he climbed out. "I'm sure you'll survive five minutes squished next to me."

"Doubt it, I'll probably contract a disease," Nicola muttered, shooting him a glare as she slid over to make room.

Alexander held out a hand to help me out of the car, and my stomach flipped as our fingers touched. The memory of his kiss after the race flashed in my mind like a neon sign I couldn't turn off. I glanced up at him, but his expression was unreadable as he waited for me to climb into Matteo and Nicola's car.

Matteo gave me an exaggerated grin as I slid into the backseat. "Welcome to the party, Luce!" he said, as if this were some kind of exclusive VIP lounge instead of a crowded car.

"Thanks for the invitation," I said dryly, squeezing into the middle seat as Alexander climbed in beside me.

Nicola, sitting on Matteo's other side, shot him a withering look. "If you make one more joke about me enjoying this, I swear to God, DeLuca—"

"You'll fall madly in love with me?" Matteo cut in, waggling his eyebrows.

"No," she snapped. "I'll throw you out of the car while it's moving."

Alexander laughed quietly beside me, leaning closer so only I could hear him. "How long do you think before they're fucking? Tonight?"

"Ew, but yeah, by end of season for sure," I whispered back, trying not to laugh. I had been watching them the whole time I had been here, and no one ever got under Matteo's skin because most people adored him. Nicola, however, seemed dead set on annoying him at any free moment, and Matteo had never had anyone not like him.

"Hey, what are you two whispering about over there?" Matteo asked, narrowing his eyes at us in the rearview mirror.

"Nothing," Alexander said smoothly, leaning back in his seat like he didn't have a care in the world. "Just enjoying the show."

Matteo huffed, but before he could fire back, the car pulled up in front of the nightclub. The bass from the music inside was already vibrating through the air, and a line of people stretched around the block.

Nicola didn't wait for anyone else, opening her door and hopping out. "Finally," she muttered, straightening her jacket as Matteo slid out after her.

I stepped onto the curb, taking a deep breath. The night was electric, the lights of the city glowing around us, and for once, I wasn't overwhelmed. I wasn't the nervous, out-of-place mom who didn't belong here. I was *me*, and for the first time in a long time, I felt confident.

Alexander came up beside me, his presence steadying in a way I couldn't explain. He glanced down at me, a small smile tugging at his lips. "Ready for this?"

I tilted my chin up, matching his smile. "More than ready."

The four of us headed inside, bypassing the line with ease, thanks to Matteo and Alexander's names on the list. The music hit me like a wave—loud, pulsing, and alive. I couldn't stop the smile spreading across my face as we made our way to a booth near the dance floor.

Drinks were ordered, jokes were exchanged, everything felt easy. But as the night wore on, my thoughts kept drifting back to Alexander. The kiss after the race. The way he looked at me when he thought I wasn't paying attention.

Did it mean anything to him, or was I reading too much into it?

I pushed the thoughts away with a sip of my drink, determined to enjoy myself. When the music shifted to a faster beat, I grabbed Nicola's hand. "Come on. Let's dance."

She hesitated, then nodded, dragging me toward the dance floor. The rhythm of the music took over, and I let it drown out my doubts, my worries, and the stupid flutter in my chest every time Alexander smiled at me.

But even as I danced, I couldn't shake the feeling of his eyes on me, every time I glanced over, they met mine.

"You should ask him to dance," Nicola said, raising a brow.

"Who, Alex?" I asked.

"Yeah, you know, the one you're eye fucking."

"Am not!" I yelled.

"Sure, sure. Anyway, I gotta go...do something." She trailed off, and with an evil smirk, danced away. Alexander was already making his way over to me.

"Hey," he said over the music.

"Hey." I smiled and reached out for him, closing my eyes. We danced like that, some part of our bodies connected throughout the next few songs. Each song that passed, we grew closer. Maybe it was the crowd, maybe it was us.

The music pulsed around us, the bass thrumming in time with my heartbeat as Alexander's hand slid to my waist. My arms looped around his neck, and the world outside the dance floor ceased to exist. It was just us, swaying together, the energy between us crackling like static.

I opened my eyes to find his gaze fixed on me, intense and unwavering. His hand on my waist tightened slightly, pulling me just a fraction closer.

"You're really something else," he murmured, his voice low enough that I had to lean in to hear him.

"Is that so?" I teased, my lips quirking into a smile.

He nodded, his expression serious despite the playful tone. "Yeah. I don't think you realize it, though."

I swallowed hard, trying to ignore the way his words made my chest flutter. "Careful, Wright. You're starting to sound like you're trying to charm me."

"Who says I'm not?" He smirked, his face inching closer to mine.

I could feel his breath against my cheek, the air between us charged. My heart was racing, and I wasn't sure if it was the music, the drinks, or just *him*.

The crowd around us kept shifting, but Alexander didn't move.

"I like us," he said, his voice quieter now.

"Yeah?" I said, trying to keep my voice light even as my pulse hammered in my ears. He slid his other hand to my waist.

I let out a shaky breath, nodding as I stepped even closer. Our movements slowed, matching the beat of the song. His forehead dipped toward mine, our noses almost brushing.

"Lucia," he murmured, his voice almost lost in the music.

"Yes?" I asked, my voice barely above a whisper.

"I want to kiss you again," he admitted, his eyes searching mine. No cameras here I could see, just us.

My heart leaped into my throat. "Alexander—"

"Tell me no if you don't want to," he said, cutting me off gently.

The honesty in his voice made my knees weak. I couldn't look away, couldn't think straight with him so close. And then, before I could second-guess myself, I tilted my head up.

"Kiss me," I whispered.

He didn't hesitate. His lips found mine in a kiss that was both deliberate and consuming, his hand sliding to the small of my back as he pulled me flush against him. The music faded into the background, and all I could feel was him—his warmth, his strength, and the way he kissed me like he'd been waiting for this moment as long as I had.

When we finally pulled apart, his forehead rested against mine, his breath ragged. My heart felt like it might jump right out of my chest. I wanted more, I wanted him.

"I've been wanting to do that all night," he admitted with a soft laugh.

Before either of us could say more, a loud wolf whistle cut

through the moment. We turned to see Matteo standing on the edge of the dance floor, his arms crossed and a smug grin plastered on his face.

"Took you long enough!" he called, raising his drink in mock celebration.

Alexander groaned, his head dropping to my shoulder. "Your brother's timing is impeccable."

I laughed, my hands still resting on his shoulders. "The worst."

"Good thing I'm not easily deterred," Alexander said, pulling back just enough to meet my gaze, his smile soft and sincere.

"Good thing," I echoed, my heart still racing as we stayed locked in the moment, the world around us a distant hum, as he leaned in again to kiss me.

The night continued, a blur of laughter, music, and fleeting touches that set my skin alight. Alexander stayed close, his presence magnetic. Eventually I was pulled away by Nicola and her knowing smile. She gave me a little nudge with her elbow and tilted her head toward the bar.

"Come on," she said, her tone laced with mischief.

I hesitated, glancing over my shoulder at Alexander, who was talking to Matteo and a few others. Nicola rolled her eyes and tugged me forward.

"He'll survive without you for five minutes. Besides, we need to talk."

We weaved through the crowd, the air buzzing with energy, and found an empty spot near the bar. Nicola flagged down the bartender, ordering something fruity for me and a tequila shot for herself.

"Okay," she started, handing me my drink. "Spill."

I raised an eyebrow, feigning innocence. "Spill what?"

"Don't play dumb, Lucia. I saw that kiss." She leaned against the bar, her smirk practically glowing under the neon lights.

Heat crept up my neck. "It wasn't a big deal."

"Oh sure, just a casual kiss with one of the most famous drivers in the world, with no cameras around, might I add," she teased, throwing back her shot with practiced ease.

I sipped my drink, the tart sweetness doing little to cool the fire in my chest. "It's complicated."

"Complicated, my ass." Nicola set her glass down with a dramatic clink. "You like him. He *definitely* likes you. So what's the problem?"

"The problem," I said, lowering my voice, "is that this whole thing started as fake."

Nicola waved a dismissive hand. "Yeah, and now it's not fake. Congratulations, you've graduated to the real deal."

I gave her a pointed look. "It's not that simple."

"Why not?" she asked, genuinely curious.

"Because," I said, glancing at Alexander across the room. He caught my eye and sent me a quick, heart-stopping smile. "He's...a lot. And I'm just—"

"A catch," Nicola interrupted firmly. "You're hot, you're the kindest person I have ever met, you're an amazing mother. If anything, he's lucky to have you."

I sighed, swirling my drink. "What if it's all too much? The media, traveling, the...everything. It's not just about me...it's about Gianna too."

Nicola softened, her teasing demeanor giving way to something more serious. "Look, I get it. You've got more to think about than most people. But that doesn't mean you don't deserve this, Lucia. You deserve to be happy."

Her words hit me hard, cutting through the noise in my head.

"And," she added, her smirk returning, "I don't know if you've noticed, but Alexander looks at you like you hung the moon. I say, stop overthinking and enjoy it."

I laughed, despite myself. "You make it sound so easy."

"Maybe it is," she said with a shrug. "Or maybe you're just scared it's real."

I didn't have an answer to that, so I just sipped my drink and watched as Alexander made his way across the room, his eyes locked on mine.

Nicola leaned in, her voice low and conspiratorial. "He's coming over here. I'm gonna disappear and leave you to it."

Before I could protest, Nicola smirked, gave me a playful wink, and disappeared into the pulsing crowd. I barely had time to process her words before Alexander appeared, his tall frame cutting through the throng of people with ease.

"Hey," he said, his voice soft but clear despite the pounding music around us.

"Hey," I replied, my pulse quickening at the sight of him.

His gaze searched mine, his brows drawing together slightly. "Everything okay?"

I nodded quickly, setting my drink on the nearest high-top table. "Yeah. Just girl talk."

"Should I be worried?" he teased, his smile warm and easy, the kind that made my knees feel a little weak.

"Not at all." I stepped closer, the space between us growing smaller. "Nicola's just...blunt."

"Mm-hm," he hummed, his gaze dropping to my lips like a magnet.

"What?" I asked, suddenly self-conscious under his scrutiny. My fingers brushed my hair back instinctively, even though nothing was out of place.

"You look so beautiful," he said, the words soft but weighted, cutting straight through the haze of noise and lights around us.

The words were simple but hit me like a punch to the chest. It shouldn't have taken me by surprise—Alexander had always been the type to give compliments freely, unapologetically honest about how he felt and who he cared about. But the way he said it now, low and earnest, felt different.

I barely managed to whisper, "Thank you," before he stepped closer, sending shivers down my spine.

"I want to kiss you again."

My breath hitched, my mind momentarily blanking.

"No cameras around here," I murmured, trying to lighten the moment even though my heart was racing.

"Fuck that, I already told you," he said firmly, stepping closer, his eyes locking onto mine with an intensity that left no room for misinterpretation. "I want to kiss you because I want to. Nothing else. Understand?"

"Oh," I managed to squeak, my voice embarrassingly weak.

He smiled faintly at my reaction, his hand brushing against mine like a silent invitation. His touch sent a spark through me, and suddenly Nicola's words echoed in my mind: *Stop overthinking and enjoy it.*

For tonight, at least, I decided to do just that.

"I'll remind you as many times as you need me to, pretty girl."

A slow smile spread across my lips as I tilted my head to meet his gaze. "Want to get out of here?" I asked, surprising even myself with the boldness of my words.

Alexander paused, his eyes darkening slightly. "More than anything," he replied, his voice thick with something that made my stomach flutter.

Without hesitation, I reached for his hand, lacing my fingers with his as we made our way through the crowd. The music and lights faded into the background, my world narrowing to the warmth of his hand in mine and the way my heart raced with anticipation. We loaded into the first cab we found, Alexander flagging it down. The ride was short on the way but felt so long on the way back. He asked for the aux cord and played cheesy songs as we bet the other couldn't remember all the words. I won every bet.

We stumbled into the hotel lobby, our laughter echoing against the polished marble floors. My cheeks ached from smiling so much, my heart thrumming with a mix of nerves and excitement. Everything felt heightened—the buzz of the night still thrumming in my veins, the warmth of Alexander's hand brushing against mine as we walked side by side, and the way his voice dipped low when he leaned in to speak, like it was meant just for me.

The elevator doors slid open with a quiet chime, and we stepped inside. I pressed the button for our floor, and Alexander leaned casually against the mirrored wall, his gaze fixed on me.

"You had fun tonight," he said, his voice soft, a faint smile tugging at his lips.

"I did," I admitted, glancing at him. "It's been a while since I've felt...like this."

"Like what?" he asked, stepping closer.

I hesitated, the words caught somewhere between my chest and throat. "Light," I said finally. "Free."

His hand brushed against mine, his fingers curling gently around mine. "I'm glad," he murmured, his thumb stroking the back of my hand in slow circles.

The elevator dinged, and the doors opened to our floor. I stepped out, my pulse quickening as I felt him follow close behind me. We walked down the quiet hallway, his presence steady and reassuring, and when we reached our hallway, I turned to face him. Anna was watching Gianna for the night in my room, and all I wanted was this night not to end. We neared our doors, across the hall from each other's.

"So," I said softly.

Alexander's hand found mine, stilling my nervous movements. His touch was warm, grounding, and when I looked up, his eyes were locked on mine, the intensity in his gaze stealing the breath from my lungs.

"Come inside?" he asked, his voice low and rough, like he was struggling to find the right words, holding up his hotel key card.

I swallowed hard, unsure of what to say, what to do. The air between us felt electric, charged with all the things we weren't saying. I plucked the key card from his hand and unlocked his door. Once inside, the door shut quickly and his hands were on me.

He leaned in and I followed, our lips meeting.

It wasn't rushed or frantic, it was gentle, deliberate, like he was giving me time to pull away if I wanted to. But I didn't want to.

His lips brushed against mine, soft and warm, and everything else fell away. The world narrowed to just this moment, just him, and I felt myself leaning into him, my hands finding their way to his chest. His thumb traced the curve of my jaw, before it slid back into my hair. Shivers erupted through me.

"You're incredible, you know that?" he said, his voice barely above a whisper, once inside his room. "I've dreamed of kissing you."

"You have kissed me before," I replied.

"No, kissing you for real, not for PR stunts, or pictures or to put on a show. Kissing you and knowing without a single doubt that it was real, because this"—he pointed to the two of us—"is maybe the most important thing to me." He paused, holding my face in his hands. "I don't want to lose this, to lose you," he admitted, and I melted. Right there, a pile of mush on the ground.

"You couldn't, even if you tried," I replied softly, then kissed him again. This time it wasn't soft or slow or chaste. It was a punishing kiss, a hard one, lips pressing into his, opening for him.

29

LUCIA

Alexander groaned as he kissed me back. His lips were as soft and perfect as I remembered, and I doubted there was anything in the world better than this. Tilting his head to the side, Alex kissed me slowly. He took his time, the palms of his hands going up and down my back, holding me to him and exploring me all at the same time.

There was no awkwardness. No hesitation. His hands mapped my body like they already knew it. His palm caressed over my mini dress, up my bare skin, fingers stretched wide. So I did the same, sneaking my hand up under his side, palming the solid mass of muscles there and the skin over his ribs, earning a soft groan that I swallowed because I sure as hell didn't want to stop kissing him again any time soon. Or maybe ever.

The last time I had felt like this, or had even been touched like this was so long ago, I had almost forgotten. This man wouldn't use me like my ex, would never make me feel trapped or isolated. He liked having me around, spent intentional time with Gianna, and showed up in a way no one else had before. He made me feel seen, and most of all, he just made me happy. His subtle smiles, or winks. The way he was always tuned into my feelings, leaving me notes, getting me those damn flowers right after we talked about them, ordering food to my room so he knew me and Gianna wouldn't be hungry. It was the way to an Italian girl's heart. When his fingers brushed mine, even when it couldn't be seen. A soft hand on the small of my back around the circuit or at events, grounding me. Holding out his hand for me, just finding the excuses to touch me, it felt all so obvious to me now. It all meant the world to me. He made me happy. A callused palm ran up my thighs to my hips, pushing up the mini dress as he went, grasping there.

Alex growled, tilting me back in his lap just enough so he could look right into my eyes as he said, "You have no idea how long I've wanted to do this." His voice was a low murmur, filled with longing, before his lips captured mine again. The kiss was unhurried, deep, and intoxicatingly sweet, pulling me under like a warm tide. My hands slid up his back, fingers brushing over smooth, heated skin, the muscles shifting under my touch.

His fingers pulled at the hem of my dress, lingering there, and he pulled back just enough to speak, his voice rough and unsteady. "Can I?"

I nodded, my breath catching, but he didn't move.

"I need your words, angel," he said, his breath grazing my cheek. The rasp of his voice sent a shiver down my spine, and my heart stuttered at the name, so soft and intimate.

"Yes," I confirmed. He gently spun me around, and his hand went to the zipper, fingers lingering on my skin before unzipping the dress at a deliciously slow pace. My heart fluttered as his lips touched my neck, peppering soft kisses down my spine as he unzipped the dress. I felt like everything had led up to this, my feelings for him had begun so long ago now, but I had pressed them down and down. The dress fell the the floor and a hand went to my chin.

"Come here, pretty girl." I turned to face him and waited. He tilted my chin up and kissed me, long and intentional. I reached up my hands, placing one on his neck and the other on the back of his head, pulling him toward me. Sealing our kiss more as I rolled my hips into him. He groaned while I pressed against him, breaking the kiss and kissing a spot between my neck and collarbone that had me whimpering. Alexander leaned away for a moment, his throat bobbing, his breath heavy. His gaze traveled slowly from my face, lingering on the delicate curve of my collarbone before dipping lower to my breasts, framed perfectly by the purple lace bra I'd thrown on in a rushed, last-minute decision earlier tonight. Something I was even shocked I had packed. But the one matching lace set made me feel pretty, so I had added it when I packed it months ago, never expecting anyone to even see it. An excellent decision, as it turned out.

"Jesus," he whispered, his voice strained as his throat worked in a hard swallow. Every nerve in my body buzzed. I was ready, so damn ready. I was almost certain I heard him murmur a low, guttural *fuck* under his breath as he slid the bra off and tossed it aside without a second thought. In a second his hands were at my waist, and he was lifting me up and setting me on the bed. One of his thighs between me, I rolled into him, needing the friction. His mouth dove down and his lips sucked a nipple between them. I moaned and arched my back, pushing my breast deeper into his mouth before he gave it another suck and moved over, suckling at that nipple, too, hard and then softly, two hard pulls and then one gentle one. Not wanting to lose the feel of him but desperate to see more, I tugged at the hem of his shirt, pulling it over his head in one swift motion. He was even more breathtaking than I'd imagined, just like he looked in the tight undergarments drivers wore beneath their race suits. His stomach was taut and sculpted, every muscle defined. His pants hung low, teasingly, just beneath that perfect line. I ran my hands down his chest and fumbled with the buttons, pulling his pants down, then gently gave a push of my hands on his chest.

"I want to be on top," I muttered, and his hungry gaze flared as he let his body fall to the side, then onto the mattress as I climbed on top of him. I lowered myself down onto his lap, settling on top of him and grinding into him. His mouth met mine at the same time my breasts brushed his chest, and I swore my nipples got even harder at each movement when they grazed the hair on his pecs. I touched him everywhere, and he touched me everywhere. Sneaking my hand down into his underwear, my fingertips brushed his length. The wide, hard base. The smooth skin covering it all, and he grunted under my touch.

I kissed the line of his jaw, the tip of his chin, and moved my hand up and down his length, gaining confidence at his own moans. I took my time, long and languid strokes. Then, pulling my hands up his chest and hooking one around the back of his neck, I kissed him hard.

"You're doing so good, angel." His mouth gave my neck a soft kiss that had me shivering under his praise.

"I've been thinking about this for so long," I told him, stroking both hands up and down him, gaining confidence.

"You don't even know how many times I've made myself come thinking about you on top of me, just like this. The dreams I've had." He panted between strokes.

"Good," was all I replied before leaning down and teasing the tip of him with my tongue, swirling before taking him fully. One of his hands reached out, brushing away the hair that fell in front of my face. He scooped it up and held it in one palm, his eyes on me. I looked up at him as I went.

"Fuck, angel, my turn." He tugged gently on my hair to tell me to stop. I released with a pop and he dragged me back to his mouth. Kissing me fully. Then an arm encircled my waist, flipping us so my back was on the mattress again. I let myself melt into each kiss. His hands wandered down my exposed stomach, pushing into my underwear and finding the wetness between my legs. Teasing touches until my groans grew louder in frustration.

"Alex!" I gasped as he pushed a finger in, then two, and

pumped. He sucked and licked at my breasts, making me squirm. Then his hands held my waist, the other pulling out of me, a whimper leaving me as he did. I reached out for him and stroked up and down the thick cock, rubbing my thumb over the top.

"Fuck." He moaned, then his hand stopped my own. "But I said, my turn," he mumbled and began kissing down my body, leaving a trail of shivers. Slowly when one of his fingers finally dipped between my lips and pushed inside again, his tongue followed after. I'd been wet from the moment he started kissing me, and I tried to not be self-conscious. I had never had anyone go down on me before, and this, *this* was life changing.

"You taste like perfection, angel," Alexander muttered, coming up for air.

Angel.

It made butterflies swarm in my stomach and I wanted to hear it a million times more.

"I've never had anyone—" I panted, "down there before."

"Fuck," he groaned, his voice rough as he leaned up and kissed me deeply. "Knowing I'm the first is definitely going to help my ego," he added with a smirk. A laugh burst out of me, light and soft, because of course this man would make me feel utterly at ease in the middle of sex. He pulled himself back down, his short cropped beard tickling my thighs. I let my hands roam his tattooed arms, squeezing when it felt overwhelmingly good. I pulled him back up eventually, needing to touch him again, needing to kiss him again. I wanted to be closer, I wanted more.

"Alexander, please," I begged. "More, I need more."

"Are you sure, angel?"

"Yes," I replied. "I've never been more sure." His smile was blinding, even in the dimly lit room. The moonlight poured in through the window, the floor-length curtains blowing with the soft evening wind from the open doors. Alexander reached over into the drawer of the nightstand, grabbing a condom and ripping it open. He rolled it over his length, his eyes burning into mine, as if nothing could take him from this moment.

"The balcony is open," I mention, nodding at it. Alexander looked at me, his hips dipped down between my legs, and I wrapped them around his hips, and with my hand around his dick, guiding him where we both wanted him, he pressed into me. A wicked smile curved his lips, his eyes shadowed and heavy lidded.

"Good. Let them hear you scream for me."

I squeezed my thighs around his sides tightly, wrapping my arms around his shoulders and tilting up my hips a little. He pushed in and out slowly, letting me adjust. It felt euphoric, like I was leaving my body entirely. I didn't know it could feel like this. Feel *this* good. Then Alexander took my thighs and pulled them up to sit on his shoulders, pushing forward more and pounding into me, and I couldn't help but scream out his name. A proud smile was on his lips.

"That's right, angel."

I dragged my palms up and down his back, and he kissed his groans across my lips. We sank into each other like this was fleeting. I muffled my mouth against his shoulder.

"You're perfect," he whispered. "You feel so damn good." His hips picked up speed just as I started to feel the heat building at the center of my body. Alexander's hips thrusted forward, holding me off the bed and on top of his thighs, and I squeezed my legs tight around his neck as he ground and ground right against where I wanted him. I cried out my orgasm.

"Come for me," he gritted out, voice thick.

His hands gripped my waist hard as he pushed in and out at a punishing speed as I kept crying out, "Faster, faster." I felt my orgasm crescendo, the electricity rushing through me. Then he was there again, moving again slowly then building up and pulling me into another one. His lips devoured me as he went, sweaty forehead touching in the slower moments, his eyes finding mine over and over again. Turning my chin to look at him. It was all just *so* much.

I had never, not once, finished multiple times in one go, but here we were, quickly coming up on a third time. His own grunts were like music to my ears, hot and enticing music. His thrusts became erratic as he came, pulsing and groaning so deep from his chest. His body slumped against mine as he lowered us onto the bed. Alexander laid his cheek against the top of my head, pressing a kiss there. I let myself take in the moment, really commit it to memory. I want to stay here, in this feeling. I want to live in it.

"That…" I sighed deeply, fully and completely content. He pulled me into his side, an arm wrapping around my waist and dipping a kiss to my forehead.

"Let's get you cleaned up," he muttered, guiding me up and to the bathroom door.

Soon the bathroom was fogging up with the warmth of the shower. He led me into it, grabbing soap and slowly dragging his soapy hands over my limbs. I was drunk on his touches when I spun around to face him, looking up through wet eyelashes and smiling.

"Round two?"

⋘∙━◌━∙⋙

I woke slowly, the faint light of dawn peeking through the curtains, casting a soft glow over the room. For a moment, I stayed still, letting my senses catch up with me. The cool sheets tangled around my legs, the gentle hum of the world in the background, and the warmth of Alexander's body pressed against mine.

My heart skipped a beat when I realized where I was. His arm was draped over my waist, his chest rising and falling in a steady rhythm as he slept beside me. His breath was soft against the back of my neck, and I could feel the faintest beat of his heart and focused on the calming rhythm. He felt so solid, so real, and so... safe.

I shifted slightly, careful not to disturb him, and glanced over at the clock on the nightstand. It was early, much earlier than I would normally be awake, but I couldn't bring myself to move just yet. Everything about this moment was so peaceful, so calm. My mind, still foggy with sleep, pieced back together the events of the night before. We'd gone out with our friends, laughed, and danced. Then he made me see the damn stars three times before we fell asleep.

His hand was resting on my hip, his thumb lightly brushing my skin, as if he was holding me closer in his sleep. I felt a flutter of warmth in my chest at the simplicity of it. A feeling I hadn't allowed myself to acknowledge.

I tried to breathe quietly, not wanting to disturb him, but as the minutes passed, my thoughts began to rush in. Was this real? Everything had moved so fast, and yet this felt so right. I'd been trying to push away the growing feelings I had for him, but it was becoming impossible. I tried to shake my own negative thoughts away.

I turned my head slightly, just enough to see his face. His features were relaxed in sleep, his dark hair slightly tousled, the faintest stubble on his jaw. He looked peaceful. Perfect, even.

But as my gaze softened, I realized I didn't want to rush this. Whatever this was, I wanted to savor it. To let it unfold, without overthinking or second-guessing. Feeling the weight of his arm around me, his steady presence grounding me in the moment and sending butterflies through me. His warmth surrounded me like a protective cocoon, making me feel completely at ease.

"Morning," his voice rumbled softly, barely above a whisper, as if he, too, had just woken up. I looked up, meeting his gaze for the first time that morning. His eyes were still heavy with sleep, but there was something else in them now, something deeper, a tenderness that made my chest tighten.

"Morning," I replied, my voice soft and a little unsure, but not in a bad way.

He smiled, a slow, lazy smile that made my heart do a little flip. His hand gently brushed my hair back from my face, and he tucked a loose strand behind my ear.

"You look beautiful," he murmured, his voice low and sincere. "Want to stay here or go get our girl?"

Our girl.

Anna had stayed the night with her, knowing we would all be out late celebrating. What she didn't know was that I was here, down the hall, naked and wrapped up in Alexander Wright's bedsheets. I let out a hum of approval nonetheless.

"Yeah, let's go get Gia."

ALEXANDER

When we arrived at Anna's, Gia came barreling toward Lucia the second the door opened, her little arms outstretched.

"Mama!" she squealed, wrapping herself around Lucia's legs.

Lucia scooped her up, peppering kisses all over her face. "Hey, baby girl. Were you good for Anna?"

Gia nodded vigorously, her curls bouncing. "We had a tea party!"

Anna appeared behind her, looking exhausted but smiling. "She's a whirlwind, but she's a sweetheart."

"Thank you," Lucia said sincerely. "I owe you one."

Anna waved her off. "You owe me nothing. Go enjoy your day."

I reached out to ruffle Gia's hair. "You ready to hang out with us, kiddo?"

She grinned at me, her big green eyes lighting up. "Yes! Can we go to the park?

"Park it is," I said, glancing at Lucia. "What do you think?"

She nodded, her smile soft but full of something that made my chest feel too tight again. "Sounds perfect."

The day passed in a blur of laughter and easy moments. At the park, Gia dragged me onto the swings and made Lucia push us both, her giggles filling the air. We built a castle out of sand, which Gia declared was "the best ever." I didn't have the heart to correct her.

Lucia watched us with that quiet, loving expression that melted me every time. She joined in, of course, chasing Gia around the grass until they both collapsed in a heap, laughing.

By the time the sun started to dip, the three of us were sprawled out on a picnic blanket, Gia half asleep against Lucia's side, clutching her favorite stuffed bunny.

"This," I said, glancing between them, "is a pretty good day."

Lucia smiled at me, her eyes soft. "Yeah. It really is."

I didn't know what the future held, but at that moment, I didn't care. All I knew was that I wanted more days like this. More mornings waking up beside her. More afternoons with Gia's laughter filling the air. More moments where everything felt this simple and right.

It was interrupted by my phone ringing. I peered over, wondering who would be calling when I had had Anna clear my schedule for the day.

"Hello?" I said into the phone.

"Wright, it's Paul. I am here with Claudia and the rest of the team. We wanted to officially tell you the good news." I felt my heart rate pick up.

"The contract will be hitting your inbox soon, but the Belen team would like to extend a two-year renewal to you as a valued member of our team."

"Thank you so much, sir," I replied. "It's an honor, I'll be sure to look over the contract as soon as possible."

"We look forward to hearing back from you."

"What is it?" Lucia whispered to me, nudging my shoulder. I pulled the phone down after saying goodbye.

"I got it." I sighed, and her eyes widened. "I fucking got the contract!"

"You did!" She jumped up, her eyes were gleaming, and she jumped into my arms. I smiled in surprise, holding her close. "You did it." She whispered it this time into my ear.

I took her into my arms, squeezing her close, then pulled back and kissed her. Kissing Lucia was like stepping into a moment that the world seemed to create just for us. It wasn't hurried or uncertain; it was intentional, magnetic. The first brush of her lips was soft, tentative, like she was testing the waters, but even that small touch sent a charge through me.

She tasted like something familiar and entirely new all at once—sweet, warm, and intoxicating. Her lips were impossibly soft, but there was strength in the way she kissed me back, like she wasn't holding back anymore. It made my chest tighten, my pulse spike, because I'd never wanted anything more than to be right here with her.

The way she leaned into me, her fingers curling into the fabric of my shirt, made every nerve in my body come alive. I let my hands rest on her waist, feeling the subtle curve of her body and the warmth of her skin beneath my fingertips. I couldn't help but pull her closer, like I needed her to know how much I wanted her in this moment.

When she sighed softly against my mouth, it was like the last bit of restraint I had dissolved. It wasn't just a kiss anymore—it was a language, a way of saying everything I hadn't found the courage to put into words yet.

You're incredible.

You're all I think about.

I'm so damn lucky.

But it wasn't just about me; it was about her too. The way she kissed back, the little hesitations, and then the boldness—it felt like she was saying something too. Maybe it was, *I trust you.* Maybe it was, *I want this too.*

When we finally pulled back, her eyes fluttered open, and she looked at me like I was the only person in the world. Her lips were a little swollen, her cheeks pink, and it was impossible not to grin at her.

"I don't think I'm ever going to get tired of that," I murmured, my thumb brushing over her cheek.

Her shy smile grew into something brighter, and damn, it was like I was seeing the sun for the first time. She didn't say anything, but she didn't need to. Her hand slipped into mine, and that quiet, unspoken connection between us said everything.

"Alex, Alex!" Gianna's voice broke through my thoughts as she ran over to us. I smiled at the little blonde whirlwind and reached out for her. "Look!" Gia's excited voice brought me back to the moment. She had managed to build a surprisingly tall tower, her little hands holding the precariously balanced blocks in place.

"Whoa, look at that, Gia! That's taller than you!" I said, making a show of how impressed I was. She giggled, delighted with herself.

"Taller than you too!" she said with a mischievous glint in her eyes, her gaze traveling up my seated frame.

"Are you saying I'm short?" I teased, raising an eyebrow. "Because I don't know about that. I think I might still have you beat."

Gia giggled even harder and dramatically shook her head. "No, silly! You're huuuuge."

I leaned forward conspiratorially, dropping my voice to a whisper. "Well, I am a giant, then. Do you know what that means?"

Her eyes widened, and she leaned closer, utterly captivated. "What?"

"I'm the best at knocking down towers!" I growled, and with one swift motion, I toppled the blocks with a playful swipe. Gia let out a delighted squeal and immediately set to rebuilding.

From the blanket, Lucia laughed again, shaking her head at the two of us. "Really, Alex? You couldn't let her bask in her victory for more than ten seconds?"

"She's a competitive spirit," I said, shrugging with mock seriousness. "Gotta keep her sharp."

Gia puffed out her cheeks at me. "I'm gonna build a bigger one this time, and you can't knock it over!"

"Oh, it's on," I said, crossing my arms and pretending to look skeptical. "But it better be strong, or it'll meet the wrath of the Block Destroyer!"

She gasped dramatically, her tiny hands flying to her cheeks before she dissolved into giggles. "Mama, help me! He's too strong!"

Lucia got up and joined us, kneeling beside Gia and whispering some strategy into her ear. The sight of the two of them, heads close together, plotting against me, made my chest tighten in the best way. This was it—this was the kind of simple, unfiltered joy I didn't know I needed until now.

Lucia glanced up at me with a smirk, her eyes sparkling. "We're forming an alliance. You don't stand a chance."

I held up my hands in surrender, grinning. "All right, all right. I'll let you two geniuses have this one."

Gia cheered, and Lucia laughed, leaning back on her heels. Watching them like this, the ease they brought to my life, I couldn't help but feel a sense of gratitude. The track, the pressure, the spotlight—they all felt miles away in moments like these.

As Gia threw herself into the task of rebuilding, glancing up at me with determined little smiles, I realized something else: I didn't just care about Lucia. I cared about this—about them.

It was qualifying day in Brazil, and the energy in the garage was electric. The team buzzed with anticipation, fine-tuning the car after some upgrades that promised to push us higher in the standings. Qualifying well today could mean a podium tomorrow, and everyone was dialed in, myself included.

I was mid-conversation with Simon, mapping out race strategy, when I caught sight of her. My blonde whirlwind. Lucia walked into the garage, wearing a Belen Racing jacket that fit her like it had been made for her. My heart kicked up a gear. The way she moved, her confident stride, the easy smile on her face. It did something to me every single time. We hadn't had a real conversation about this fake-to-very-much-not-fake thing we had going, but I had every intention of making that crystal fucking clear after the race. I wanted her to be mine.

Then there was Gianna, beaming up at everyone, clutching a Barbie dressed in a racing suit I'd found for her weeks ago. She held it high like a trophy as they weaved their way toward me, the crew parting like the Red Sea to make way for them.

"My favorite girls," I said, a grin splitting my face as they closed the distance. Gianna didn't hesitate, launching herself into my arms with the kind of boundless energy only a toddler could manage.

"How's my girl?" I asked, poking her chubby little cheek.

"Good!" she squealed, her laugh filling the space around us. Her tiny hands latched onto my neck, her fingers brushing over the tattoo spread across my throat. She poked at the inky wings etched into my skin, her big eyes full of wonder.

"Will your wings help you win?" she asked earnestly.

"I sure hope so," I said, trying to keep a straight face as my heart melted a little.

Lucia reached us then, her smile soft as she watched us. I extended an arm toward her, and she didn't hesitate to step into me, her warmth pressing against my side. With Gianna in one arm and Lucia tucked into the other, the rest of the world faded away. It was just us—my two favorite girls.

Here, like this, I felt unstoppable.

"Good luck out there." Lucia raised up on her tiptoes, brushing a kiss to my cheek, but I didn't want a chaste kiss on my cheek, I wanted her lips, so I trailed my finger along her jaw and tipped her chin to me and kissed her.

"Thanks, angel," I said lowly before kissing her forehead and turning to face Gianna. "All right, princess, be good for your mum, okay?" Gianna nodded as she held out her arms for Lucia, who took her.

"We'll be cheering you on from here!" She waved.

The moments before a race were always the same: the controlled chaos of the grid, the hum of engines warming up, and my own heartbeat, steady but electric. This was my world. As I settled into the cockpit, the weight of the helmet pressing against my head felt grounding. I was exactly where I needed to be.

The engineer's voice came through the radio, crisp and clear. "Final checks complete. You're good to go, Alex."

I flipped the switches on the steering wheel, my gloves firm against the grip, my focus narrowing as the lights on the gantry began to light up, one by one. The roar of the crowd melted away, leaving only the pulsing red lights in front of me and the snarling engine beneath me.

When the lights went out, the car roared to life. The wheels spun for a fraction of a second before finding grip, launching me forward. The g-forces pushed me back into the seat as I surged toward turn one.

The opening laps were a blur of precision and aggression. I slipped into a rhythm, each corner a calculated move—braking late, clipping apexes, and throttling out onto the straights. The car felt incredible, perfectly balanced, as if it were glued to the track.

The corners came fast, each one demanding complete focus.

By the final laps of qualifying, it was me versus another driver, fighting for P1. Every move was a gamble.

The last lap was a crescendo. My hands were steady on the wheel, but my heart pounded. Coming out of the final corner, the crowd was a deafening blur of color and sound. The car in front of me made a slight mistake, a wobble on exit. I held my breath as we nearly touched.

"P1, Alex! Incredible drive!"

I let out a yell, a flood of adrenaline and triumph coursing through me. The cooldown lap was a blur.

When I pulled into the *parc fermé* behind the P1 marker, I climbed out of the car, standing on top of it to soak in the cheers. Now everything came down to tomorrow; if I won one more time, then my points would be well ahead of Theo, making the sixth world title just a little closer.

31

ALEXANDER

It was race day, the world felt too loud, too bright. My chest tightened as the noise of the paddock swirled around me—the buzz of the crowd, the clanging of tools, the hum of engines. It all pressed in, like a vice squeezing my ribs.

I tried to focus on the routine. Gloves on, helmet in hand. But my fingers fumbled, the tremor too obvious. My breath came in short, uneven bursts, and the walls of the motorhome felt like they were closing in.

I sat down heavily on the bench, pressing my palms into my thighs, trying to will myself back to normal. Deep breaths, I told myself. But they wouldn't come. My head spun, and I gripped the edge of the bench until my knuckles went white. I needed to get it together, I needed to calm the fuck down.

"Alex?"

Her voice cut through the noise. Gentle, steady, familiar. Lucia.

I couldn't bring myself to look at her. My vision blurred as I stared down at my hands, still trembling.

"Hey," she said softly, kneeling in front of me. "What's going on?"

"I can't...breathe," I managed, my voice barely audible. "It's too much."

Her hand found mine, warm and grounding and she pulled me to a corner, away from the buzzing crew members. "Okay, listen to me," she said softly, her tone calm but firm. "You're having a panic attack again, that's okay. It's okay, but we're going to work through it together. Can you look at me?"

I turned my head slowly, her face coming into focus. Her eyes were steady, locked on mine, and it felt like an anchor in the storm.

"Good," she said, her voice low and soothing. "Now, breathe with me. In through your nose for four counts." She exaggerated the motion, taking a long, slow breath in.

I followed her lead, though my inhale was shaky and shallow.

"That's okay," she said. "Let's try again. In...one, two, three, four. Now out through your mouth, slow and steady."

She demonstrated, and I mimicked her, my exhale hitching at first but gradually smoothing out.

"Keep going," she encouraged. "You're doing great."

Her hand stayed on mine, her thumb brushing back and forth in a rhythm that matched our breathing. The noise around me started to dull, the edges of my panic blurring into something softer.

"That's it," she said after a few minutes. "You're getting there."

I nodded, my breaths finally evening out. The tightness in my chest loosened, replaced by a heavy exhaustion that left me slumping forward.

"Better?" she asked, her other hand brushing a stray lock of hair from my forehead.

"Yeah," I croaked. "Thanks."

She smiled gently, her hand lingering on my cheek for a moment before dropping away. "You don't have to thank me. I'm here for you, remember?"

I let out a shaky laugh, rubbing my hands over my face. "I don't know what happened. It just...hit me out of nowhere."

"It happens," she said softly. "But you don't have to face it alone. Not last time, not now, not ever."

Her words settled in my chest, grounding me even further.

The call came through the radio, time to get to the car. I stood up, and so did Lucia, her hand slipping into mine for a brief moment before letting go.

"Go out there and do what you do best," she said with a wink. "And remember, I'll be right here, rooting for you. Win me a trophy, would ya?"

I nodded, the panic replaced by a renewed sense of calm. "All right." I smirked and leaned in for a quick kiss, and Lucia pulled her hands to my face.

"Go get 'em," she whispered, squeezing my arm. I took one last deep breath and nodded, I knew how to do this next part. Racing was in my blood. I sent a wink to her, squaring my shoulders and getting in the zone.

The roar of the engine vibrated through me as I slid into the cockpit. Qualifying had gone well, the car felt dialed in, I just needed to translate that to a win today. Everything about the setup needed to click. The balance, the grip, the sheer power. My nerves were always sharp before the start, but this time I took an extra moment to pause. Remembering those affirmation cards I kept in my bag that Lucia had given me. I knew it was cheesy, and my team would totally make fun of me if they saw them, but they meant the world to me. Plus, they worked. Lucia called it manifesting, even if you didn't feel it, say it and bring it into the world. I went over a few in my head as I slid into my seat.

When the lights went out, instinct took over. The car launched off the line. My team's strategy was on point, and by Lap 10, I was holding first, and fifteen seconds ahead of Theo in second place according to my last update from Simon over the coms. The track was alive under me, every corner flowing into the next as if the car and I were one.

The radio crackled with Simon's familiar voice. "You're in a good rhythm, Alex. Keep this pace, and manage those tires."

I acknowledged with a double click on the button, my focus razor sharp. Then the rain began. It wasn't in the forecast and I only got a warning over the radio ten minutes out. Two crashes had been reported behind me and the gap between me and Theo was rapidly closing as he caught up to me while the safety cars came out, but the moment it was cleared I zoned in. The laps blurred as I fought to maintain position. Every overtake, every defensive move—it all felt perfect. The car was an extension of me, responding to every subtle input.

The crowd noise barely registered, but I knew the stands were alive even now as the rain poured down. Brazil had a way of amplifying the atmosphere, and I could feel it even through my helmet. Everything was lining up for a strong finish. Until it wasn't.

It happened in an instant. Coming out of a high-speed section, the track ahead erupted into chaos. Debris scattered across the asphalt like shrapnel, glinting under the harsh sun. My spotter's voice crackled in my ear, sharp and urgent: "Debris on track. Collision ahead!"

But it was too late.

A car spun wildly just ahead, smoke billowing from its tires. I had mere seconds to react. Instinct took over—I yanked the wheel hard to the left, trying to swerve clear of the wreckage. The tires locked briefly, the car shuddering beneath me as I fought for control. At this speed, though, control was a fragile illusion.

The back end snapped out, and before I could correct it, the world twisted violently. My car spun, and then something clipped me—hard.

The force launched the car into a roll, flipping end over end. Time seemed to warp, stretching into disjointed moments as gravity abandoned me. I was weightless and trapped all at once, my body thrown against the restraints. My head slammed into the padding as the car turned upside down, metal groaning and screaming around me.

Another jarring impact sent me flying into the barriers. The deafening crunch of steel colliding with steel reverberated through the cockpit, followed by a series of sharp alarms and the acrid smell of burning rubber. The car came to a gut-wrenching stop, mangled and lifeless.

For a moment, all I could hear was my breathing—ragged, shallow, desperate.

Then the radio crackled back to life.

"Alex, are you okay?!" The voice was panicked, cutting through the haze in my mind.

"Alex! Please report."

I swallowed hard, forcing my mouth to form words. "I'm...I'm fine," I croaked, though I wasn't sure if it was entirely true. My hands moved on autopilot, patting down my body, checking for pain or anything out of place. Adrenaline surged, numbing everything but the roaring in my head.

"Medical team is on their way," the voice assured, but I barely registered.

I leaned my head back against the seat, squeezing my eyes shut for a moment. The noise of the crowd outside had shifted, the collective gasps and murmurs of thousands rippling like waves. One thought cut through the fog: *Lucia and Gianna. They're watching.*

I couldn't let them see me like this—not trapped, not broken. I had to move.

Taking a steadying breath, I blinked my eyes open and tried to focus on the outside world. Shapes blurred, shifting into clarity. A familiar figure emerged through the chaos—Matteo. *Why was he here? What was he doing?*

The medical team swarmed the wreck, their shouts mixing into the ringing in my ears. Matteo was shouting something, his face pale beneath his racing cap, but I couldn't make out the words. Everything felt muffled, like I was underwater.

Hands reached into the cockpit, steady and efficient, guiding me out. I was lightheaded, my legs unsteady as they hauled me to the medical car. My eyes flicked back to the wreckage, and what was left of my car. The halo above the cockpit was dented but intact, the only thing that had kept this from being so much worse.

I sank into the seat of the medical vehicle, Matteo climbing in beside me. His lips were moving, his hands gripping my shoulder, but all I could hear was the dull thrum of blood rushing in my ears.

I turned my head to him, blinking slowly as the haze began to lift. "I'm okay," I whispered, the words more for myself than anyone else.

He exhaled, his grip tightening briefly. "You scared the hell out of us," he said, his voice breaking through the fog at last.

I let my head fall back, staring at the ceiling of the medical car. *I'm alive.* That singular thought rooted itself in my mind, overriding everything else.

32

LUCIA

It happened so fast that I didn't have time to process what I was seeing.

One second, I was leaning against the garage wall, Gianna perched on my lap as we watched the screen showing the race, our matching Belen headsets covering our ears. The next, a flash of debris scattered across the track, and chaos unfolded in the high-speed section.

My heart stopped. Matteo's car spun out of control, his tires smoking as he skidded toward the runoff area. My hand flew to my mouth, stifling a scream as Gianna clutched at me, her tiny fingers digging into my jacket. The screen cut to a different angle. My brother's car came to a stop, smoke curling from the back, but he was moving. I exhaled a shaky breath as he climbed out, pulling his helmet off and throwing it aside. Relief hit me like a wave, but it was short-lived.

Because then I saw Alexander.

His car collided with another, debris clipping the nose, sending him into a spin. My stomach twisted into knots as the car flipped, the tires catching just enough to launch it into the air. It tumbled violently, end over end, before slamming into the barrier.

On the screen, Matteo was running—no, sprinting—toward the wreckage. His face was pale, his expression unreadable, but I knew. He was running for Alexander.

The crowd noise in the background turned into a dull roar, a wave of gasps and murmurs rippling through the grandstands. My pulse hammered in my ears as the medical team swarmed the scene, their fluorescent vests a blur of motion around the crumpled car.

"Mommy," Gianna's tiny voice quivered, pulling my attention back. Her eyes were wide, filled with fear, as she looked up at me. "What's wrong?"

I swallowed hard, fighting back the lump rising in my throat. I didn't know what to say. My lips moved, but no words came out. Instead, I hugged her close, my hand trembling as I ran it over her curls. Staying brave for her, staying brave for him.

Through my headset, the radio crackled faintly. For a few agonizing seconds, there was nothing but static. Then, finally, "I'm...I'm fine."

Alexander's voice. Shaky, but there.

I exhaled a sob of relief, gripping the headset as if I could will him to hear me. "He's okay," I whispered, mostly to myself. "He's okay."

The screen showed Matteo crouched beside the medical team, his hand on Alexander's shoulder as they pulled him from the wreck. Alexander looked dazed, his movements sluggish, but he was upright. He was alive.

Tears blurred my vision as I clutched Gianna tighter. I wanted to run to him, to see him with my own eyes, to reassure myself that he was really okay. But all I could do was sit there, my body shaking as the adrenaline coursed through me.

He was okay. But I wouldn't feel whole again until I could see him, touch him with my own two hands.

"Mommy?" Gianna asked again, her small voice grounding me.

I kissed the top of her head, my lips brushing her soft curls. "It's okay, sweetheart. There was a crash, but everyone is okay."

The time spent waiting for Alexander was agonizing. Both he and Matteo were retired from the race, along with two other drivers, one being Alex's competitor, Theo. The medical team had taken Alexander for evaluation, and Matteo had gone with him, leaving me in the pit with Gianna clinging to my side. Every second felt like an eternity, my mind running through worst-case scenarios no matter how many times I told myself he had said he was fine.

The atmosphere in the garage was subdued, the earlier energy snuffed out. The crew moved quietly, their usual chatter silenced as they focused on packing up equipment. Occasionally, someone would glance at me, their expressions filled with concern, but I couldn't bring myself to meet their eyes.

Gianna was unusually quiet, her small hand clutching mine as she pressed against my side. Her Barbie, dressed in its tiny racing suit, sat forgotten on the workbench nearby.

"Mommy, when can we see Alex?" she asked, her voice soft but steady.

"Soon, sweetheart," I promised, though I didn't know if it was true. "They're just making sure he's okay."

The words felt hollow, even to me. I had seen the crash. The car flipping, the force of the impact. My mind kept replaying it, each rotation of the car etched in vivid detail.

The minutes ticked by until finally, Matteo appeared at the entrance to the garage. His face was drawn, his hair a mess from running his hands through it, but his eyes softened when they met mine.

"He's okay," he said, his voice breaking the heavy silence.

Relief hit me so hard that my knees buckled slightly. Matteo was at my side in an instant, his hands steadying me.

"He's bruised up, maybe a mild concussion, but the halo did its job," Matteo continued, his voice gentler now. "He's asking for you."

I didn't need to hear anything else. Scooping Gianna into my arms, I followed Matteo out of the garage and through the maze of hallways to the medical center.

When I stepped into the room, the sight of Alexander sitting on the edge of the bed, his hair tousled and a few smudges of dirt still on his face, made my chest tighten.

"Hey," he said, his voice softer than usual. His eyes lit up when he saw us, and his smile, though faint, was genuine.

Gianna wriggled out of my arms and ran to him, her small arms wrapping around his waist. "Alex!" she cried, her voice muffled against his chest.

"Hey, little racer," he murmured, his hand gently brushing her hair. "I'm okay, see?"

I stood there for a moment, my feet rooted to the spot as emotion welled up inside me.

He was here.

He was alive.

Alexander looked up at me, his gaze warm despite the exhaustion etched across his features. "Come here," he said softly, holding out his free arm.

I crossed the room in a few quick strides, wrapping my arms around both of them as a tear slipped down my cheek. His hand came up to cradle the back of my head.

"You scared the hell out of me," I whispered, tears breaking free.

"I know," he replied, his voice tinged with regret. "Scared the hell out of me as well."

Anna walked into the room, typing away on her phone, checking in with the aides and crew in the room. She walked over, a sullen expression on her face.

"Hey," she said gently to Alexander, "how are you feeling?"

"Been better," Alexander replied with a small smirk. She rolled her eyes, Gianna traced the tattoos on his hand.

"They want a post-race interview so the fans can see you are okay. Simon is requesting to see you as soon as possible, as well as a meeting post interview with the team." She rattled off the list, dragging down her finger on the screen. Alexander only nodded.

"Shouldn't you rest?" I asked. Alex looked up to me with soft eyes.

"Yeah, that's after." He shrugged but let out a groan from moving. He was mostly stiff from the impact. The doctor had mentioned that the stiffness would be the biggest issue within the next few days but otherwise he was cleared.

So the day went on as normal. Or what was normal for a high-performance race car driver. Alexander did his interviews. Matteo left with a reassuring smile and a forehead kiss for Gianna before going to meet with his own team. Gianna and I eventually made our way into our own lounge room. I sat in a bit of a daze, worrying. Matteo had been in crashes but nothing this big, and watching Alexander's car flip on screen had been the worst feeling in the world.

The door creaked open, and Nicola slipped in, the crew key card and VIP tag around her neck on a lanyard. I vaguely noticed how dressed up she was today, the tailored vest and matching trousers, the click of her heels.

"Hey," she said gently, sitting down next to me. Gianna ran over, giving her a hug before going back to her toys and happily entertaining herself.

"You okay?" she asked after I didn't reply.

I nodded slowly. "Yeah." I sighed.

"It's a lot to watch," Nicola said, leaning back, kicking off her heels and huddling under the blanket with me. I smiled as she leaned in, resting on my shoulder. I tipped my head to lean on hers in response.

"Mm-hm," I said halfheartedly.

"But it is a part of the job, Alex has had a big crash before, so have many other drivers. They know the risks, and there's so much in place, like the halo for the driver's safety." Nicola kept going.

Reassuring me with facts and experiences, making my heart calm down eventually.

"Thank you," I said after she was done. I squeezed her tight and she brushed it off with a laugh.

"I know, what would you do without me, huh?" Her million dollar smile was on display and I rolled my eyes at her. Amazed that only a few short months ago I didn't even know her. That in that small amount of time she had somehow wormed her way into my life, and into my heart. It felt so healing to have a friend, an adult friend. Because that shit was hard.

I took the time in the lounge with my two favorite girls and let my thoughts roam. The whole point of me coming on the road with Matteo had been to get out of my comfort zone, to find what excited me, find my spark again. And along the way Alexander had gone from my brother's best friend, to my own friend, to my fake boyfriend, to wherever we were now. I knew one thing for sure, I wasn't faking any feelings anymore, not for the cameras or the tabloids. I wanted to be in his life for real. Today had all but cemented that. Feeling like I was watching his life flash before my eyes, then him walking away with hardly a scratch. Life was too damn short to not take exactly what you wanted.

I wanted us.

33

LUCIA

We had all forced Alexander to rest the next day. He wasn't happy about it. The Brazil Grand Prix had been crucial, a chance to secure enough points to cement him as the world champion in the Drivers' Championship. Now, with the crash taking him out of the race, those points were out of reach, and he'd need stellar finishes in the next two races to claim the title. It was eating at him.

All morning, he'd been sulking, scrolling endlessly on his phone. The tabloids were merciless: *Reckless or Resilient? Wright's Costly Crash* and *Is Belen Racing Betting on the Wrong Driver?* Headlines like those gnawed at him, even though we all knew better than to believe the nonsense.

The tension in the room shifted the moment Matteo bounded in, Nicola hot on his heels. His energy was loud, chaotic, and entirely Matteo.

"All right," he declared, clapping his hands dramatically. "I have a master plan."

"That's what you're calling it?" Nicola asked skeptically, crossing her arms.

"No one asked for your opinion," Matteo shot back, sending her a halfhearted glare.

"Don't be rude," I cut in, narrowing my eyes at him.

Matteo sighed, his expression softening. "Okay, okay. But seriously, I have a plan." He waved his hands like he was unveiling a great secret.

Alexander, who had been doom-scrolling himself into a dark hole, didn't even glance up. "And what exactly is this so-called plan?" he asked flatly, his voice edged with exhaustion. Matteo strode over, plucked the phone from Alexander's hand, and tossed it across the room.

"Seriously, mate?" Alexander barked, his head snapping up. "You had to bloody throw it?"

Matteo ignored him, grinning like he'd just solved world peace. "Right, so in conclusion, since you two are in love and refusing to admit it—"

"Wait, what?" I blurted, my jaw dropping.

"—Nicola here is miserable or moody or whatever—"

"Hey!" Nicola protested, looking genuinely offended.

"—and Gianna is clearly a Moretti fan, not a Belen fan. Red is better, come on." Matteo grinned smugly, clearly proud of his convoluted logic. "The only solution is obvious: we should all go on vacation."

"I'm sorry—what?" I asked, completely thrown. "Did you just say we're in love? Where the hell did that come from?"

"And how does any of this even connect?" Alexander added, rolling his eyes.

Nicola muttered from the corner, "I am a ray of sunshine."

"Way to just jump the gun, bud," Alexander added dryly.

From my arms, Gianna perked up, her big, curious eyes darting between us. "Who's in love?"

"It's nothing, baby," I said quickly, scooping her up and heading for the door. My face was on fire, and I couldn't stand to look at Alexander. Behind me, I could hear Matteo rambling, trying to justify his "master plan."

As I stepped onto the balcony, the cool breeze hit my face, helping calm the storm of emotions swirling inside me. The view of the city stretched out before me, bustling with life beneath the golden sun. It was a picture-perfect day, yet all I could focus on was Matteo's stupid comment.

"Hey," Alexander's voice broke through my thoughts, soft and gentle. I turned to see him standing in the doorway, his expression unreadable. He stepped closer, his hand brushing against my arm. My body responded instinctively, leaning into his touch.

"Hey," I managed, forcing a small smile.

Gianna wiggled in my arms, reaching out for him. "Me too, me too!"

"Obviously," Alexander said, his smile finally reaching his eyes as he took her from me, cradling her against his chest. He kissed her temple and gave her a little squeeze before setting her down.

"I'm gonna show Zio and Nicola my princess dress!" she announced before dashing back inside.

Alexander chuckled, watching her go before turning back to me. "You okay?"

"Yeah!" I replied too quickly, my voice unnaturally high-pitched. Clearing my throat, I tried again. "Yes, I'm fine."

"Want to talk about Matteo's comment?" he asked, his gaze steady but cautious.

I looked out over the edge of the balcony, avoiding his eyes. The view was breathtaking, but it couldn't distract me from the weight of his question. Finally, I felt his hand slip into mine.

"Well…" I began, my voice faltering as I tried to put my tangled thoughts into words. "The last week—everything between us has been so good. *So good*. I don't want to mess that up, but this whole fake relationship, then it turning into *this*. My heart's all wrapped up in it now, and I just don't want to get hurt, but…"

I sighed, finally meeting his eyes. They were softer than I'd expected, brimming with something that made my stomach twist. "I love our time together, Alex—all of it."

He winced, like he was bracing himself for whatever I might say next. My words caught in my throat, so I stopped.

"What were you going to say?" I asked, desperate for a shift in focus.

He took a steadying breath, his gaze dropping for a moment before returning to mine. "First of all, these past few months have been incredible. Having you and Gia here...it's been like nothing I've ever had before. For the first time, it feels like I have a family rooting for me." He paused, his voice growing quieter. "But the thing is—"

My heart stuttered. Here it was, the letdown. The inevitable rejection. This wasn't real to him, not like it was to me. Why would it be? He's Alexander Wright, for God's sake. He could have anyone in the world. I felt the sting of tears threatening, but before the spiral could consume me, his hand came up to cup my cheek, his thumb brushing gently against my skin. His touch was warm, grounding, and I couldn't help leaning into it.

"I can see that pretty mind of yours working overtime," he murmured, his voice so soft it sent shivers down my spine. "Will you let me say something before you spiral any further?"

I nodded, my throat too tight to trust myself with words.

"The thing is, Lucia," he began, his voice steady and sure, "I don't want this to be fake. My feelings for you are the most real thing I've ever felt. I know my life isn't the safest or the easiest—I know bringing a toddler into this world isn't ideal—but I would do anything to keep you here, by my side. I want this, I want us."

I blinked up at him, stunned, as he went on.

"I don't have all the answers, and I can't promise it'll always be smooth, but I know without a doubt that I want you, Lucia. Exactly as you are. As you grow, as you change, every version of you. I want to be there for all of it."

Oh. Tears were definitely coming. I tried to fight them,

chanting *don't cry, don't cry, don't cry* in my head like a mantra. But my throat was dry, my chest too full, and my voice failed me completely.

So I just nodded, furiously, over and over, hoping he understood.

A smile broke across his face, crooked and boyish with a glimmer in his eyes that made my knees weak. "So, what do you say, Lucia DeLuca?" he asked, his tone lighter now, teasing, as his hand slid down to intertwine with mine. "Want to be my girlfriend?"

All I could do was nod again, this time with a watery laugh escaping my lips. "Yes," I finally managed to whisper, my voice breaking. "Very much."

And when he leaned down to kiss me, his lips capturing mine with a tenderness that made my chest ache, I knew I was exactly where I was meant to be.

"About damn time," Nicola said as we broke apart. We glanced over to see Matteo with a shit-eating grin plastered on his face, Nicola next to him, hands on her hips and a smirk.

Then, without missing a beat, Matteo smirks again. "So I booked us all on a flight in an hour to Italy."

Because, of course he did.

ALEXANDER

The drive to the Italian seaside resort was peaceful, the kind of quiet that felt like a deep exhale after weeks of chaos. The sun kissed the coastline as we arrived, golden light glittering off the waves. Gianna talked excitedly in the backseat, her tiny hands gripping her favorite stuffed bunny as she stared out the window.

Lucia's smile was soft, content, as she looked over at me. It was a rare sight—her shoulders relaxed, her hair loose around her face. Moments like this, when she wasn't carrying the weight of the world, made me fall for her even more.

When we pulled up to the resort, the concierge greeted us with a warm smile and a quiet assurance of privacy. That was the whole reason I'd okayed this place when Matteo mentioned a last-minute vacation. No prying eyes, no cameras, just a chance for the four of us to breathe.

That was until we got to the check-in desk.

"Ah, Mr. Wright," the attendant began apologetically. "We've had a slight issue with the room allocations. Unfortunately, only two suites are available, and each has just one king-sized bed."

Lucia's eyes widened, her lips parting as if to protest, but I was already suppressing a grin.

"That's fine," I said easily, my hand brushing hers. "We'll make it work."

Nicola, standing beside Matteo, didn't look nearly as thrilled. "Excuse me?" she said sharply.

Matteo smirked, the picture of smugness. "Guess we're bunking together, Nic."

Her glare could have melted steel. "Don't call me that, and no, we're *not* sharing a bed."

"Well, there's always the floor," he said, shrugging. "But I'd hate for you to hurt your back."

Nicola groaned, muttering something under her breath about unbearable idiots, while Matteo only grinned wider.

Meanwhile, Lucia's gaze flicked nervously to me. "Alex...are you sure?" she whispered. "About us? What about Gianna? She's not great at sleeping through the night sometimes, and I don't want to keep you up or—"

"Hey," I interrupted gently, lowering my voice so only she could hear. "It's fine, Lucia. I'll help. If she wakes up, I'll get up with her, okay? We're a team."

Her eyes softened, her lips pressing together as she nodded. "Okay." Gianna, oblivious to the logistics, tugged on Lucia's hand. "Mama, can we go see the water now?"

"Soon, baby," Lucia said, brushing a kiss over her daughter's head.

The suites were beautiful, each with a balcony overlooking the turquoise sea. Lucia and I settled in, unpacking our things while Gianna explored every corner of the room. I felt a little *thrum thrum* in my chest at the sight. The three of us in our own hotel room. Sure, we were constantly in each other's rooms with our friends or each other, but this felt different. This felt real. When it came time to discuss the sleeping arrangements, Lucia was hesitant again.

"Sometimes when she can't sleep the only way I can get her back down is by sleeping next to me," she said, glancing at the king-sized bed. "What if she won't settle?"

I crouched down beside Gianna, who was busy arranging her bunny and blanket on the pillows. "Hey, kid," I said with a smile. "Think you can share the bed with Mama and me tonight?"

She nodded eagerly. "Like a big sleepover?"

"Exactly."

Lucia exhaled a laugh, her hand brushing over my shoulder as I stood. "You're so good with her," she said softly.

"Comes naturally when you're around," I teased, earning a roll of her eyes but a faint blush on her cheeks.

Meanwhile, from the adjoining suite, Nicola's exasperated voice carried through the wall. "Matteo, if you snore, I swear I will smother you with a pillow."

"Noted," came Matteo's amused reply. "But don't worry— you'll be too busy dreaming about me to notice."

Lucia and I burst into quiet laughter, sharing a look of mutual understanding. The vacation was already off to a chaotic, ridiculous, *perfect* start.

Turning my phone off and leaving it in the hotel room had been a great decision. We were lounging on the beach. Nicola had stormed off into the ocean after Matteo said something stupid. I was building a sand castle with Gianna while Lucia was taking a well-deserved break. Deserved because she looked so beautiful lying there sunbathing and the view was too nice to disturb.

"Alex, can we make a princess tower?" Gia asked.

"Sure, G," I replied, prying my eyes away from her mother.

"I'm hungry," Matteo whined, making Gia sit up.

"Me too!" She matched his whine. God, they are the same person, it was kind of terrifying.

"Let's go, principessa. *Andiamo*!" Gianna ran over to him, her body covered in sand. I laughed at them, Matteo was also covered in sand as he had just emerged from being covered in it when Gianna made him into a mermaid.

They walked away, hand in hand, covered in sand, and I only smiled and looked to Lucia. She had pulled her sunglasses down to look after Gianna and Matteo, waving goodbye to them. Then her eyes tracked over to me. Gleaming under the Italian sun. God, she was beautiful.

"What are you thinking about, angel?" I asked.

"That I have the best village." She smiled, and I cocked my head a bit. "They always say it takes a village to raise a kid, and at home I had my parents. And don't get me wrong, they were amazing and wonderful, but it still felt so lonely. Out here with you guys. I'm just really thankful, is all," she mused. I strode over to her and leaned down, kissing her.

"You're getting sand on me!" she complained. I only laughed and brushed my hands together to make more sand fall.

"You're the worst!" she grumbled, shaking her head.

"Wanna go rinse off?" I asked, raising a brow and nodding toward the ocean.

"It's going to be freezing." She groaned. The sun was out, which was amazing, but she was right, the ocean was freezing.

"Come on, this is your yes year." I poked her.

"Don't use that against me!"

"Have you ever jumped in a winter ocean?" I asked, knowing she hadn't.

"No..." she trailed off, looking at the ocean. Nicola was swimming, but Nicola was kind of insane like that.

"Let's try new things then," I said, dragging her up.

"Fine, okay, I'll put my feet in." She conceded. I only laughed and shook my head, then reached down and pulled her up, throwing her over my shoulder.

"Alexander! Put me down!" she screamed.

"I don't think so," I replied and ran us to the ocean. The closer we got, the more she shrieked.

"Alexander, I swear you will regret this!"

"Worth it," I said before launching both of us into the ocean. I pulled us back up above the water quickly, a shit-eating grin plastered on my face.

"Fuck you!" she screamed, splashing water at me, a huge smile on her face. "It's so, so cold, oh my god," she cried, bringing her arms into herself. I reached out and pulled her toward me easily. Her legs wrapped around me, as if on instinct.

"Want me to warm you up?" I smirked.

"Gross." She glared halfheartedly. I leaned in and crashed my lips onto hers. I could kiss her for hours, weeks, years. I would never get tired of it. Her hands wrapped around my neck and into my hair. Before I knew it, she was dragging me to our hotel room.

35

LUCIA

$\mathcal{A}$lexander kissed me like he'd spent too long holding back and couldn't stand it anymore. His lips are demanding. I sighed against him, the sound swallowed by the heat of his kiss. His grip tangled in my hair, gently pulling just enough to make my head tilt back. The shift deepened the kiss, and his tongue stroked into my mouth, a shiver racing along my skin.

There was no hesitation, just raw, unfiltered need. The pressure of his lips, the way he held me like I might slip away if he let go, was intoxicating. Sparks of pleasure rippled through me, and when I lightly sucked on his tongue, he groaned, low and guttural, like he was coming undone.

It was messy, consuming, and absolutely everything.

My hand came up to the hem of his T-shirt, pushing it up to tell him I wanted it off. I felt him smirk under my lips.

"So bossy." His voice was gravelly, his breath on my lips. Our eyes met and that mischievous glint was back. He pulled back for only a moment, reached one hand back, and pulled off his shirt in an easy motion. Alexander might be lean, like any other Formula One driver, but he was pure lean muscle. I palmed down his chest and abs. I tried not to blush at the sight, him laying himself bare for me, making my heart race a million miles a minute. He leaned back to me, the ghost of a touch on my chin, tipping my head up toward him. Every time he did it, I swore a part of me screamed inside; it made my heart beat, and the swarm of butterflies in my belly erupt. It was everything.

Our kisses slowed down. I savored them. I savored our time alone like this, even if it was us sneaking away from the beach while Gianna was with her uncle. This time felt golden; I wanted to keep it, bottle it, and have it with me always.

He pulled off my beach cover-up, only the string bikini in his way now.

"What do you want?" he said between kisses. I loved the way he asked, checked in with little looks, words, or nods to me, putting me first in a way no one had ever done before.

"You," I whispered gently. His hand traveled down my body, making my brain fog at the need washing over me. He smirked and let his hands roam, a palm taking a breast in his hand before he removed his lips from mine. He pushed the thin fabric to the side and teased me, moving to the next before reaching and untying the bikini, plucking it off my body. I let out an involuntary gasp. His hands continued to roam so slowly, mapping out every curve of my body, squeezing gently when he caressed my hips.

"Hmm." His voice was so deep, so rough, it sent chills coursing through me. The corner of his mouth tipped up, but his eyes were dark, like he was enjoying torturing me like this. A hand dragged down my stomach slowly, so close to where I needed him. He kissed me again, his nose nudging mine, then kissed my neck, then my collarbone.

"Does this feel good, angel?" I nodded. "You want this?" He barely dragged a finger over the material covering my sensitive clit, making me shiver. I nodded again, hands tensing on his broad chest. His eyebrow cocked up.

"Please," I gasped out, absolutely at his mercy.

"Good girl." He stared down at me, searching my face as he

moved my bikini aside and stroked his long fingers over me, circling my clit. I pressed my lips together to hold in a moan as he glided over my sensitive nerves. I was breathing hard as he dipped one finger inside me, then the next.

"Fuck," he muttered, and my eyes fell closed at the delicious, tight feeling. "So fucking wet for me, Luce. This is all for me?" I nodded, my eyes closing and head falling back before a hand clasped at my chin, sending shivers down my spine.

"Eyes on me, angel," he whispered. I bit my lip, swallowing a moan, which earned me a look.

"I want to hear it," he said, pulling my lip down with his thumb. I gasped at the gesture. He stopped moving and I let out a groan of disapproval, desperately wanting him to move again. He shook his head.

"I want to hear it," he said again. I nodded slowly, keeping my eyes on him as he pumped his fingers, in and out slowly, making me squirm.

"Alexander." My voice was scratchy, coming out like a beg. I was a mess, needing and wanting him.

More, more, more, my mind chants. As if he could hear me, he picked up the pace. Faster, until he was pounding into me with three fingers, curling up and hitting the just right spot to make me see stars. I swear this man had magic in his fingers. I had always been self-conscious about having a hard time orgasming, but Alexander had blown that out of the water. Obviously that wasn't a me problem if the man knew what he was doing. And Alexander Wright knew exactly what he was doing. His thumb hit my clit, circling again, teasing enough to send me over the edge as he pumped in and out and I felt the pressure building, felt myself go breathless.

"That's right," he said as I let out a cry. "Ride it out, angel." My breath came in short little gasps, my eyes rolling back.

"I'm-I," I stuttered out.

"Come for me, angel. Come for me." Warmth wrapped

around me as I found my release. He kept moving, letting me ride it out. When I was breathless and spent, he pulled out and a contented smirk looked down at me.

"Damn, angel," he murmured.

"Mm-hm," I agreed. He leaned down, peppering sweet kisses along my neck and up my cheek before finding my lips again. He kissed me softly, and I melted again.

"I like when you call me that," I said, ducking my head and blushing. It was new territory to speak up during sex for me. But Alexander encouraged it, wanted to hear my thoughts, what I liked and didn't like.

"Good," he replied with a kiss. "Because you're my angel." My heart stuttered and I sighed, leaning down and kissing him back, then I found myself climbing on top of him. I layered his stomach in kisses, slowly dragging myself down his body. He groaned in response and I felt satisfaction and excitement fly through me. I liked this, feeling in control and making him feel good. I reached out and grabbed his hard cock through the fabric of his swim trunks. His short swim trunks that made me want to climb him like a tree when he joined us on the beach.

He shook his head. "You don't have to," he assured me.

"I want to," I replied, dragging my hand up and down in the same torturously slow way he teased me earlier. He let his head fall back on the pillow. I pulled at the strings of the trunks and pushed them down slowly.

"Hmmm." I leaned down to him and let my tongue caress him from the base up and he let out another groan, fueling my confidence.

"Fuck," he mumbled as I took his length in my mouth. "You are perfect," he said, looking down at me. I kept my eyes on him as I sucked him, high on the power. I gently let my teeth trail as I pulled back up, making him groan even louder. And damn, a man who groaned and responded to your touch like this? The hottest thing I have ever experienced. I felt so powerful in that moment.

I kept going until a hand reached down, pulling my hair together out of my face, then tugged.

"Come here," he commanded, voice dark. In a trance, I nodded and did as I was told. My heart beat so hard I could hear it, drunk in anticipation. He kissed me long and slow, one of those toe-curling, heart-fluttering kisses. Then our foreheads touched for a moment.

"I'll go get a condom." He walked toward the bathroom. When he came back, his eyes were dark and clouded, it was intoxicating to see. He looked me up and down, drank me in as he reached me, and held out the condom with a smirk. I leveled him with my own look, chin high, feeling so beautiful and strong under his gaze. I took it from him and climbed on top, a hand to his chest to push him down, straddling him as I ripped open the foil with my teeth, pulled it out, and rolled it on his thick length. He hesitated, watching my reaction, and I smiled, because Alexander's subtle check-in made my heart soar. I nodded and tilted against him in the sheer need to have him touching me again. He pushed inside me, his jaw tight as he shut his eyes.

Oh God.

A moan slipped out of me as I stretched around him. The pressure grew, and I gasped as he hit every nerve inside me.

"So fucking tight." His voice was a low rumble, his eyes flashed with heat as he kept pushing. His hand drifted to my breast, toying with my nipple as he slid in farther. The sensation of him is all-consuming. Our hips are pressed tight against each other, my knees on the mattress, and another moan of pleasure slipped out of me as heat raced up my spine.

"That's right, angel." He brushed the hair out of my face, a thumb brushing my cheek. "Such a good fucking girl, taking my cock so well." His voice was tight with emotion, a flush coloring his cheekbones. His eyes burned with a mix of heat, longing, and adoration all at once. The way he looked at me like that, it made my heart skip, my head dizzy. I wanted it. I wanted it all the time.

He pushed in deeper, his jaw still clenched and gorgeous. The pressure built and he gave me a second to adjust before he moved again, faster and harder. And I melted into him. Our groans melted together, our bodies tangled. He flipped us over, him behind me, and he wrapped my hair around his fist. So gently and yet just the smallest tug sent me over the top. I felt the pleasure flooding my body, my back arching into his touch as he readjusted and started moving again.

"Harder." I gasped out and he did just as I asked.

"You feel so fucking good, angel," he said between thrusts. I gasped in response, and turned to look behind me, his fist still wrapped around my hair.

"Like the view, hotshot?" I asked, feeling confident. I could've sworn his eyes rolled back into his head at those words.

"Best damn view I've ever seen," he responded, slowing down. His breathing was ragged as he tried to regain control.

"More, please," I begged, and it was enough for his eyes to darken and to resume. "I'm so close," I cried out. Pleasure flooded me again, building and building before the pressure popped and my orgasm rolled through me in a final crescendo.

"Fuck," he groaned out, coming down with me. We collapsed afterward, limbs tangled and hearts racing. I rolled over to face him. His espresso eyes were soft and contented. He reached out his hand, gently brushing his thumb over my chin, then cheek, and placing a kiss on the side of my head. He pulled me to him and drew circles on my skin with his fingers while he muttered, "Fucking perfect."

I love him. I love him more than the stars in the sky. He is my sky.

The thing about vacations is you never really want them to end. Then when they do end, you kind of feel like you've been hit by a truck.

I was half asleep with my head in Alexander's lap, his arm wrapped around my waist. Alexander had been asleep since takeoff. Gianna was knocked out in Matteo's arms and Nicola had contorted her body into a ball, reading on her Kindle.

Gianna had woken up in the middle of the night, but it was Alexander who got her, who rocked her gently for an hour, trying to get her back down in her crib before eventually bringing her to bed with us. She curled into my side easily, and I don't think I have ever slept better. My heart grew ten sizes that night.

As I sat on the plane, I felt so overwhelmed with the amount of love there was here. The amount of people who would go to bat for my daughter. Who would love her and protect her. I had always felt this deep guilt about raising her by myself. That maybe I wasn't enough. But the thing I was realizing, especially over the last few months, was that I wasn't alone. That it was okay to feel those things. Anna had opened up to me about feeling the same, about feeling the loss of self to motherhood. How she felt guilty for going back to work even though she loved what she did. Most of all, that it was all normal. It was all things we would feel and grow through. And that it was hard, really fucking hard. But if you had your village, then the days would get easier and you could cherish every moment no matter how hard the days were or how little sleep you got. Granted, it was easier said than done, but I was readjusting and really enjoying the little moments of every day.

DRIVER CHAMPIONSHIP STANDINGS

1. **Theo Bauer** — 364 pts
   Kaz Energy Racing
2. **Alexander Wright** — 352 pts
   Belen Racing
3. **Carlos Torres** — 272 pts
   Moretti Racing
4. **James Hansson** — 203 pts
   Belen Racing
5. **Matteo DeLuca** — 167 pts
   Moretti Racing

36

ALEXANDER

The atmosphere at the Las Vegas Grand Prix was electric. The lights of the Strip shimmered in the distance, casting a neon glow over the track. Even as I strapped into the car, the buzz of the crowd was palpable, charging the air with adrenaline. But beneath the excitement, I could feel the lingering edge of last week's crash tugging at my confidence. The images of the impact replayed in my mind when I closed my eyes, but I couldn't let that get to me now. *Not here. Not tonight.*

Qualifying hadn't been ideal. I placed mid-grid, eighth, but a necessary penalty for the much-needed car upgrades pushed me back to twelfth. A gut punch, sure, but I knew I had a strong car under me. Simon had reminded me of that a dozen times this weekend. I was buzzing with energy; I had woken up with Lucia in my arms, looking like a painting with her blonde hair cascading down her bare back. I had left rather early. Nicola had brought Gianna back over from their sleepover. Lucia had been getting dressed for the race, tugging a light blue dress on before I left. I barely had time to scribble on the hotel stationery and hide it under her phone on the nightstand before she noticed.

You look pretty today. I like you in blue.

I liked leaving her notes; they were my own version of her affirmation cards. So she could be reminded of how amazing she was, even if it was little things.

"All right, Alex, starting from P12," Simon's voice came through the comms as I reviewed the track map one last time in the garage. "You've got the pace to make it to the front. Clean overtakes, smart moves, and we can turn this around, points are close."

"I'm not just making it to the front. I'm taking the whole thing." My tone was confident, but inside, I was still grappling with the what-ifs. Simon caught my hesitation.

"You've done it before," he said firmly. "You can do it again."

The start was everything in a race like this, and I nailed mine. Off the line, I squeezed into P10 by the first turn, narrowly avoiding a scrap with another driver. The upgrades to the car felt incredible. Responsive and fast, just the edge I needed to claw my way up. Each lap was a calculated attack: late braking here, finding extra grip there, threading the needle through tight gaps, and managing my tires.

By the halfway mark, I'd pushed into P4, the adrenaline drowning out every doubt. My crew was on point, a lightning-fast pit stop setting me up to chase the lead pack. The final laps were a blur of precision and chaos. Overtaking the car in P2 took everything I had. My tires screaming, the car dancing on the edge of control, but it was worth it.

And then, with two laps to go, I saw my opportunity. The leader hesitated coming out of the second chicane, and I pounced. Timing it perfectly, I took the inside line and surged ahead. My heart thundered in my chest as I crossed the finish line in P1, the roar of the crowd exploding in my ears.

The victory was massive. Coming from P12 to P1 wasn't just a statement, it was damn redemption. The pit crew was already cheering as I pulled into the paddock, and my thoughts immediately jumped to Lucia and Gia.

I climbed out of the car, standing in the front and cheering with the crowd. Pulling my helmet off, I looked. My eyes scanned the crowd at the barrier, and then I saw her. Lucia, her smile brighter than all the Vegas lights combined, with Gia perched on her hip, waving excitedly.

I didn't think; I just moved. Closing the distance to the barrier, I reached out for her. She passed Gia to Nicola and leaned into my outstretched arms, her laughter mixing with my own exhilarated shouts.

"Come here," I said, hauling her over the low wall in one smooth motion. She barely had time to protest before I wrapped my arms around her, spinning her around.

"You did it!" she exclaimed, her voice thick with pride and emotion.

Instead of responding, I took her face in my hands and kissed her. Hard, deep, and with every ounce of adrenaline still coursing through me. Her hands gripped my shoulders, steadying us both as the world roared around us. The moment was ours, untouchable and perfect.

When I pulled back, her cheeks were flushed, her eyes shining. "You're incredible," she whispered.

"With my girls by my side?" I grinned. "Anything's possible."

As I held Lucia in my arms, the world around us seemed to blur. The noise of the crowd, the cheers of the crew, the cameras flashing—it all faded into the background. It was just her, her smile, her warmth grounding me in a way nothing else could.

My heart was still racing, though not just from the victory. There was something about her, about this moment, that made me feel untouchable. Invincible. Like I could take on anything the world threw at me. The crash from last week, the doubts that had crept in—they were gone. It didn't matter anymore. All that mattered was this high, this unshakable certainty that I could do it. I *would* do it.

The thought of the championship flickered through my mind, and a fire lit in my chest.

One more podium.

That was all I needed to secure my sixth world title. Those points would shoot me high enough in front of Theo Bauer to claim the drivers championship for the year.

It felt surreal to even think about it. I'd dreamed of this as a kid, racing go-karts on dusty tracks, pretending the stakes were as high as they were now. My dad cheering me on from the sidelines. I felt that ache of missing him so frequently. It felt like a permanent hole in my life and probably would always be, but it was quelled by Lucia and Gianna being here for me. In a way, I knew I would make my dad proud. I called him every week even though it had been over a year since he remembered who I was. At this point, I think he thought I was just a man who did weekly check-ins. He talked about his art classes and how he hated the new oatmeal in the mornings. Every time I called was different. This week he told me about his son, and how he had won his first F3 title.

"My boy, he's going to be one of the greats one day," my dad's voice cracked over the phone.

"I have no doubt." I cleared my throat.

"Look him up, Alexander Wright. First Black man to make it to Formula One. You'll see, he'll be there in no time."

"World Champion even?"

"Absolutely."

And here I was, on the brink of history. One more race, one more perfect performance, and it was mine. The sixth title would cement everything I'd worked for, the sleepless nights, the sacrifices, the risks.

I could see it so clearly: Lucia and Gia in the paddock, celebrating that sixth title with me. Gia wearing her little racing suit, Lucia's laugh filling the air as I lifted the trophy. It wasn't just a dream, it was a promise I'd make to myself right here, right now.

"One more," I whispered under my breath, my arms

tightening around Lucia. She beamed up at me, and I could've sworn her smile was emitting sunlight.

"One more race," I said, my voice steadier now. "One more podium, and then champion."

She placed her hand over my chest, right where my heart was pounding. "You've got this," she said simply.

One more race. Just one more. Everything I've worked for, sacrificed for, was within reach. I've imagined this moment a thousand times: crossing that finish line, hearing the roar of the crowd, the weight of the championship finally mine. And yet, it felt heavier now than it ever had. The pressure, the expectations, the whispers of doubt that crept in when no one else was watching. They already claimed I was a legend, but legends are only as good as their last race. What if I failed? What if all the work, all the years, came down to a single mistake?

But then I thought of her. Of Lucia. Her faith in me was unwavering, steady in a way I'd never known. It was not loud or demanding, but it was there, a constant undercurrent that carried me when I felt like I was sinking. She didn't care about the trophies or the records. She just...believed in me. Not the driver, not the champion, but me, the man behind the wheel, flaws and all. When she looked at me, I saw a future that wasn't tied to podiums and champagne. I saw home. And that faith? It was more powerful than any engine. It made me want this even more, not for the glory or the legacy, but because she deserved to see me win. To see me cross that line and know she was right to believe in me.

This race wasn't just for me, it was an accumulation of so much work, for my dad, for my team, for myself. I'd give it everything I had because, if there was one thing I knew, it was that Lucia already made me feel like a champion. No matter what happened out there, I'd get to go home with my girls. But God, I wanted this. I wanted to win. For her. For Gia. For the version of me they made me want to be.

37

LUCIA

The lights above the track in Qatar racetrack burned bright, reflecting the chaos and glory of the moment. Fireworks exploded in rapid bursts, painting the night sky in dazzling colors, but even they couldn't outshine the man standing in the spotlight.

He did it.

The crowd roared, a thunderous, unrelenting wave of cheers that rolled through the circuit, louder than any engine on the grid. Tears stung my eyes, unbidden and unstoppable, but I didn't bother wiping them away. There was no shame in this. Not tonight.

Gianna had stayed back at the hotel with Nicola, but Anna and I had been glued to the screen in the paddock club, barely breathing through those final laps. My fingers still ached from gripping the edge of the counter so tightly, and my heart had been pounding in rhythm with the race. I knew from the beginning, knew that he'd make it. He was Alexander Wright. Nothing stopped him.

But when that checkered flag waved and he crossed the finish line, securing not just the win but his sixth world championship, the air left my lungs. The garage erupted around me, cheers, shouts, hugs, but all I could do was stare at the screen. He was there, climbing out of his car, throwing his arms in the air with that blinding grin.

He did it.

Pride surged in my chest, so overwhelming it nearly knocked me off my feet. It wasn't just pride for his achievement. It was for him, the man behind the wheel, the man I loved. He'd poured his heart and soul into this, and now, it was his moment.

The crew spilled out of the garage in a flurry of excitement, and before I knew it, my feet were moving. The noise around me blurred as I sprinted toward the podium area, my pulse racing with every step. I didn't see the cameras or hear the cheers; all I saw was him.

And there he was, standing near the barrier, in his race suit, looking every inch the champion he was. His face was flushed with victory, hair damp with sweat, but his smile...God, that smile. It was pure joy, pure Alexander.

Without thinking, I broke into a run and threw myself into his arms. He caught me without hesitation, his grip strong and steady as he spun us around. My hands clutched at his shoulders, and my legs instinctively wrapped around his waist.

"Hey!" I laughed breathlessly, holding on tighter as he twirled me. "You did it!"

His laughter joined mine, bright and carefree, as he set me down but didn't let go. His hands settled on my waist, grounding me in the storm of emotions swirling around us.

"I did it," he said, his voice low but filled with wonder. His eyes locked on mine, wild and alive, but there was something else in them—something softer, just for me. "And you were right here with me, Lucia. Every step of the way. I couldn't have done it without you."

The weight of his words hit me, and tears welled up again. My hands found his face, fingers tracing the sharp lines of his jaw, as if trying to memorize him at this moment. My heart thundered in my chest, the three little words begging to be let out. Maybe it was the excitement of the night, the championship win, every single moment from when I joined them on the road in the Netherlands. But finding this feeling, finding my person, here among the high-speed life of Formula One, I couldn't help but let the words slip from my lips.

"I love you, Alex," I whispered, my voice breaking. "I'm so proud of you."

Alexander froze at first, then his smile softened, and he leaned down, pressing his forehead to mine and closing his eyes. "I love you, too, angel."

He kissed my forehead, the gentlest brush of his lips, but it was enough to make the world fade away. The crowd and the cameras, the fireworks and the noise—all of it melted.

I rested my head against his chest, breathing him in. There was still the faint scent of sweat and race fuel, but underneath it all was something that was simply him, the man who had captured my heart in ways I had never thought possible. I squeezed him tight before dropping my feet back to the ground.

"You're amazing," I murmured into his suit, a small smile pulling at my lips. "Six-time World Champion. I'm never going to get used to saying that."

He chuckled, the sound vibrating through me. "I'm just getting started."

I leaned back to look at him, my grin matching his. "Well, don't forget about me when you're winning the seventh."

He laughed, that full, unrestrained sound that I loved. "And where will you be?"

"Right here," I said, as if it were the most obvious thing in the world.

EPILOGUE
LUCIA

Speckled sunlight shined on the balloons that floated tied with bows to chairs around an extra long wooden table in my parents'. Olive trees framed the yard, silver leaves swaying in the wind. My mother was bringing out ornate dishes filled with food, plates of cheeses and perfectly crafted savory pastry bites. She had fused all day over having every single one of my favorite foods to celebrate my birthday today. After the final race of the season, Gianna and I had flown back on Alexander's private jet. He arranged a personal car to pick us up from the small local airport and everything. Being back home was wrapped up in some complicated emotions. It was so amazing to be back, the county breeze pushing my hair along with the wind, the endless rows of vineyards around my parents' stone-covered house. But being back in my childhood room, the same room all those hard months after having Gianna, held heavier emotions than I had expected. This morning, I had been sitting on the bed, the familiar floral pink sheets under my legs, when my mom had walked in, a worn apron tied around her waist, leaning against the door frame.

"You know, my love, you have done all your growing here. I am proud of the woman you are, the mother you are, the person you have grown to be." She smiled her warm smile. Tears glimmered in her eyes. And I was starting to understand it now, being a mother. The days stretched on, but the years breezed by. Gianna was already almost three years old, her birthday not far from my own.

Today I was twenty-nine years old. I had an amazing daughter, a full life, a dreamy boyfriend, friends who I considered family. I was proud of myself too. Proud of not giving up, of finding myself again in this new version of life.

"The boys get in in a few days, yes?" she asked. I nodded. I was sad to not have them here for my birthday, but they were busy with end of season things. And my mother, ever the planner, had gone all out and made more food than the four of us could ever eat on our own, tied balloons to the chairs, and cut fresh flowers from the garden, placing them in different colored glass vases.

The golden glow of the afternoon bathed the vineyard as my father stepped into the garden, Gianna perched in his arms. Her tiny hands were full, one clutching a fistful of wildflowers, the other wrapped around the plush bunny Alexander had given her. My heart squeezed. It had only been a week since we'd come home, but I already missed it—the hum of the track, the friends who had become family, the thrill of it all. But I also loved this. The quiet. The familiarity. I craved both.

"*Tanti auguri*, principessa," my father greeted, his voice warm. He pulled me into a side embrace, Gianna giggling between us.

"Tanti auguri, Mama!" she chirped, thrusting her flowers toward me.

"*Grazie*, my love," I murmured, accepting them with a kiss to her curls.

"Shall we eat?" My mother's voice carried across the garden, a knowing glint in her eye as she placed the last dish on the long wooden table. The spread was beautiful. Sun-kissed dishes painted with yellow daisies, a pitcher of wine, glasses filled to their brims. But something tugged at me. Seven plates, when there were only four of us. My phone buzzed,

ALEXANDER

That dress is a knockout, angel.

"Mama, why are there—" The iron gate creaked behind me.

A chorus of voices rang out, "Tanti auguri!"

I spun around, already knowing before I saw him.

Alexander.

Matteo got to me first, sweeping me into a tight hug before ruffling my hair like I was ten again. I shoved him with a laugh just as Gianna let out a delighted shriek.

"MONTY!"

She wiggled free from my father's arms, barreling toward the golden retriever, who wagged his tail so hard his whole body moved. Nicola barely had time to steady herself before Gia crashed into her legs.

Matteo clutched his chest in mock pain. "Damn, that stings."

Nicola grinned, victorious. "Hey, kid," she greeted Gia warmly.

And then—

"Hey, angel."

That voice. Smooth, warm, laced in my favorite British accent.

I turned, smirking. "Hey, hotshot."

Alexander kissed my cheek, his touch easy, familiar, but I wasn't satisfied with that. I pulled him into a hug, feeling the steady beat of his heart beneath my hands.

A throat cleared.

We turned to find my father watching us, expression unreadable. Alexander straightened instinctively, extending a tattooed hand.

"Hello, sir."

A pause. Then, my father shook it, his lips curving ever so slightly. "Alex. Welcome back. Got your place all settled?"

I blinked. *His place?*

"Yes, sir," Alexander replied smoothly.

"Good." My father gave a nod before turning toward my mother, who had already begun fussing over Nicola, pulling her into a long embrace.

Nicola shot me a look over my mother's shoulder, a bit panicked. I grinned. My mother had more love to give than space in her arms. By the time we were all seated, passing plates and wine around, I leaned into Alexander.

"What were you talking about with my dad?" I asked, keeping my voice low.

"Hmm?" He feigned innocence.

"Your place? Are you not staying here with us?"

"You'll see." A smirk tugged at his lips.

I narrowed my eyes. "Alexander Wright, I hate surprises."

"You liked me showing up early," he countered.

"Well, yeah, but you can't just drop something like that and not tell me what it is!"

He leaned in, pressing a kiss to my cheek. "Be patient, angel. I know you'll love it."

I grumbled, knowing he wouldn't budge. There weren't any houses for miles, just rolling hills and sprawling vineyards.

The meal passed in a blur of laughter and warmth. My heart felt full, surrounded by my people, my family. The sky had begun to melt into gold and lavender when Alexander touched my arm.

"I want to take you somewhere," he murmured. His voice was soft, intimate.

I glanced toward Gianna, who was happily playing with Monty as Nicola and Matteo looked on.

"She's having a sleepover with Nicola," Alexander assured me with a grin. "And Monty, of course."

"A sleepover?" My brow lifted.

"She's very excited about it. Now, say your good nights. I'm stealing you away for the night." My heart thudded.

After thanking my family for the wonderful meal and pressing a kiss to Gianna's curls, I followed Alexander to the cobblestone driveway, where a sleek black Alfa Romeo awaited. He opened the door for me before sliding into the driver's seat, and soon, we were gliding down the winding road. I let my hand drift out the window, fingers dancing in the cool night air.

We drove for a while, the familiar landscape slipping past, until Alexander slowed, turning onto a side road I didn't recognize. A large iron gate loomed ahead. He pressed a button on the call box, and with a creak, the gates parted.

"Alex..." My voice trailed off.

"Few more minutes, angel."

The car rolled up a newly paved road, twisting through the hills. And then—

A house came into view.

It sat perched atop a hill, glowing in the dimming light. Tall windows reflected the fading sunset, stone walls softened by warm wooden inlets. It was stunning, breathtaking, but more than that—something about it felt familiar.

"Alexander," I whispered. "Where are we?"

He turned to me, smiling. "Home."

My heart lurched.

"I closed on the land last summer," he explained. "It's the lot next to your parents'. I worked with a local architect and designers to have it ready by the end of the season. There's a lit path through the vineyard to your parents' place—we can add a road later if we want to. There are extra rooms, an office, a wraparound porch in the back where you can sit and read." His fingers fidgeted together as we approached the front door. "I-I started adding things, maybe unconsciously, for you and Gianna. I want to get some animals, make this a real home. Every other place, none of them ever felt right. Nothing did until I started spending summers here. This is where I want to be, where I want to raise a family one day."

Emotion thickened my throat as he unlocked the door, revealing a breathtaking entryway that opened into a cozy living space. Floor-to-ceiling bookshelves lined one wall, framing an oversized, impossibly comfortable-looking couch. Warm light pooled from vintage sconces, the scent of fresh wood lingering in the air.

Alexander rubbed the back of his neck. "Your mum helped with the decorating."

I laughed, blinking back tears. "That explains why it feels like home."

We wandered through the house, my mind spinning with images—baking cookies with Gianna in the sunlit kitchen, curling up on the porch swing with a book, movie nights snuggled under blankets.

Three years ago, I had driven through the night, pregnant and terrified of the future. I never could have imagined that summer would change everything—that I'd find a family, love, a place where I truly belonged.

And yet, here I was.

Later, we opened a bottle of wine and settled onto the porch's swinging daybed. The stars burned brilliantly above as we talked about it all, how I could visit as often as I wanted during the season with the private jet, how he wanted me and Gianna to move in when I was ready.

"I'll build or change anything you want," he promised, his voice thick with sincerity. "I just want to make it perfect for you."

I curled against him, listening to the steady beat of his heart.

It already was.

ACKNOWLEDGMENTS

We did it! I have had this little story in my head for so so long, it's gone through many versions and I am genuinely so proud of where it landed and what it formed into!

First and foremost, thank you to my sweet readers and bookstagram community, I wouldn't be here without you!

Writing Lucia's story is so deeply special to me. Coming out of a horrible relationship then tumbling into another huge life change. I always used to say things come in threes. But honestly sometimes they're double digits and you just can not catch a break. That's where Lucia is at the beginning, you see her raw and broken self for a minute in the first chapter. By the time we meet up with her again three years later, she had done the work, healed her soul and now wants to meet herself again. That journey is so deeply special. Lucia is so vulnerable, so real with herself and her emotions. She knows she's an over-thinker, we see hints of her dealing with anxiety and panic attacks as she helps Alexander through his own. She gets the time to blossom into a mother but also herself! And Alexander, my MAN. He's just is a magnet for chaos and the poor man just wants to slow down! Writing Alexander's journey through anxiety was so special to me because he truly has to learn what it is. having a panic attack for the first time is so confusing, and then can continue to be before you figure out what is happening. Writing from that perspective was so personal to me, basically solidifying him as one of my favorite MMC's I've written. I started to experience debilitating panic attacks in high school, I was lucky enough to have friends who knew what they looked like, who talked me through it and calmed me down. Who would grab my headphones and put them in my ears in the middle of class to help ground me. A sweet friend that would meet me in the hallway and sit on the ground with me, and just be there. Anxiety is so different for everyone, so really pulled from my own experiences and tried to channel someone who didn't know it was panic but was in that haze filled state.

So thank you to those little guardian angels that appeared in my life and helped me through it.

Thank you to my WONDERFUL beta readers: Grace, Chloe, Bailey for seeing the chaos of the first round of what FTTOIA looked like and still loving it. For my second round beta readers: Kalina and Logan, your words and encouragement fueled me! For EVERY single member of the Booksta community that commented, shared and loved on this book in ALL of its stages. VROOM VROOM baby.

Thank you to my wonderful Dev editor Kay Morton. You have been a constant in every stage of writing and editing. Thank you for continuing to agree to edit the dyslexic mess that is my drafts. You're a wonder.

Thank you to my amazing Copyeditor, Paisley McNab at PerfectlyWrite for your patience and absolute love you put into my book baby.

To the Cameron and Ferris to my Sloane - *"Life moves pretty fast. If you don't stop and look around once in a while, you could miss it"*.

To my sister, Kathryn, for being such a source of encouragement and love through my writing processes. For inspiring Gianna's entire character with your perfect daughters. Gianna was written while Daisy was the most precious 2-3 year old, but every there's a piece of every Martin girl in her. I love you my Martin Girls.

Thank you to my OG fangirls of this book, Dayna and Jen (@daynas.bookshelf + @dearwritten). Your unwavering faith in me and the amount of love you sent my way while writing is literally how I finished drafting this baby!! Love you so much!

To MR Elliana Rose for being my rock and anchor in the world, I love you always.

To my family who's loud Italian-ness are basically the DeLuca Family.

I dedicate this book to my stand in grandmother of my childhood, Elena Maggetti, who passed away right as I finished the first draft. I hope I have you in every lifetime.

Per quelli che volano.

WHAT'S NEXT?

Want to read Matteo & Nicola's story?

Heart Racing is book two in the Sparks Fly series and available here: Heart Racing: A Formula One Boss's Daughter Romance

Follow Elliana on instagram @authorelliana for the most up to date news and releases.

ABOUT THE AUTHOR

Elliana Rose is a lover of romcoms, hoarder of books and personal photographer to her German Shepard "Gremlin". When she is not writing she is making bookish graphics and designs for her shop Primrose&CoDesign, reading in the sunshine, and probably dreaming up a new idea. She also writes Fantasy under the pen name E.R.Maggetti.